THE PARANORMAL CASEBOOK OF JEREMIAH THORNE

James Barr

Please keep in touch with the author via twitter: @JamesBarrJT

CONTENTS

TALE NUMBER ONE – DEAD END CONVERSATION

It was intriguing to receive a call from an NHS nurse sounding quite as desperate as this Susie girl. Maybe all NHS nurses are desperate given the headlines in the newspapers about workloads, poor pay and hospital viruses. However there certainly was a panic, perhaps one might almost call it a *fear* in her voice. As usual, I did initially wonder if it was another practical joker. I do, after all, get all kinds of strange people giving feedback and commenting on the forum section of my little paranormal website. Although there was something pretty genuine sounding about this Susie. Oh yes, there was also guilt. That was something else I detected in her voice. Granted, she did actually say, 'this is all my fault' at least three times during our ten-minute conversation, so to be fair, it was a bit of a giveaway.

I took down a brief outline of the nature of her potential paranormal incident and based on the phone information provided, it seemed to hold my interest. Of course, the vast majority of my calls can be dismissed as non-paranormal within the first thirty seconds. For instance, 'Excuse me, I think my house is haunted – things are going bang in the night' can usually be answered by asking if they've just started their annual central heating usage. Then of course, the ethereal scratching at the window is normally the result of someone's unkempt garden foliage. Nothing worse than an untidy bush I always say. My non-politically correct character would normally make me ask if they've checked their undergrowth recently. Invariably they then slam the telephone receiver down but not before calling me a pervert or worse, but such things appeal to my wicked side. I don't much like conforming. I'm an aging rebel without a cause. Don't get me wrong, I do take my craft seriously though and when my old nose senses it's on to something, I leap into action and give it one hundred percent. Admittedly, my aging body means the degree of my leaping and exuberance of action is somewhat restricted these days but the mind is always willing even if the rest of me has trouble keeping up. Plus, with the help of my somewhat over energetic young niece on some of my cases, I have managed to scrape together some pleasing finds in my field of paranormal research over the years. No actual proof I admit, but I'm not a miracle worker unfortunately, or even the remotest bit lucky, it would seem. Amateur ghost hunters and professional parapsychologists have been searching for proof of the existence of paranormal phenomena for the scientific community and the world alike for decades and decades, yet we are still none the wiser. After all my years of having a slight obsession on this subject, I know, I just *know*, that ghosts and hauntings exist. I've seen, I've heard and I've experienced. However, as for actual evidence that would convince even the hardest hearted, that, I cannot provide, despite all the best efforts of myself and several other thousand people the world over. Spirits, phantoms, call them what you like, are perhaps mischievous or even shy and as such simply do not play ball when we need them to. I know, how unreasonable! Either that, or there's some higher force, maybe God or Gods, if you believe in him, her or them, not allowing their discovery in case us mere mortals go crazed with this additional knowledge of divinity, creation and the world beyond our own. Bit like seeing a genuine UFO or extra-terrestrial I suppose. Could you imagine the worldwide hubbub if you got proof of that?

Anyway, now that I've started to go all philosophical, I'll stop immediately and get back to the strange telephone call from this nurse called Susie.

It was mid-afternoon and I was down in my 'den'. By this I mean my office in the garden, my centre of investigative excellence as it were, down amongst the shrubbery. And it was while I was down there, I had my first introduction to Nurse Susie. She certainly sounded pleasant enough, but at the same time somewhat nervous of our communication and I could certainly pick up on some unease in her speech. Mind you, I'm always a bit wary I'll find myself talking to timewasters or spaced out freaks who get my mobile number off the internet site my niece Francesca set up for me. However, there was certainly something authentic and indeed, genuinely fearful in the voice of this hospital angel. After the usual pleasantries and introductions of strangers on the telephone, it wasn't long before the first of the 'it's all my fault' statements, followed by a pause and then a deep intake of breath. I think it was safe to say she was a tad weepy but composed herself enough to convince me to meet her and more specifically her friend, housemate and co-worker Jane, who seemed to be the chief victim of their little spot of trouble. Therefore, as I wasn't at the 'day job' the next morning and as they were both on the hospital 'late' shift, an appointment for such a rendezvous was set. Having spent a dire lifetime employed as a civil servant trying to work out what to do with my life, before I knew it, I'd passed the half century, still none the wiser as to who or what I was meant to be on this earth. So, to give me the time and space I needed to figure that one out, my radical mid-life crisis made me take a part time job instead, at the big library in town. Yes, I wish I could've said I was a lion tamer or vampire slayer to impress you, but I can't. Anyhow, the part time working hours gave me the much-needed extra free time to think philosophically about who I am, or more importantly, more time to investigate hauntings and the paranormal.

This little enquiry raised the necessity for niece Fran to tag along. I thought as a young, trendy wee thing, she may well help my interaction with the youthful nursing staff I was set to meet. Fran could be my guardian and protector given I was about to get together with these female nurses within the confines of their National Health Service accommodation block. As for all I know, they may have had a 'thing' for the older man, and as such jumped on me as soon as the door was closed and ravaged my manly body. Apologies, that was just a bit of a short daydream fantasy I had after the phone call but at my age, daydreams tend to be as good as it gets in that department. I'll try and buck my ideas up.

I sent my Frankie a text to ask her to be free in the morning and went off to mull over my phone call with the nurse. She'd managed to pass on her anguish and distress to me during the call, to the extent that I was now feeling somewhat uneasy as well. Annoyingly, for whatever reason, she wouldn't go into too much detail on the phone. But it wasn't her saying it was all her fault which troubled me. I remembered after the call, she whispered something guiltily like, 'I think we've done a terrible thing'. For a second, I wondered if it was really the police she needed, not me. However, there must've been a reason for going to the trouble of finding and then contacting a paranormal researcher instead. So, reservations put to one side, I began to look forward to our post breakfast meet up and finding out what on earth they'd done which was apparently so terrible.

~ ~ ~

The following morning, I heard the sound of Fran's Moped pull up on the gravel outside the house, despite me being sat in the kitchen which is more towards the side of my not-so-happy home. That's the thing with Mopeds; their high-pitched glorified lawnmower style engine seems to ring out for miles. My wife Cynthia had long since gone out, being someone who gets up at dawn for no good reason whatsoever, which suits me anyway as it means we don't then need to try and force a conversation. Being a 'drag me out of bed if you must' sort of guy it was already after nine and I had only just finished the morning cornflakes.

Therefore, whilst being dressed, I was still an unwashed sloth but enjoying my first cigarette of the day with a cup of my favourite filtered coffee. The back door flung open and in came Francesca looking as usual like a 'wild child', sporting her hot pants and black leather jacket combo which she wears more often than not and somehow seems to suit her personality.

"Ah, you're actually up then," came her typical opener.

"Good Morning to you too, oh beloved niece among nieces," I retorted, nonchalantly blowing my cigarette smoke in her general direction.

"Thought for one horrible moment I'd have to make conversation with the dreaded Auntie Cynthia. Not sure I can face that at this time of the morning."

I knew exactly what she meant.

"You want to try living here," came my despondent reply.

Although, as for her initial greeting, my niece has an uncanny knack of mocking me for exactly the same sort of sins as she lives by. Being up by nine in the morning on a non-work day is for her, exactly like me, an early start. I offered her a restorative café noir which she duly poured and sat herself down beside me helping herself to one of my ciggies, as such is her way.

"So, what's this job you texted me about? Not more time wasters I hope?"

Fran and I sometimes referred to our little assignments as 'jobs' but despite the title we never took a penny from people because we were more what you might call, researchers. We didn't offer a service as such although sometimes we did give individuals peace of mind by letting them know they didn't have a ghost or for that matter if they did, we helped them understand more, except for one or two cases where we had to throw water on the hysterical and perhaps slap them across the cheek. But I'm not in the business of exorcisms and if that's what people want, they need to get on the blower to a trusted servant of the Pope.

"Well," stubbing out my spent fag, "we're off to a nurse's home."

"Have you finally realised you're getting on a bit and need putting away? Did you want me to come and help you pick a room? Hope you've sorted out power of attorney!"

"Nurses home, not nursing home," knowing full and well she heard me properly in the first place. "As in a nurse accommodation house near the main hospital."

I told Fran about my previous day's conversation with this Susie girl, then popped upstairs for a quick face in a flannel session, a brush of the hair and like any man of action, a generous splash of Old Spice aftershave for luck.

"You only want us to go and meet these women because they're nurses and you're hoping to see them in their uniforms. You've probably got some kind of fantasy like that haven't you?" joked Fran sporting a cheeky grin, as we got into my 1975 Rover P6 saloon. I don't hold with modern cars, so many buttons, microchips, electric this and that, too much to go wrong say I. Keep life simple thank you very much.

"I do not wish to perve on anyone, thank you, uniforms or no uniforms. And if that's all I wanted to do, I'd just have a day trip to the Casualty department. For one thing, these girls we're seeing may look like the back of a bus for all I know and for another; they won't be in their work attire because they don't start their shift until this afternoon." Such was my grumpy retort as I turned the key and fired up the 3500cc V8 beast that powered my old mustard cruiser. Fran just gave a mischievous smirk, a habit which she has carried with her since early childhood, naughty little toddler, then unruly child, then wayward teenager that she was, but I ignored her, moved the car gear selector into 'drive' and commenced the journey to this initial interview.

I followed the directions from my enquirer to the part of the hospital campus which had the accommodation block for the nursing staff and in reasonable time we pulled up outside the appropriate building.

"Nothing much is very scary about this place. I suppose that doesn't necessarily mean anything but you are sure we're not dealing with some joker?" enquired Frankie.

"Guess we'll soon find out," I responded but I could see what she meant. It was mid-morning but the general area looked calm and peaceful. There was winter sunshine brightening all around us, rich verdant grass surrounding the buildings and with nothing but a gentle breeze and occasional caw from a crow, you could happily imagine that all was right with the world. Admittedly you could also hear the distant activities and fuss of a major hospital several hundred yards away, but this little corner, secluded by many shrubs and young trees, was all right by me.

The building we were set to enter had no age or architectural interest to it, being modern in construction, but its newness meant it was smart and presentable and as such I could entirely concur with the view Fran had expressed, that nothing in the surrounding area felt very spooky. There were no hideous gargoyles staring down at us, no circling vultures overhead and no dark, hooded figures holding a scythe in one hand and a parking penalty ticket machine in the other. Of course, there is nothing in the rule book that says paranormal activity doesn't happen in or around the walls of a new building. And ghost sightings aren't always in old manor houses, castles and moors after all. In fact, nearly half of my investigations have been at modern buildings.

"I suppose we better go and get the full story. Apparently, their rooms are up on the second floor," and so I pressed the intercom and we were subsequently allowed to enter, so that we could find out what happened to make a once happy nurse named Susie racked with guilt and fear.

~ ~ ~

The corridors and staircase must have recently been refurbished as was evident by the smell inside of the newly laid plastic floor covering. Or whatever this industrial type of material is, making the hall and stairway cold and echoey. It certainly didn't have the homely smell of a woollen carpet that's for sure. But after a short climb of stairs, we were greeted by two casually dressed and welcoming girls who, age wise, were something in the region of their mid-twenties. A full figured, down to earth looking brunette introduced herself as Susie who gave me the call a day earlier. With her was Jane, the woman she had briefly mentioned as being the one with whom there were the current difficulties, whatever they may be, because the somewhat confused telephone conversation hadn't really cleared that one up. Jane was a pleasant looking blonde-haired lady, although there was clearly something troubling her behind the convivial greeting. There was no sparkle to her eyes, in fact her face seemed grey with fatigue and I rather suspected that despite her fair complexion she was not normally quite this pale.

"I didn't realise you'd be coming with anyone Mr. Thorne, is this your daughter?" asked Susie.

"No, no, this is Francesca my niece. She sometimes helps me out on the odd case."

"Call me Frankie," she interrupted, as informal as ever and mildly abrupt, giving me the impression, she thought this whole business was a nonsense.

"Sorry, I should have said I'd be bringing her along." This time Jane spoke up. She sounded as drained as she looked and within her lovely husky tones I detected a slight Irish accent.

"It really isn't a problem, I'm afraid we're just going to be wasting your time anyway, so please, well, forgive us I suppose. Come on in."

I wasn't sure why Fran seemed to have taken an instant dislike to them, but she was a bit thin on banter or reassurance.

"Well, we'll hear what you've got to say and take it from there shall we?" Her tone with the two nurses was still a bit brusque so I thought I'd better do the honours on the pleasantries front.

We were invited through to a communal lounge area and there were a couple of other young women there who immediately made polite excuses and darted off. So, the pair of us sat down on an aging sky-blue couch, which was lower than my old legs are comfortable with these days given my backside felt like it was about two inches off the floor. Jane disappeared off to make some coffee, leaving us with Susie.

Such an arrangement was clearly orchestrated by the aforementioned brunette as there was evidently something she wanted to say without her friend being within earshot. In the few seconds Jane was exiting the room, I had a moment to take in my surroundings and get a feel for the place. I suppose you would say the room was 'tired' but perhaps that's just how it goes with staff housing. The magnolia emulsion which adorned the walls had had its fair share of knocks and scrapes while the blue carpet tiles on the floor were hardwearing, almost industrial, but not especially homely. Granted it was only basic, live-in accommodation for a number of NHS staff members. But it would be fair to say a suite at The Ritz would have a significantly more luxurious décor.

I was brought to attention by Susie giving a light cough and as she did so she moved forward, clearly wanting to be nearer to myself and Fran so her vocals could be at a lower level.

"Look Mr. Thorne, I know you must have to deal with your fair share of spurious claims and weirdoes but please don't include us in that. What we're about to tell you happened... I mean it *really* happened. I'll admit, if someone tried to convince me about the bizarre things that have been going on in this place, if I hadn't been here to see for myself, then I'd tell them they were either a liar or full of crap." To be fair to the girl, she was earnest with a capital E and that was clear. I thought this young lady needed my reassurance. I also thought she had lovely eyes. Sorry, just thought I'd mention that.

"Listen Susie, firstly, I believe you've obviously been affected by something here but I'm not saying it's anything paranormal without all the facts, and making my own little investigation is paramount. Secondly, call me Jerry, don't stand on ceremony for my sake."

"OK, Jerry it is. As for getting the facts, you shall have them." She took a deep intake of breath and shook her head with self-reproval.

"How I wish I could turn the clock back and not have organised that stupid game. I feel so responsible! This really is my fault and poor Jane seems to be the one doing most of the suffering," she added, and the look of disgrace that filled her face was with true remorse.

Just as Jane was returning with the caffeine supply, Fran started her forthright interrogation.

"So, what do you mean by stupid game?" coming straight to the point, tact and diplomacy going straight out of the window.

"I had this crazy idea of having a séance here on Halloween night – well, our version of one anyway. We fancied doing something a bit different you see. There were probably several Halloween parties going on that we could've gone to, or silly themed nights at the clubs in town but none of us felt like doing any of that this year. And so, as we all had that night off together for a change, we decided we would have a bit of a girl's night in. A few drinks, pizza delivery, just have a bit of a laugh. Our mate Judy had been reading up on that sort of thing recently – she's a bit of a closet hippie, you know."

"Clarify 'that sort of thing'," I asked, wondering if this Judy girl had been researching pizza or alcohol.

"Oh sorry, I'm getting ahead of myself. Judy's been getting a lot of books about séances, witchcraft, Ouija boards, all that."

"Almost into the realm of the Dark Arts then," said Fran with a somewhat brusque undertone. I thought I should support the loyal niece. I had a feeling I knew where these girls were going and I've seen some bad stuff happen over the years when individuals dabbled in this sort of caper.

"In our experience, not really things amateurs should mess with for fun, assuming none of you knew anything about the subject," I added.

"As I said, Judy had read a book or two on it and said it would be a laugh. Well, we all thought it would be fun."

I looked at Fran, she looked at me and without a word, we both looked back at the two nursing staff. Jane was looking down at the floor and chewing her lip nervously. Susie continued.

"Anyway, the night went on its merry way and we were all having a good time until we tried our hand at having a séance, around that table over there." She gestured toward a tatty pine dining table & chairs that were positioned near the doorway to what I presume was a small kitchen area, given that was where Jane had gone to make the coffee.

"We pulled it away from the wall and five of us, me, Judy, Jane and a couple of our pals – the ones you saw just as you arrived - sat round it. Then it sort of went, well, a bit sour."

When anyone recites their tales to me I do my own type of shorthand notes. Nothing like professional shorthand you understand, but the Jerry Thorne version, i.e. to anyone other than me it just looks like a lot of squiggly lines and therefore, they can't read it. Although, rather worryingly on more than one occasion, when I've tried to translate my own shorthand later I've had to drink two or three whiskies to even come close to understanding it. Still, it's a good excuse for a wee drinkie. My attention however, was drawn upwards again at the husky sound of Jane's gentle Irish tone joining the story telling.

"Jerry, I should say this tale of stupidity didn't exactly start that night. Something really odd happened that morning." She turned towards Susie. "We need to tell him about when I went to work..."

Her friend held her hand and moved closer.

"Hun, are you sure you want to mention that? You know I believe you but, you know, others..." at this point she nodded in our general direction. "Well, others might just think you were imagining things."

I thought I'd offer a bit of reassurance.

"Ladies, you can tell us anything. I can guarantee we've heard a lot worse. We're not here to make judgements on you, but we'll need all the facts, however odd you may think they are."

Jane gave a little smile, which really showed off her natural beauty.

"That's settled then," she said defiantly, "OK Susie?"

"Of course it is," she replied with much care and compassion for her friend. "It just gives me the creeps hearing about it again. And oddly, it spooks me out more than everything that went on in the evening."

"So, what did happen then?" Fran chipping in impatiently.

Jane took a few seconds drawing air into her lungs as if for support and a brief moment later, in her beautiful soft Irish accent, began to relay the strange event from early in the morning of the day these foolhardy nurses had their ill-fated evening séance.

~~~

"'I was on an early shift, the day we had the séance. So, it wasn't particularly light outside when I was walking across to the hospital and I happened to notice an elderly lady walking slowly along an adjacent path. I immediately thought how odd it was that someone of her age, particularly given how tiny and frail she looked, was walking around in this area of the hospital grounds but also that she was there at all, so early in the morning. I just assumed she was a bit lost and looked away thinking nothing more about it. At that time of day, I'm not thinking about much to be honest with you, I'm usually half asleep. Then I heard the sound of someone falling over, so I looked back at her and there she was on the floor, in a bit of a state. Obviously, I ran over to help.

"Oh hell, are you all right?" I asked and the sweet old thing that I assumed she was – how wrong was I – said to me, "Yes dear. Thank you, what a silly old fool I am." So, I helped her up. "Don't ever get old dear," she added as I slowly managed to get her to her feet.

"Are you sure you don't want me to take you over to the hospital?" As I said this she stopped and just stared into space with a glazed look in her eyes. I wondered what the hell she was doing or what on earth was wrong with her."

At this point Jane paused and she too was staring into space as if stunned by something.

"Jane?" queried a quizzical looking Susie, "you all right?"

Jane suddenly came to and apologised. "Sorry, I was just playing it over again in my mind."

"What was the big deal? An old dear fell over, it happens," dismissed Fran who by now was impatiently keen to hear exactly what happened to our pretty, but tortured Irish nurse. Jane continued and for a moment even shook her head as she spoke, as if she didn't believe herself what she was saying.

"She grabbed my arm, incredibly tight, with such force and such grip that I was completely taken aback, given she seemed so old and frail. But then a complete contrast came over her face, one minute she's this kindly old girl, then her expression was as hard as nails. But worst of all she looked me straight in the eyes and commanded with such ferocity, "Don't play with the spirits Jane! You're lucky enough to be given a warning and that warning is coming from me, to you, now, at this instance!"

"How do you know my name?" I screamed, "What are you talking about?" Then I remembered our scheduled evening's entertainment but thought, no, we're just going to have a laugh, this is surely someone having a wind-up. Or I'm dreaming still and I'm going to wake up soon in my nice warm bed. But still this old woman clutched at my arm with such force it was red and sore for two days afterwards. Then she started again, "Jane, there's evil about tonight, don't play at things you don't understand, they don't like being messed with Jane, please, I beg you dear, leave them be, leave them be...!" All the while her voice was getting louder and more insistent; she'd taken hold of my other arm and had started to shake me. I couldn't stand it, I simply couldn't stand it!"

"Who are you? Leave me alone you crazy bitch!" I screamed, managing to break away and I ran off. I looked back at her and she just stood there, arms held out towards me with anguish and horror on her face, "Jane!" she shrieked.

I turned away, ran a few steps more, realising my handbag was back on the path where the confrontation had taken place. Not two or three seconds passed before I looked back again at where she stood, and sure enough there was my bag on the ground where I had dropped it, but the old woman was gone. Completely vanished. There was nowhere she could have gone in that space of time or in that part of the grounds. No bushes to hide behind, no buildings, no nothing. She was gone, vanished into thin air, and yes, I know it's not possible, but it happened and a shiver went down my spine so cold that I couldn't get to that hospital quick enough. And when I did, I fainted within a second of being there. Now you tell me Jerry, how the hell could that have happened? I didn't dream it, mores the pity. Am I mad? Is that what you're going to tell me?"

She had upset herself so much in the recounting of her unpleasant experience that by now she was practically shouting at me. I thought it a good idea to calm the atmosphere and with amazing diplomatic judgement retorted,

"Got any biscuits?"

Not brilliant, but the best I could come up with at the time. I needed to say something to break the tension.

"Afraid not. Any biscuits in this place seem to disappear within minutes of a packet being opened, not bad really considering we're all permanently on diets. We must have the cookie monster living under the sink," answered Susie, attempting to lighten the mood, who by now had her arm around Jane, comforting her as she had started to quietly weep.

"I'm afraid that isn't the end of the story," continued Jane, wiping away some of the moisture from her eyes with a tissue. "You should've been here in the evening when we actually had the séance."

"You went ahead with it despite this strange business in the morning?" I asked.

"I'm afraid we did," Susie replied.

"So what happened?"

"Well, we'd managed to convince Jane she had nothing to worry about and her mind was just playing tricks on her. She's been overdoing it a bit recently and I honestly thought, well, we all did, that she was just tired out and an evening to let her hair down would do her good."

"What time was it?" asked Fran.

"I guess it was about seven when we ordered a couple of pizzas. The Vodka was opened before that I'm afraid to say. The five of us – me, Jane, Tracy, Shona – those were our two friends who left when you arrived – and of course Judy. She's our friend who thought up the idea. A couple of books from the library and she thinks she's Mystic Meg."

I primed my propelling pencil, took a new page in my notebook and urged Susie to continue, leaving no detail out of her report.

"I guess it was about half eight when we went to sit around the table over there. We pulled it away from the wall, cleared the junk off and all sat round it. Oh, and Tracy lit a few candles and turned the light off. We were merry but I wouldn't say any of us were drunk. Judy got us to lay our hands out on the table with our little fingers touching and it didn't get off to a good start because all of us bar Judy, who was taking it very seriously, had a fit of the giggles. Then, when we'd composed ourselves and she closed her eyes and said 'Is there anybody there?' Shona kicked the table leg three times before bursting out in a fit of laughter again. Judy had a strop and started to get up to go but we pulled her back, bribed her with chocolate and then she started again but not before she made us all promise to behave."

Susie had a slight smile as she reported this early part of her narrative and looking across to Jane it was reciprocated. But the smiles soon faded away as she continued her story and seriousness and gravity filled both their faces.

"Anyway, Judy started again, asking 'if anyone was with us', 'was there anybody there', 'was there a message from the spirit world', blah, blah, and all that sort of thing. She went on like that for about ten minutes and to be honest I think the rest of us were getting a bit bored with it. And I began to wonder if we should've gone to a club after all. But then the first really spooky thing happened. We had one of those thick, church style candles lit in the middle of the table. And the flame started to flicker."

"Nothing unusual in that" piped up Fran. "Candles can do that, with or without any draught."

"Well there wasn't any draught and it didn't just flicker. It started to go wild for nearly a minute and then it went out. We all just looked at one another and I think we were all a bit freaked out, even if we didn't say so at the time. If Tracy hadn't put lots of other candles around the room we would've been sitting in darkness. Then it started to get a bit chilly, so much so that Shona put her cardy back on. Judy snapped at her for breaking the circle and shouted that she thought we were on to something and boy, did she have that right! We heard a noise and all looked toward that shelf over there. One of us had left their empty glass on it when we cleared off the table, and this glass was literally moving along the shelf by itself! It simply moved along the shelf, knocking off everything in its path! We all just sat there, open mouthed with total disbelief, staring at it."

I thought I ought to ask an intelligent question but I struggled a bit and could only ask if she knew which one of them the glass belonged to.

"No, sorry, I can't. The heat of the moment has clouded my memory a bit, if that's the right phrase given how cold it became in here. But something none of us will forget in a hurry was when the glass lifted off that shelf, moved three feet away from it, hovered in mid air for what seemed like ages, and then flew with the angriest of force at that picture over there."

She pointed toward a big photographic poster such that you can get nowadays from one of those trendy stores which sell that sort of thing. It was a photo of a young gentleman with his shirt off.

"It's Robbie Williams, Uncle. He's a singer," clarified my Fran in a slightly mocking tone. Although the clarification was appreciated as I didn't actually know who the young gentleman posing in the poster was. However, I've subsequently heard this chap is rather successful in his chosen field and when I've since heard a couple of his songs, whilst I didn't think he was up there with my beloved Elvis, Sinatra or Harrison, I thought he could hold a tune quite well.

"If you did actually have a brief visitation from a Spirit, it obviously wasn't a fan of his," I suggested.

"One of us cracked that joke on the night," replied Jane. "Which broke the silence. We were all too scared to move until then. We just didn't believe or understand what on earth was going on! And I'm afraid at that point; I lost it completely and ran to my room."

She had my sympathy. I think if I was sitting in a candlelit room, with hovering glasses smashing against walls, with no physical presence being responsible for it, there'd be windy noises in my underwear too. I glanced toward Fran who was deep in thought for a moment.

"Just say for a second, you actually managed to open a pathway to some sort of Spirit dimension... Did this Judy or whoever was in charge, actually close any link to the spirit world, if of course, one was actually opened in the first place?" she asked, maintaining her somewhat abrupt manner.

Susie was picking up Frans vibe and responded in kind.

"Listen I don't know about Spirit dimensions or anything like that, but at that point I asked Judy if there was anything we should be doing to finish. She just said she needed to thank the spirit for visiting and say bye to it. So I told her to tell it goodbye, although my version had three f's in it if you know what I mean, and then I went to check on Jane. I was pretty annoyed with myself because this whole night in was my idea and I don't mind telling you it ended on a pretty sorry note and we were all really upset by it."

I didn't want a lady fight on my hands, so I butted in.

"Thinking back to the glass moving, I don't suppose any of you are telekinetic or anything like that?" I enquired.

"No of course not. And we wouldn't play this sort of trick on one another even if we were."

"Have either of you any thoughts on what might've caused this odd occurrence?"

Both Susie and Jane were shaking their heads.

"No idea. I thought at first, that one of us was having a wind up but now I'm absolutely sure, that none of us would do anything like this to the rest of us," said Susie forthrightly.

"None of us would know how to!" chipped in Jane, "I mean a glass travelling along a shelf by itself, hovering in mid-air, before flying across the room and into the wall! No way Jerry, beyond our area of knowledge! We just wouldn't know where to start."

"And has anything happened since?"

"Not as such no," said Jane but there was hesitation.

"You're not convincing me," I replied.

"Well nothing has *happened*. Physically that is. It just feels different here now. It's probably just me; I'm the only one who feels like this." Jane then held her head in her hands.

Susie put her arm around her again.

"Look, I've known Jane for more years than I can remember, and whilst none of the rest of us have felt or noticed anything odd since that night, if Jane says she has, then I believe her. So that's why I searched the web for answers and that's when I found your site, and so that's why I gave you a call to see if you would offer up your opinion. Are you able to help us at all?"

There was no doubt in my mind, this plea from Susie was earnest and heart felt, so if this Jane was still feeling a bit upset by the events of that evening, there was no wonder she was ill-at-ease.

"Look, I'm not saying I can help. If you're after someone to come in and do all that throwing of Holy Water about type ceremony, then I'm just not that man. But maybe I can make a little investigation into this for you. If I find nothing then I can tell you that. You may get some comfort from that, you may not, but it's up to you. Jane, where have you been having these 'feelings' and just what sort of thing are we talking about here?"

"In my room," she replied, her voice wavering like someone about to get upset again. "Or sometimes out here, but only if I'm on my own..."

"And what is it you think you feel?" Wrong choice of words and I wish I'd put it better but isn't hindsight a wonderful thing?

"I don't think I feel anything, I know it!" she retorted. I just know someone or something is with me, watching, moving my things, it's just there. There in the shadows. The times these last few days, I've put something down in my room, my locked room I might add, and then a few moments later it's moved. I know you're going to say I've just forgotten where I've left things but because I thought I was losing it I've been consciously remembering and memorising where I've been putting stuff. And minutes later, it's somewhere completely different, be it the other side of the room or even in one instance, I'd left a lipstick on my dressing table, I went to the loo, and when I came back after a lot of searching I found it in my knicker drawer. With a pair of tights literally wrapped around the tube! It's not me going mad Jerry, I'm sure it's not me…!"

"OK Jane I believe you, I really do. But to be clear, has anyone else felt any change or noticed anything out of the ordinary in your rooms, communal or otherwise, since the night of this séance?"

"No nothing at all, none of us have noticed anything. Apart from Jane here being so uneasy all the time it's driving us all mad with worry," said Susie.

"Have you thought about going away? Perhaps taking a holiday to see what happens?" Fran had now rejoined the dialogue.

"I am thinking about taking a few days off. I was going to try and book a few days at the end of this week, if they'll let me take it at such short notice." replied Jane.

"How do you feel about maybe Fran and I staying over in your room when you're away. See if we can record any activity? And if your friends don't mind, we could perhaps check out these communal areas too while we're here?"

"I certainly don't mind," said Jane with great enthusiasm, "I'll be pleased to have some time away from this place and I'll be happy to have someone prove to me I'm just being an over sensitive, idiotic, wet blonde."

"I don't think it'll be a problem with any of the girls here Jerry," added Susie. "I think they'll be cool about it. Even if you just came here and said at the end of it we're all fretting over nothing and to get a grip of ourselves!"

Fran emitted a polite, attention drawing cough. "You're volunteering both of us but I might not be available. I do have a job you know!" she stated in a rather defiant manner.

"Yes, dearest niece," I retorted, conscious that any little spat between us didn't develop given we had an audience in front of us. "So do I, but I'm sure all parties can organise a mutually convenient evening."

"Yes, but an overnighter like this will mean I'll need two days off from work, won't it?" she said through somewhat gritted teeth.

"Well..." gritting mine too, "I'm sure we can sort something."

"Look we don't want to cause any trouble for you..." offered Jane most courteously.

"You're not! Not at all, we'll sort something out," I replied and turning to Fran muttered, "Won't we Francesca?"

"Yes, Uncle Jerry," she responded in a sarcastic and mocking voice, sporting a false, almost chilling, smile across her face.

And after our temporary farewell to the two nurses, we made our way downstairs to the exit in silence as I knew Fran was in a strop and years of marital disharmony has taught me that if I utter a single word to a lady in a mood it would open up a torrent of abuse in my direction. Although, no doubt the lady in question would feel I heartily deserved it.

~ ~ ~

"You could've checked with me before booking us out on a job!" she shrieked as soon as we were outside.

Slight amendment to my theory – sometimes you don't need to utter a single word, and you still get shouted at.

"You don't normally mind and I did say it would have to be a mutually convenient time. Anyway, you don't have to come along."

"And who's going to be the dogsbody if I don't come?"

"True. That's what I like about you Frankie, you tell it like it is. Ciggie?" I offered a peacekeeping cancer tube and she readily accepted and instantly calmed down.

"So what's with you grumpy? I mean, you always are but this morning you're worse than normal."

Drawing back hard as she lit her cigarette, she replied, "Oh it's perfect princess girls like them up there. Goodie two shoes girlies who flutter their eyelids and the men come running."

"Where on earth has that come from?"

"A bit of a sob story and you soon came running to their aid, didn't you?"

"My interest is in their paranormal predicament. If, of course, there is one. I take it you weren't convinced?" I queried as I unlocked the car doors, nonchalantly flicking some ash off my own fag so it didn't go all over my leather upholstery. "Besides, I don't know why you're complaining. When you go out clubbing and whatever you youngsters do, the lads are normally round you like flies around the smelly brown stuff."

"Yeh but the men I attract are all losers, after what they can get. Oh, forget it; I guess I'm just in a bad mood. And as for your other question, no, I don't think I am convinced," she said slamming the car door behind her.

"Why? Just because you don't like them?" I started up 'old faithful' and slotted it into reverse, as I was keen to get going, or more specifically my empty belly was.

"That's got nothing to do with it. For instance, remember when that Jane told us she saw the old lady early in the morning but she admitted she was half asleep? Who's to say she wasn't actually sleep walking, or just not with it? She could've imagined the whole thing"

"Granted," I concurred.

"We should have asked her if she was on any long-term medication as well. She might just be having side effects."

I began to think Fran was taking objectivity too far.

"Oh come on, do behave!" I said.

"So why, out of all of them, did she get this old lady's warning? Why not this Judy girl, if she was the one who thought she was the great and wondrous medium?"

"An interesting point and one to chew on," I agreed.

"And what about when she said that since the séance, only she has felt anything? None of the others have, have they?"

"Of course, but that could go both ways. It's not uncommon that a spirit may concentrate its energies on just the one person is it?"

This, Fran had to concede.

"S'pose."

"Besides, you can't deny that we have five people who saw the floating and flying glass activity can you? That is more than a little strange, assuming they are all telling the truth of course."

"Or they were all so utterly legless, they believed they saw something when in actual fact, they were just completely drunk with gallons of Vodka."

"Let's just see what happens in a few days' time when we can stay over there and do some official recordings. Then we can make a proper judgement."

I was so busy saying this while throwing my cigarette butt out of the window I nearly drove the motor in to a post box.

"That's if we last until the end of the week," muttered my niece sarcastically, who looked a little unnerved at our near miss. "Will you be inviting any of the local ghost club to come along on this one?"

I should explain that we sometimes go along to organised ghost hunting events with a small paranormal club in the area. There is a lovely comradery with the gang, even if some of them can at best be described as thrill-seekers, rather than scientifically disposed researchers. For instance, one member, a charming lady whose identity shall remain concealed I'm afraid, will see a shadow, which in all probability will be her own, and then promptly run for the hills, screaming her head off. This for her, is a good night out. Still, it takes all sorts to make a world and at least she adds some drama to our all-night vigils. Trouble is, one person's hysteria tends to spread and then we all get a fright over nothing. Goodness only knows what she'd do if she actually ever saw a ghost, but unfortunately, she doesn't last long enough at any investigation to get that far.

Sometimes, I might invite one or two members to my own, private little investigations which, I hope, are of a more serious and structured nature, and sometimes I might invite a medium along. I know a couple and they are lovely, genuine people but the information they provide would probably not be considered serious enough for the scientific community and so therefore I do have to weigh up whether it is worth involving a medium on a case by case basis. Although there's no guarantee what they report via their 'spirit world guides' is true, it can be quite entertaining and if the stories they relate are historically possible, then more often than not, I try and find a place for them on the team.

"I'm not sure I'll ask any of the gang to come along in case we're wasting their time, given that you have your doubts and I suppose I'm not entirely convinced we're going to discover anything. Still it's worth a punt, but maybe just for us this time."

"Tell you what though," said Fran, who now seemed chirpier.

"What?"

"This Judy woman, who was doing the séance. A completely untrained amateur, right? Well, when I asked Susie if her mate had properly closed down her link or connection to the spirit world, assuming this might be the problem, she didn't convince me it had been done."

"I don't follow."

"Oh, get with it Unc! Bunch of vodka fuelled night-off nurses somehow open a link to the spirit world. Out pops a nasty, glass throwing, Robbie Williams hating spirit. They all wet their NHS starched panties. But séance mistress is an amateur, who doesn't close the link properly, so Mr. Bad-Spirit doesn't get sent on his way back home to spirit land like he should and ends up staying behind."

"No... Do you think that's possible then?"

"Why not?"

"No... And this spirit is latching on to young Jane?

"Could be."

"No... Honestly, your imagination. Mind you, she's a fine-looking young girl. If I was a spirit, I'd aim for someone who looks as good as her."

"I knew you'd have the hots for them. You're old enough to be their dad. Anyhow, moving away from your lechery, you obviously don't like my theory then?"

"Whatever gave you that idea? It's a masterpiece girl! Sometimes you amaze even me." Credit where credit's due, I did actually think that maybe the beloved niece had a sound theory going on there.

And so we headed homeward, debating when might be a convenient night for the both of us to go back with our equipment to do a formal analysis into the torments of Nurse Jane. And also, what to have for lunch.

~~~

After treating Frankie to a burger at the drive-thru, yes, I'm a master of generosity, I dropped her back to her flat, as she had to get ready for her afternoon/evening shift at the bar and restaurant she slaves at in town. I headed home and saw my wife Cynthia's car was in the drive. Such is our jolly marriage that my heart gave its normal sinking motion at the sight but I was strong and parked up alongside.

I went in and found her sat in the drawing room doing her needlework.

"Hello dearest," I offered with conviviality.

"You're back then," she muttered, stating the blasted obvious again, not even looking up from what she was doing.

"Yes, it is I, your darling husband in the flesh." She didn't comment on that bit.

"You left your mobile phone behind," she said. "It went off, so I answered it. That all right is it?"

"Of course, my little angel, I have no secrets from you. Anybody interesting?"

"If it's anything you're involved in Jeremiah, it's just plain odd, not interesting," she squawked with her usual love and warmth. "Some Vicar or Curate. Stephen Light, he said his name was. Don't tell me after all these years you've found religion?"

"Not that I'm aware of dearest, but I keep my eyes open. Did this chap say what he wanted?"

"He wanted to speak to you."

There she went again. Stating the bloody obvious.

"Yes, I had sort of assumed that given he'd rung my mobile phone. Having said that I really don't recall his name.

Did he state his reason for phoning?" Sometimes speaking to Cynthia is like extracting teeth.

"Said he'd seen your website and as he didn't live far from here, he wanted to come and interview you."

She thrust the scrap of paper with the details on in my direction along with my mobile itself and carried on with her latest needlework project. This was a sign of hers that my allotted time slot in her presence was at an end, so I left her worshipful majesty to it, after bowing first of course, and looking at the note as I went.

Well, what an odd thing. I wondered what on earth a clergyman would want with me. And to 'interview me' as well. Don't recall applying for a job in the Church of England, as I'm happily enough employed with my part time library job. Still, I got myself a restorative cuppa, sat down in the kitchen and gave the guy a call.

It turned out this Rev Stephen Light had come across my website by chance, having an interest himself in the paranormal and seeing that I was not far from him, he fancied a chat on the subject. However, I then started to fret that maybe he was a sceptic who was more interested in making his name as the man who goes down in history who proves there are no such things as ghosts. Whatever floats your boat, say I, and I wish him well if that is the case, but find it hard to believe he'll be successful. Having said that, he seemed a pleasant enough bloke to talk to and so the following day, after my 4-hour morning shift at the library, I agreed to drive across to the other side of town to the 'homeless centre' where he was helping out for a few hours that afternoon.

~ ~ ~

The following morning, I was woken at the positively silly hour of eight o'clock. Cynthia was violently shaking my shoulder shouting 'Jeremiah, Jeremiah' endlessly. Now, it was one of those nights I had chosen to sleep inside the house, rather than my garden den, although mine is a separate bedroom to my wife which suits us both admirably. I have the little box bedroom, as the decent ones, other than the master room, she keeps back for her guests. Regrettably she had not appeared at my door with a delicious early morning brew in one hand and the morning newspaper in the other, whilst gently, nay softly, calling my name between terms of love and endearment. The only thing she had in her hand was the cordless house phone which she was repeatedly thrusting at me like a serial murderer might lunge a ten-inch blade.

"Come on wake up you stupid old man, I'm not your secretary. Jeremiah, wake up, there's some emotional wreck on the line and I've no interest in dealing with your trail of destruction." Well, what a nerve.

"What? What? Who is it? It's the middle of the night damn it!"

"I don't know, just take the blasted thing. I was watching the breakfast news!" Oh, I'm sorry dearest, I thought, but I wasn't awake enough or brave enough for that matter, to utter my retort until she was long gone, having dropped the phone handset down on my head. I picked it up and tried to make sense of the situation.

"Hello?" I said down the receiver, somewhat feebly.

"Jerry! It's Jane. Oh my God, you've got to help me!"

Gracious! A damsel in distress so soon in the day and I wasn't even out of my jimjams.

"Jane, what is it!? What's the matter!?" By this time, I had sat up with a bolt and was awake on adrenalin.

"Jerry! There is definitely something in this place. I've never been so sure of anything in my life!"

The poor woman was hysterical.

"Calm down, deep breaths. Is Susie there with you?" I enquired; a bit shell shocked that Jane had called me. How I wished I was not still half asleep!

"No, she's on an early start over at the hospital," by this time sniffing heavily as if crying.

"Look, calm yourself down and tell me exactly what's happened." And she did and as far as I can remember, her description was something like this....

~~~

"I'd just had a soak in the bath and got back to my room. I went in and shut the door and started drying myself off. Then out of the corner of my eye I'm sure I saw some sort of black shadow move quickly across the room in the mirror reflection. I stopped and looked round but there was absolutely nothing there. I just assumed I was being irrational again so carried on drying off, while walking to the back of the door where my dressing gown hangs up. I took it off the door and threw it down on the bed, then went to my dressing table to get out the hair dryer. Jerry, I had my back to the bed for ten seconds and when I turned back round that dressing gown was back on the door hook!"

"But can you be sure you actually moved it? Maybe you just thought you did?" I suggested, trying my best to sound coherent in my sleepy state.

"No! I know I did, seconds before. And then I realised how utterly cold the room was. Like being in a fridge, in fact I had goose bumps all over me and it was just like that night at the séance. So I asked if anyone was in there and then I heard a man say 'Sarah', in a long drawn out, husky voice!"

"Sarah?" I exclaimed, "who's Sarah?!"

"How the hell do I know?!" She paused realising she'd been a bit short. "Sorry I don't mean to snap, I'm just so scared."

"You are sure the voice was inside the room? Did it say anything else?" I asked.

"Yes, it was definitely in the room, like a whisper coming from nowhere. It said it again, only with more urgency this time. I mean, who the hell is Sarah anyway? I screamed 'get out of here!' but I felt such a fool, I mean there was nothing there! Well, nothing I could see, just this voice! I ran out of there so damn fast the towel I had around me got hooked on the door handle but I was in such a rush I just kept running and I couldn't care less that I didn't have stitch on. Thankfully because I was screaming so much Shona came running out of her bedroom to see what was going on and she went back and got me a coat to put on."

"I'm not sure what to say Jane, it all sounds pretty horrid."

"Oh but you haven't heard the worst of it Jerry! When I was hooked on to the door handle I had to turn around and look into my room and what I saw will fill my nightmares 'til I die. I could just make out a misty figure! A figure of a stockily built fella with such an aged, disfigured face it makes me shiver just thinking about it. He was a giant of a man, and as I was stuck to that door, the figure slowly moved toward me and his eyes, so black and deep just staring at me!"

At this point poor Jane really started to cry but composed herself enough to finish her account. Which was just as well, because I wasn't much good at consoling the unfortunate girl.

"After that I don't know what happened really, as somehow, I'd got out to the lounge, with my towel still attached to the bloody bedroom door handle, screaming and freaking out like some mad woman, some mad naked woman at that. And like I said, that was when Shona came running out."

"Jane, you poor thing," I said in my most compassionate voice, trying hard to concentrate on her terrifying experience and not on mental images of her with no clothes on.

"What a story, I just don't know what to say to you. How are you doing now? Is there someone with you?"

"No, I don't want anyone to see me like this. I'm beginning to think they reckon I'm losing the plot and going doolally. The only person I can trust is Susie but she's on duty and won't be back for a few hours yet."

"Did you want me to come over there?"

"No, it's fine honestly. I think I just needed to get it off my chest. I just hope you'll be able to make some sense of all this for me Jerry. I can't carry on like I am."

And that's pretty much how we left it. I think, if anything, the poor lamb was a bit embarrassed about bothering me, but it was certainly an interesting update to the knowledge base on this case. Although, I had a growing sense of unease as to whether nurse Jane was going to be able to ride the course without experiencing a worrying degree of mental torture.

~ ~ ~

I went to meet the Rev Stephen Light as arranged, at the homeless centre in town which I believe he regularly helps out at. Whilst powering along in the old motor, musing as the V8 rumbled away under the bonnet, I thought what an appropriate name for his profession – 'Light', perhaps as in, making people 'see the light'. He'd have his work cut out if he tried that on me. Anyhow, I wandered in and found the guy. He was as friendly in life as indeed he was during our phone call, and my first impression was that he was not as I imagined him to be. I just assumed he would be a slight, intellectual looking sort of fellow, quietly spoken and devout. Of course, he may well be devout, but I wasn't expecting a grip like a vice when we shook hands, or that he would be a burly, muscular sort of chap with handsome square jawed face and the look of a hero detective from a 1950's crime novel. That is if he was wearing a tweed suit, rather than a dog collar.

And clothing leads me on to the other thing that struck me. Some of the homeless people looked better dressed than me. That is no criticism of them, I hasten to add, more that I realised how scruffy I'm getting these days. I had always thought I cut quite a dash in my brown bushman's hat and dark green wax jacket, but there you go.

We went off to a quiet corner and he made me a mug of welcome tea.

"It's good to meet you Jerry, I found your website very interesting," he said in a softly spoken, but still manly tone of voice.

"Thanks. Anything in particular?" I enquired, fishing for compliments.

"No, not really," he replied, as I listened, hopes dashed.

"I'll try harder," I retorted, trying not to sound indignant, "but my computer savviness isn't up there with Bill Gates and the like, although I do what I can."

"Sorry, didn't mean to offend. It's just that I was half thinking about the reason why I was even searching for paranormal information websites in the first place, so wasn't concentrating on how I word things."

"You haven't got spooks in the vestry by any chance?" I said, trying to make [Rev] light of things, excuse pun.

"Actually, I let down one of my parishioners and I feel pretty bad about it I can tell you," he replied somewhat downcast.

Poor chap; he seemed a decent bloke, so I could see in his face that these things hit him hard.

"You see, a young single mum came to me asking for help about some trouble she was having in her newly rented house."

"Tell me all," I asked encouragingly.

"It's just that, she'd put her little girl to bed each night and you know those video baby monitors?"

"Yes," I said, "I'm not a big follower of new fancy mod cons, but I have seen those things for sale. The ones where you can see as well as hear your child?"

"Exactly. Now, bear in mind this poor mum was single so she was on her own during the night, making it all the more unpleasant for her. Imagine if you will that she's downstairs alone, young child in bed, when she regularly starts to hear odd sounds over the baby monitor. She would look at the camera, or even go up to the room, but see or find nothing."

"What sort of sounds?" I enquired, slurping my tea.

"She struggled to describe it, although sometimes she said it sounded like sibilant whispering, even when the girl was asleep."

"We all talk in our sleep sometimes, maybe it was the child talking."

"She thought the same at first, but said it never sounded 'quite right'. But after a while it seemed to get worse, to the extent the child would wake and get upset. Saying that 'a dark figure' wouldn't let her sleep... Wouldn't leave her alone..."

"I'm guessing the mum didn't see anything on the video monitor?" I enquired.

"Oh well, that's just it. Eventually she did. One night, she looked at the monitor screen and she said that she too saw a dark figure, as plain as day, standing by the girl's cot-bed, which then began to bend over and look like it was reaching it's arms out toward the child. Like it was going to pick it up. Needless to say, she was terrified and went running upstairs to the child's room, and there was nothing there. So she took the kiddie into her own bedroom, and from that point onwards the child only ever slept with her. That's when she got in touch with the church and I was sent round."

"Bloody hell," I said, adding "sorry Stephen, I got a bit chilled by your narrative."

He chuckled in good humour.

"I guess you only really understand her horror and despair if you're a parent too. You got any little ones Jerry?"

"No, just a niece who I'm close to, my sister's girl. Although not so much of a girl now. She's almost like a daughter to me, but thankfully I was always able to give her back! Anyhow, what happened to this single mum?"

"I failed her, that's what. We're not big on exorcisms in the C of E, so maybe I didn't take things seriously enough. I went around there, said a few prayers, tried blessing the house, you know, followed the procedure book. But even after that, the noises and bangs in the night got so bad, she had to move out. Poor woman lost a lot of rent money, which she could ill afford. I went to see her, thought maybe I could help her on the money front, but they were both gone. No forwarding address, nothing. So I've no idea what happened to her. I do know there have been two short lived tenants since mind you."

He looked visibly annoyed with himself, so it was clear he was a curate of high working standards.

"I don't think you should be too hard on yourself, you did what you could. Sounds an interesting case mind you, would've been something I wouldn't have minded being involved in."

"If anything else like that comes up I'll be sure to call you. But it's all too infrequent, which is a shame because I would love to have more exposure to this kind of thing. I've always been interested. Ever since I was a child. Loved ghost stories since I was about eight years old."

"You're not one of these sceptics out to prove people like me are charlatans, are you?" I enquired suspiciously.

"Are you a charlatan Jerry?" he replied with a twinkle in his eye.

"No, I'm not. Tell me, are you allowed, given your profession, to be interested in the paranormal? Thought it would be frowned upon."

"I'm sure I don't need to tell you how many members of the clergy have recounted their own true ghost accounts through the decades, or indeed the small selection of published ghost photos which have been taken by Reverend This, That or the Other."

"True. And I'm impressed by your knowledge. Maybe I was just worried your Bishop would beat you round the head with his psalm book for even talking to the likes of me." I hoped my concern for my new-found friend would be appreciated.

"I don't think he'll be too worried. So long as he has a case of good Amontillado in his cellar, he's generally content."

Consequently, I took the opportunity to fill Stephen in on my latest case. Clearly, as a naturally caring man, he was most concerned to hear the plight of poor nurse Jane. Then his face lit up, as if he was struck by a light bulb moment.

"Look, it's a bit of a cheek given we've only just met, but when you do your vigil, any chance I could tag along? I'd stay out of your way, and wouldn't interfere or butt in. You could put me in charge of coffee and cheese sarnies."

It all sounded good to me and how could I refuse a curate with a catering talent. Oh, and a mutual interest of course. Not sure how well a man of the cloth would rub up with my feisty niece mind you, but I'd cross that bridge when I came to it.

~ ~ ~

The next evening, I had just finished my four-hour shift at the library and was driving home through town. It was a little after five thirty, so given the time of year it was pretty dark, but as I was waiting at the traffic lights, quite by chance I saw nurse Jane coming out of the high street wine shop; even more coincidental really, given I was literally just thinking about her. I gave a toot-ta-toot on the old car horn and caught her eye, so she came over. Conscious as I was the traffic lights were about to change, I offered her a ride back to her 'national health service staff accommodation'.

"Thanks for the lift, I've a feeling it's going to rain," she remarked in her mellifluous Irish tone.

"Stocking up on essentials I see," I replied, gesturing towards the bottle of wine she had clearly just purchased.

"Let's just say, I need a lot of this every night now, just to get off to sleep."

"Oh dear, things that bad?" She didn't reply, but I knew what was going through her mind. Clearly, my fears about Jane were justified, although drinking herself to sleep at night was a bit of a worry. "Funnily enough, I was going to give you a call later anyway to sort out the vigil tomorrow night."

"OK, that's great. I'm still up for it. As far as I'm concerned I need all the help I can get right now."

We sorted out the details for the following evening; times, who was coming, etc, and that Jane could go off with her friend Judy to a nearby room should things with us get too much for her. Other than that, small talk was a struggle. She was clearly troubled and her mind was elsewhere. I don't think it was me, but of course she may well have just been uncomfortable in my company, a bit like my wife. Or being a passenger in my car, again, a bit like my wife...

Anyhow, we pulled up outside her residential block and I offered to walk in with her as it was dark. It gave me some reassurance to my pride that she was very keen for me to walk with her, given the stifled atmosphere in the car. Perhaps I wasn't quite the ogre I was worried she saw me as.

"You know Jerry; my stomach turns somersaults as soon as I see this building now."

"You've had some bizarre occurrences here," I said, trying to comfort. "It's not really very surprising you'd be uneasy; anyone else would too in the circumstances. It'll sort itself out, I'm sure." Not that I completely believed what I'd said.

"Maybe I didn't see that old lady on the way to work. And maybe there was just some pervert in my room the other morning. When I think I'm trying to put all this down to visitations from some sort of spirit world, perhaps I'm just postponing the inevitable."

"The inevitable?" I asked, not being quite on her thought process.

"The mental hospital. Padded cells and all that."

"Look, let's just see what we can record tomorrow night and take it from there. Come on; let's get you inside, in case it does rain."

We walked towards the entry door, along the poorly illuminated pathway. Now, despite what my wife says, I myself, am not ready for a padded cell and straightjacket, but as we walked along that path, my attention was drawn to some rather disturbing sounds of movement within the shrubs and bushes lining the pathway on our right. Clearly, I wasn't the only one who had noticed this because Jane had grabbed my left arm and was in a state of near terror, almost dropping her bottle of vino. Now, what was I to do? Charge into the bushes and see if it was our unwelcome spectre? Or rush into the building to get Jane inside the safety of her home and her friends?

As it was, the decision was made for me as Jane threw her wine bottle towards the shrubby area where the sound was emanating from. There immediately followed someone saying 'Ow!' very loudly.

Well now. Being a slight coward, I had taken comfort from the fact that I don't believe ghosts and spectres often say 'ouch', 'ow' or 'bother that hurt' when hit with bottles of wine. This gave me the strength to head on into the bushes and confront whatever was there.

"Who's there!?" I shouted, doing a good job I thought, of sounding quite manly. I pulled back a substantial branch, only to reveal three pimply teenage boys armed with digital cameras. The look of fear on their faces when they saw me was hilarious, as they immediately hightailed it off at a pace I thought impossible for anyone other than a trained athlete on performance enhancing drugs.

"Kids! Can you believe it!? What's that all about?" I exclaimed in complete bewilderment as I stood hanging on to the shrubs trying to see where they went, which was an impossibility given the darkness.

"Ha, they've been here loads," retorted Jane calmly. "Little pervs! Funny really, or pathetic, not sure which."

I was clearly looking a bit slow on the uptake.

"Come on Jerry, think about it!" chuckled Jane. "It's like that film from years ago, where the boys hang around outside the nurse's home hoping to catch a glimpse of one in her underwear at the window."

"Oh I see. Would've thought using the internet would be quicker," I replied, bemused by modern youth.

"There's nothing like the thrill of the real thing I guess. I think one of these days I'm going to walk back and forth in front of my bedroom window, completely starkers, just for their entertainment. And I bet they wouldn't know what to do!"

This isn't the first time Jane has referred to herself being naked in my company and it's quite a lot for my feeble, weak mind to cope with. She's a very good looking and shapely woman, and I worry these mental images aren't helping me focus...

That said, it was nice to see Jane smile. I had the feeling she hadn't done too much of that lately. So it was all the more upsetting to see her face completely drop as she turned her head towards the building. There I could see the cause of her sudden change of expression and I cannot deny, it had a similar effect on me. For looming midway on the path, between Jane and the entrance door, was the immense form of the most gargantuan, fearsome 'man' it has ever been my misfortune to see. The figure must have been a good seven feet tall, but I cannot say that was with its feet on the ground, because it did not appear to have any form below its knees! Suddenly it opened its arms out to Jane and spoke, in a singularly unnerving, deep, hoarse voice.

"Sarah, my love, why do you hide from me so?"

Shivers of fear were pulsing down my spine so it took me a second or so to ponder the question 'who in bloody hells name was Sarah?'

I looked towards Jane, who was noticeably shaking and breathing extremely fast with terror.

"I'm...I'm not...I'm not Sarah!" she stammered.

This response seemed to anger the spirit, as he flung his arms downwards in a fury, the draught of which was felt by myself even from where I was, sending me reeling backwards against the shrubbery. Then with outstretched fist he spoke again to her.

"Don't toy with me! Do you not recognise your own husband? I have come back for you my love, so we may be together... for always!"

"But my name is not Sarah!" wailed Jane, tears rolling down her cheeks, her body shaking from head to foot.

The already massive form of the spectre almost seemed to increase still further with the anger at Jane's responses, and it appeared to position itself in such a way as if it was about to attack her.

"Don't lie to me!" it bellowed, in its ghastly gravelly voice, now even louder.

I simply didn't know what to do. I am no cage fighter with the wherewithal to take on something like this, but here was poor Jane in trouble, I needed to do something. But what?

I saw the wine bottle lying in the dirt near my feet, and it was all I could think of for a weapon. Looking back, I appreciate it was probably useless but I needed something for courage. By that I mean I held it, as opposed to drank it...

I grabbed the bottle, held it high above my head and ran forward aiming straight for the apparition. I recall screaming something as I went but I can't remember what. It may have sounded a little like a Red Indian battle cry perhaps. However, although I had a good aim, I just seemed to run across the path where the spectre was, to the lawn the other side of it, whereupon I simply fell over. I must have run through the phantom, but then, lying face down in the grass as I was, I looked over my shoulder to see the towering figure had gone. It was then I'd realised the exterior lighting of the path was now back to full illumination, for I hadn't noticed how dimly lit and faded it was when the spirit was present. But there was Jane. On the path. On her knees. Head in her hands, sobbing. I picked myself up and joined her.

"Thank God you were with me Jerry," she said through tears.

"Let's get you inside," I said. I didn't like to admit it, given what a state *she* was in, but I was pretty shaken up too and my own pounding heartbeat seemed to be trying to break out of my chest. "We've got a bottle of wine here, I suggest we get in... and get it open." Yes, I know I was driving, so no, I didn't have much of it. But my goodness, didn't I quickly down the glass I did have.

~ ~ ~

The following morning, Frankie and I were in my kitchen with a constitutional coffee and cigarette. I could tell she was concerned for me after the unpleasantness of the night before, because she offered up one of her ciggies for once. Normally she cadges them off me.

"Stephen will be here soon, I can't wait for you to meet him," I said, stubbing out the nicotine tube.

"I'm not looking forward to it. What possessed you to bring in a bloody vicar to the team? You and I were the team. Crazy uncle, hot niece. Sorted. Anyhow, why are you so excited about it anyway?" she responded suspiciously.

"Because you're like chalk and cheese, so I'm wondering who will throw the first punch." I had amused myself with this statement and was chuckling away while she just looked at me stony faced.

"He's hardly likely to punch me, is he? I can see the papers now, 'local curate thumps innocent woman'."

"You're not that innocent," I replied derisively.

"Look, me and the church don't get on, all right? I can tell already I won't like him."

"How do you even know that? The last time you were in a church was at your christening. You were only a baby."

"Yeah, and I cried all through that too didn't I?"

The little madam had a point and although I wanted to argue the matter, the doorbell rang, so I went off to let the poor maligned curate in.

I returned to the kitchen a minute later with Stephen.

"Right, introductions. This is my niece, Francesca, or Frankie, or Fran, whichever you can be bothered with. Frankie, may I present the Rev Stephen Light."

To my surprise Frankie just stared at him open mouthed. I couldn't really ever remember her lost for words like this, and it took me rather by surprise. Thankfully Stephen chipped in.

"Nice to meet you. May I call you Frankie?" and he offered up his hand.

"Umm, yeah, course," came my niece's lame response.

"Goodness Fran, you're not normally this reticent." I turned back to Stephen, "normally you can't shut her up."

Fran just glared at me then looked back at Stephen.

"I didn't think good looking vicars were allowed?" she enthused.

"Umm they're not. I nearly didn't get the job for that very reason," answered Stephen, nervously attempting humour.

"What!? Seriously?" Fran replied.

"No, not seriously," said Stephen, smiling.

I laughed. Fran just gave a nod. Now you can never tell with her if that response was a good thing. Either she had a secret respect now for our new curate friend because he had a bit of spunk in him. Or she would now hold a grudge against him forever and would be looking for every opportunity to avenge herself. Anyhow, not my problem, we had the matter of Jane and her terrifying ghost to deal with. The vigil was that evening, so we had things to prepare. Having already told Frankie about the events of the previous night, I needed to give Stephen all the details, not leaving out any of the bits which showed how extremely brave I had been. Heroic even. Clearly more coffee and cigarettes were called for, and fast. Frankie had now moved onto my ciggies as per the norm. Evidently her compassion for me only stretched to the one from her own packet.

"It's odd this ghost has got it into his head, albeit dead head, that your nurse friend is his wife Sarah," Stephen mused.

"I can only assume Jane must look like this Sarah. Although from where in history this woman and her scary husband come from, is anyone's guess," I retorted.

"Well," said Fran, "there was nothing on that land before the hospital and ancillary buildings were put there. So, this guy is clearly some random spirit those silly bitches pulled through when they did their stupid séance."

"As you can see Stephen, my Fran is renowned for her caring, charitable nature."

"I can see I'm going to have to watch myself," replied Stephen with a cheeky grin.

"You better believe it," responded Fran, without any grin and giving him a hard stare. I began to think she was holding a grudge after all.

"From what you were saying, that spirit was wearing some interesting clothing. Do you think that tells us anything?" Stephen asked.

"I don't know. He was certainly built like a brick outhouse that's for sure. He had a dark cap on, waistcoat, horrible long apron, a nasty leather like apron I think, but it's hard to tell given he was hovering a foot up in the air."

Just as I said this, all three of us jumped out of our skin, as unbeknown to any of us, my wife Cynthia had silently appeared in the kitchen with us. I'll swear that woman is some kind of secret ninja, or that's what I thought as she chipped in her observation.

"Obviously you're talking about some kind of blacksmith or the like," she snorted, "although I can't imagine it's any kind of apparition or spirit. The only kind of spirits around here are the ones you consume Jeremiah to such an extent, you think you can see things like this."

And with that, off she flounced, as silently as when she had entered.

"Thank you, my love," I called after her, "as helpful and charming as ever." I then lowered my vocals to add "you old bag" to the sentence, to which Fran and I did a 'high five'. Poor Stephen just looked at us, wide eyed.

"You'll understand one day," I told him.

"Thing is, even if Auntie Cynthia is right and this ghost was a blacksmith from some distant history, how does this help us?" Fran asked.

"It doesn't," I replied, "it just shows us you were right about how an amateur séance can throw any old spirit out in to the world and those girls ended up with an extra, unwelcome guest at their party. And not necessarily a nice one."

~ ~ ~

I thought it would be a good idea to let Stephen have a look at some of the gadgets we take on our ghost hunts and all of this is down in my garden den, so I took the three of us off there. That way, my secret ninja wife can't creep up on us again as well. As you've probably gathered my wife isn't remotely keen on keeping my company and I am a happier man when I'm out of range of her nagging, abuse and generally disparaging observations of my person.

I have no doubt the feeling has become mutual over the years so when she's at home you will find her inside the house, at which point, you will no doubt find me in my garden den. It is my little haven of peace and tranquility away from her shrill, venomous tongue. Don't get me wrong, it is also my most impressive paranormal research centre of both worth and note, in my eyes anyway, probably no one else's mind you. The best for yards around is my usual joke, which no one else finds funny either. I might add though, it's not bad considering it's a just second hand, twelve foot by ten wooden summer house I bought off of eBay a few years ago. It's quite snug in there really, a real centre of operations. Maps pinned to the walls with little flags to denote locations I've investigated, dubious paranormal photos which basically means night time pictures with little dots of light in which are inconclusive but make me feel like I know what I'm doing. Then there's all my folders with procedures and test results – I can be quite organised you know, well, sometimes when I've got nothing else on and it's raining outside. And it's quite cosy too, with the old olive-green curtains I picked up at a jumble sale and there's even a power line from the house, enough for a lamp and my plug-in oil-filled radiator. I've put a big old table in the middle (covered in my notes and specialist reference books) and some drawers and things at the side full of crap, sorry, valuable research papers. Then one day some time ago I picked up a few old Windsor chairs which were going to be trashed by some pub renovators in town, so for the price of a couple of four-packs of low-brow lager I took them off their hands.

By now my old den is getting a bit tight on space but there's just room for the best bit. I managed to squeeze in an extremely comfortable camp bed in the corner complete with super snug three-inch mattress. A winters night, glass of whisky or few to aid my bodily heating system, electric radiator on, sleeping bag pulled up to the chest and it doesn't matter if it's minus one Celsius outside, there'll be more warmth there than in the vicinity of my ice-cold wife Cynthia. I don't sleep there every night, I'm not completely uncivilised, that is to say my wife and I can bear being in the same house now and then. Just not too often and not too close and not normally in the same room.

"Wow Jerry, this is absolutely amazing!" exclaimed Stephen. "It's like a military operations room."

"Thanks Stephen, all positive feedback gratefully received," I beamed, "especially as I'm not used to it."

"Hey, don't forget I helped you get a lot of this together," protested Fran.

"'Tis true Stephen, I cannot deny I've always been ably assisted by my lovely niece."

"Well I think it's brilliant," he added, which helped cheer me up no end.

"I've got some of the gear over in these cupboards Stephen. Here you go, take a look as you might want to get a feel for some of this stuff," and with this I opened various cabinet doors.

His eyes widened as he took in my little collection of digital cameras, video cameras, EMF detectors, batteries, voice recorders, walkie-talkies, motion detectors, that sort of thing.

"And some good old-fashioned bits here Stephen; compass, candles, matches, torches, notebooks, talcum powder. Even some dowsing rods! Could never get the hang of those mind you. Fran tried once, nearly poked her eye out."

"I can't believe you have all this stuff out here Jerry. And you don't even lock the cupboards!" Stephen exclaimed in shock.

"What you will eventually appreciate is the fact I have one of the best security features in the known world. A very fierce, singularly unpleasant guard dog. And her name is Cynthia," I replied.

"Unc! You're a bad man. Remember, that's a vicar you're talking to," said Frankie, feigning disapproval, although I knew she agreed.

"Yes, beloved niece, but he's young, and he'll have to start getting used to dealing with demons someday. And they don't come much more demonic than my wife..."

~ ~ ~

As Fran and I drove up to the nurse's accommodation building on the evening of our vigil I noticed Stephen had already arrived and was patiently waiting outside. No doubt he'd been looking heavenward, checking in with his guvnor and saying a quick one like the good man he is. Fran and I, like the bad people we are, simultaneously threw our fag butts out of the car windows as we pulled into the parking space.

"Hi guys," said Stephen, full of cheer and opening Fran's car door, for which he received nothing more than a sulky grunt of thanks from my stroppy niece.

"So you all set for your first investigation tonight?" I asked him.

"You bet. And just to be on the safe side, I've armed myself with my mobile, and a bible."

I looked at him quizzically, which he didn't pick up on, because to be honest I hadn't a clue what he meant by that.

"Ok, well, that's nice," I replied, not sure what I was supposed to say. Thankfully faithful Fran broke in and brought us back to the matter in hand.

"Unc, is this where you saw the apparition?"

"No, by these bushes here," I corrected, gesturing to where Jane and I had been when the menacing blacksmith, or whatever he was, had suddenly appeared to us.

"It was a good thing you were with her Jerry," said Stephen, "I should imagine at night time, this is quite a quiet corner to have ghosts with attitude jumping out on you."

"I can't deny it will certainly go down as one of my brown pants moments, I will happily admit to that. Anyway, let's get the gear and go upstairs to set up." But no sooner had I said this, Susie, the nurse who contacted me in the first place, came running out of the building in a flap.

"Ah Jerry, thank goodness you're here!"

"What's wrong?" I asked, completely taken aback.

"It's Jane. She's got herself in a right state and now she's going!" panicked Susie.

"Oh bloody hell! But I need her as bait." Susie looked at me wide eyed.

"That is to say, we'll need her help," I corrected, back tracking my story.

"You won't be able to stop her, she's too upset. I think something else has happened; I don't know... Seriously, I think she's lost it!"

After Susie made this exclamation, I turned to Fran, then I turned to Stephen, then I turned back to Susie. No one said anything intelligent during all this frantic head turning. Therefore, in frustration, I demanded we all go and find out what the hell had gone wrong.

~ ~ ~

Jane had just finished packing a second suitcase and was smoking a cigarette, busying herself from one side of her room to the next.

"I'm sorry Jerry, but I've got a train to catch in less than a quarter of an hour, so my taxi will be here any moment!" stated Jane in a very frank and to the point manner. I hadn't ever seen her so forthright.

"Can I assume you saw this spirit again?" I asked.

"Yep, you betcha," she responded, almost defiantly. "On my way to the hospital early this morning. Thankfully, an empty ambulance went past and I knew the crew, who let me ride in with them." She started to look around for somewhere to put her spent cigarette.

"Look at me!" she shouted, her eyes filling with tears. "Look what I've become! I mean, I haven't smoked for years! But I've got to get out of here. Its emergency leave for two weeks. And when I come back, it'll be with short brown hair and a whole new wardrobe. Anything! Anything to try and confuse this monster so he doesn't think I'm this bloody Sarah girl!" I tried to reassure but wasn't sure what to say. My biggest concern was that the spirit may follow her, and then she'd be without the support of her friends or us. And of course, if the spirit went with her, there was little point in the three of us spending the night in her bedroom. I really needed Jane to stay.

"You know Jane; this is clearly just a case of mistaken identity. Some distraught spirit, perhaps stuck in purgatory or whatever there is after death we humans don't understand, suddenly pulled back to this world by that séance, decades after his passing and who immediately starts searching for his loved one. By some coincidence, you happen to look like her."

"And you've experience dealing with confused ghosts, have you?" asked Jane, not without a certain degree of aggression.

"Not as such, but unless we try to communicate with him, make it understand, then how can we sort this out? That's why it would really help if you stayed Jane." I did my best 'begging Labrador puppy' face.

"No chance. Do what you like in here, but you won't be doing it with me."

And with that, she grabbed her two suitcases and was away. She didn't even say goodbye to her friends Susie and Judy, who were quietly sitting in the corner of Jane's bedroom, watching the discussion but keeping out of it.

"This is all my fault, messing about with that séance," said Judy, after a minute of us all being in steely silence.

"What's done is done," muttered Susie. To say the mood had become pretty low was an understatement.

I wasn't sure now, what to do... Should we pack up or hang around just to see what we found? I turned to Frankie and Stephen for inspiration.

"Thoughts guys?" I asked. Fran nonchalantly shrugged her shoulders, at which point Stephen just said, "don't look at me, I'm the newbie. I just brought the sandwiches, remember?"

A fat lot of good our trainee vicar was.

"OK, this is what we're going to do. We're here, so we're doing the investigation. If the phantom menace shows itself we'll try and communicate. Reason with it. Let him know he's got himself in the wrong time dimension."

"He didn't get himself in the wrong time dimension, they pulled him in to it with their stupid séance," bitched Fran, waving a desultory gesture towards Judy and Susie, who both sheepishly lowered their heads.

"Frankie, wind your neck in," I rebuked. Suddenly Susie had a look of panic.

"You don't think this thing is going to start on the rest of us now that Jane has gone!?" she cried.

"I should've thought it would keep on looking for Sarah. Sorry, I mean Jane," I replied. "What a shame no one here looks like Jane so that we could try and draw him to us this evening."

"It's shame we don't have a blonde wig with us," said Stephen casually.

"My word, Stephen, you may just have redeemed yourself!" I exclaimed, an idea bursting in my brain.

"Redeemed myself for what?" he said, looking wounded.

"For not being much use so far," was my hurtful putdown. "Yes, yes, yes! Where can we get a blonde wig, at this time of night, at such short notice!?"

"I know!" piped up Judy with a triumphant look. "There's an old woman on one of the wards I get on really well with. She has one, a really realistic jobbie. She'll lend it to me, I'm sure!"

"Brilliant Judy, head off to wig ward and retrieve!" I shouted, excited and encouraged by my own brilliance.

"So... someone wears this wig, to look like Jane, to act as bait?" asked my ever-bright niece.

"Absolutely."

"And that someone is, who?" Fran asked, taking a deep breath and folding her arms defensively.

"Well, it needs to be someone I can trust," I gushed. "Someone young, someone as pretty as Jane, someone who could make wearing a blonde wig look sensational. And to be honest, that someone ain't Stephen."

"You are so full of…"

"That's enough Fran. Your mother didn't bring you up to use swear words in quite so many of your sentences."

~ ~ ~

Two hours later and we're nearly ready for 'lock down'. Stephen and I had set up a few bits of equipment in the vain hope we might just get some bit of sound or visual activity recorded. It was good to know that Stephen is technically minded. Meanwhile Fran was sat at Jane's dressing table, as Susie and Judy had been combing and styling the wig, which was now in situ on Fran's disgruntled head.

"I look a proper idiot," moaned my niece.

"I think it suits you," replied Judy innocently, only realising the danger of her comment when Fran shot her a look that could kill.

"It's quite good quality actually and now we've combed it through like Jane has her hair, you look a lot like her," added Susie, choosing to ignore Fran's grunt.

Shortly afterwards Judy and Susie, gladly no doubt, left us to it and our little team of three were alone.

"I'm starting to get an uneasy feeling about all this Jerry," admitted Stephen, who was beginning to look a trifle unnerved.

"Come on, man up Stephen," I chastised, "a big, burly man of God like you being afraid of a little ghost. Assuming of course, it even shows up tonight."

"From what you were saying, it isn't that little," he whinged.

I decided I'd better reign in the rebellious chit-chat. "Granted, we have a disorientated ghost with a bad attitude on our hands, so there's no guarantee this will be easy. But negotiation team, that's the key! Talk to it, reason with it and politely tell it to move on."

I was therefore a little disappointed, on seeing Fran and Stephen's disbelieving faces.

"Uncle dear. Do you remember that poltergeist we investigated down in Shorefield Street? I seem to recall you saying something similar then."

Oh dear, I knew what was coming.

"And then Uncle dear, you will no doubt recall me ending up with three stitches to the back of my head."

"Here we go again, this old chestnut. Anyway, I told you to duck," I replied, indignantly.

"Yes, about one nanosecond before impact!"

At this point Stephen obviously decided to put his good trainee vicar diplomatic service hat on.

"Time out guys. Surely, we need to start? I mean, this spirit thing could turn up at any moment and none of us will be ready. Remember, this is my first time so I've not a clue what I should be doing."

Suitably chastised, I decided to get my head back to operations. Between us we got the equipment turned on, the main light turned off but with a small table lamp by Fran left on. She was sitting at the dressing table holding a brush pretending to apply makeup. Stephen and I had our waiting positions in the wardrobe. Luckily it had Louvre doors, so we could just see through the gaps.

"This could be seen as a bit dodgy, couldn't it? Being in a wardrobe with a member of the clergy."

"Watch where you're poking that coat hanger please Jerry," replied Stephen, who seemed to be having some difficulty fitting his burly body in our tiny compartment.

"Just be grateful it's only a coat hanger," I joked. "There really isn't a lot of room in here is there? I wouldn't be at all surprised if I get cramp, standing like this. Still, Jane's clothes do smell nice."

"Yes they do," agreed Stephen, "we must ask her what fabric conditioner she uses."

"Oh yes," I concurred. By this point however, there was the sound of Fran banging something down on the dressing table top.

"I'm sorry, but I thought that while I'm out here on my own, you know, in a vulnerable and dangerous situation, there were two strong, grown men in the wardrobe, ready to protect me if there's any issue. Instead it seems, there are two aging washerwomen in there, which is not very reassuring."

Stephen and I remained quiet for a moment before I had to defend ourselves.

"If a man can't admire the softness of a lady's fabrics, what's the world coming to?" I snorted, indignantly.

Stephen put on his diplomatic hat again and changed the subject.

"Will there be any signs do you think, before this entity shows itself?"

I was impressed by the intelligence of his question.

"Well Stephen, there may indeed be some indications, assuming he doesn't just appear. Rely on your senses. Is there a change in temperature? Is there a noticeable smell? An unusual sound perhaps? Does something move?" I suggested.

"Or maybe if I start to levitate six feet in the air, that's another good sign!" Francesca chuckled.

Sometimes my niece just doesn't take our work seriously.

~ ~ ~

Over two hours had passed and I wasn't sure how much longer my aged legs could cope with this standing up. The occasional twang of developing cramp was a constant threat as well, but I did my best to wiggle each foot as quietly as possible. I was sleepy too, barely able to keep my eyes open in fact, as the sweet smells of Jane's clothing wafted around my nostrils. I hadn't heard much at all from Stephen, on my left in the wardrobe. I could hear him breathing so I knew he wasn't dead, which is always handy, but I couldn't see him with all the jackets and blouses hanging up between us and of course, the darkness. As for my Fran, I made the occasional glance through the Louvre doors and she seemed to be struggling to maintain her 'pretending to put on makeup' ruse and I noticed she was making some quiet, but grumpy mutterings. I'm sure I heard her whisper something about, "and now for the thirty-fifth coat of eye-liner" but I could be mistaken. Though I suppose two hours of picking up and putting down lipsticks and the like, all for show, was beginning to rile her. She never was the most patient puppy in a basket.

And so the time went on. I was practically doing a Scottish jig in the wardrobe to keep the blood flowing, Stephen was completely motionless, probably asleep for all I knew and Fran in boredom, was making patterns in a pot of foundation. By this point to my shame, I had started to close my eyes and despite being upright apart from leaning against the back of the wardrobe, I was drifting off to sleep. That is until I suddenly realised I eventually heard Fran saying something in a loud, urgent manner.

"Crikey, isn't it cold in here now...? In fact, somewhat icy I think...! ICY!!"

I shook my head as if it would bring some life back in my brain, whilst I swiftly moved my eyes to the gaps in the door, and from hearing movement from Stephen I assumed he was doing the same his side.

At first when I started to watch, I didn't see anything other than Fran, sat upright and alert, at the dressing table in the subtle illumination of the small table lamp. Poor thing was clearly unnerved as she stared intently at her mirror, trying to see something behind her and occasionally trying to surreptitiously look over her shoulder. As a caring Uncle, I longed to call out to reassure her there was nothing there, but I couldn't risk jeopardising our vigil. I began to think this was a false alarm anyway.

That was until a minute later, when all of a sudden, I began to feel uneasy. My skin started to tingle, which I suppose may have been my bodily hair standing on end, though at first, I couldn't comprehend as to why. Then when I refocused my eyes through the door gaps, my unease was justified as I slowly began to see a dark, hazy human outline start to materialise somewhere between where Fran sat and our wardrobe hiding place! I won't deny I was afraid, although probably all the more so because it was down to me that my beloved niece was in such an exposed position. Therefore, I remained glued to one of the gaps within the louvre door as before my very eyes, this sinister, misty form had turned into a very solid and real looking figure of a man. No, a giant of a man. And a none too friendly looking one at that, which had started to slowly move toward my Fran...

"Sarah, my love. I have come back for you," it whispered in a deep, menacing tone.

At hearing his awful, unearthly drawl, Fran spun around on her stool and confronted the gargantuan spectre before her. Her eyes widened in fear and disbelief as she took in the giant, unsightly form towering in front of her. However, with a deep intake of breath she managed to blurt out a defiant, albeit untactful reply.

"Look mate, sorry and all that, but I just ain't the girl you're looking for."

There was a long, uncomfortable pause until eventually there was a reply with its formidable boom.

"Sarah, why do you lie to me? What is the meaning of this nonsense!?"

There was a definite increase in agitation coming from our other world visitor and I should really have gone to Fran's aid, but I felt rigid with terror and none of my limbs would move. And I suppose Stephen didn't move either because he was no doubt waiting for instruction from me. Or God, maybe.

"My name is not Jane! You are dead and shouldn't be here! Go back to where you came from!" she ranted.

I had to admire Frankie's bravery. Maybe it's because she has youth on her side, but to shout such a thing at a very angry spirit, took courage. And stupidity. Unfortunately though, if she was expecting our foe to calmly clear off, thanking her for her time and apologising for the inconvenience, she was very much mistaken. Her bitter retort, to a ghost which no doubt in life was probably a bit of a bully, expecting a woman to remain in her place, seemed to antagonise it somewhat and I can only describe the noise it made as being like a male lion's roar multiplied by ten. This seemed to make the whole room shake and for all I knew the whole building. In turn, it seemed to wake me out of my trance enough to realise I had the most incredible cramp in my right foot, which in turn made me steady myself on my left foot because of the pain, which in turn meant I then lost my balance and fell out through the wardrobe door landing in a pathetic heap on the floor. The spectre spun around and looked at me with his extremely ugly, corpse like face. Fran peered around him, staring at me with a surprised, querying look on *her* face. And then Stephen popped *his* face out of the wardrobe and calmly asked, "Shall I come out now too?"

~ ~ ~

"Ow! Bloody cramp!" I exclaimed, as if to explain my sudden arrival, shaking my right leg in the air prior to realising the need to stand up quickly before I made myself look anymore ridiculous.

"Surprise attack Unc, nice one!" Fran remarked facetiously.

"What means this!" bellowed the spectre, and as it did so, the room seemed to vibrate, and the lamp flickered pathetically, as if the apparition was sucking its electrical energy.

I remembered my original plan of trying to reason with the thing so I defiantly pulled myself up to my straightest, fullest height, which isn't that high unfortunately and began my negotiations.

"Good day er, sir. Jeremiah Thorne, at your service. I would like to explain the reason for us being here..." Unfortunately, our hostile spirit was not in the least bit interested in having a conversation with me, moving his massive form directly in front of Stephen and myself with a most threatening demeanour.

"You will die Jeremiah Thorne, and so will your clergyman," came his whispering, menacing reply. Bit unsporting, I thought, not allowing me time to finish my sentence and explain the situation to him. That being he was dead, he needed to clear off. Although looking back, I do wonder how well he would have responded to this information, given that Frankie had already told him and it wasn't well received then. The other thing I thought was unsporting, was that at this point our spirit-world foe, simply with a forward moving gesture of his wide arms and without even touching Stephen and I, managed to push us through the air backwards at surprising velocity. We both flew hard back against each of the louvre doors of the wardrobe we'd previously been hiding behind, with enough force that the thin strips of wood snapped with the pressure of impact.

I was a bit shell shocked for a few seconds, not really registering anything, although I have a faint recollection of Frankie calling out asking if we were all right. Stephen, I think, tried to be angry. Or angry for a cleric, I suppose is another way of looking at it.

"Hey, you, ghost man or whatever you are, that's enough now!" shouted Stephen, with great authority. However, it clearly made no difference because then various objects from around Jane's bedroom started to move into the air and fly in the direction of Stephen and me with such force we automatically put our arms up to shield our faces. In this position it was almost impossible to try and reason with the angry spectre because every time I tried to speak, some small hard object came flying towards my face. I just managed to see Fran try and hit the ghost with the dressing table stool but as she did so it just went straight through his body, whereupon it left her hands and joined everything else flying through the air, coming in our direction. To say the least, my plan was a disaster, I'd completely underestimated the power of our opponent and we were very much in a complete pickle.

It was not the easiest environment to try and think up a solution, as my concentration is not aided by hard objects flying at me, not least the stool Fran had just been sat on which really hurt my arms, as I was using them to protect my head. Thankfully, Jane's room was only so big and as such, there wasn't anything left for our nasty wraith to send in our direction in his act of war. I glanced across at Stephen who seemed to be frantically looking through his Bible, muttering that there must be a passage somewhere which he could recite to help our situation. I tutted in frustration, thinking this was a time for action, not a time for sitting down and having a nice read. Poor frightened Fran also seemed devoid of solutions, having moved herself back against the wall by the dressing table, staring intently at the spectre, blonde wig all skew-whiff.

Could I open a line of communication with the spirit? Could I, through rational discussion, calm this lost soul and reason with it? Could I resolve this paranormal crisis with courage of speech and masterful diplomacy? The room seemed calmer as the giant spectre just stood before me and Stephen, watching us, as if he was calculating his next move. I needed to reduce the intimidation, so despite shaking like a leaf, I stood up to face him eye to eye. The slight flaw in my plan was twofold. Firstly, I am not a big man, so my eye level turned out to be his lower chest level. Secondly, his deformed corpselike face was so unpleasant to look at, I was hardly able to speak, but I gave it my best shot nonetheless.

"Look. There is no need for this animosity. Talk to us and maybe we can help you," I pleaded. His head turned to one side quizzically before he replied with his most menacing but quiet tone.

"I need not your help, little man. And you will be gone away from my Sarah."

If there's one thing worse than a ghost, it's a confused one, and I was consumed with exasperation.

"But this isn't Sarah! Sarah is not here! Sarah has never been here and in fact, she's probably as dead as you are." I don't know where the bravery came from for this tirade of mine, but I was about to add more when our unsightly phantom turned and faced my Fran. She in response, looked very uneasy and my fear of what he might do quickly quieted my previous outburst.

In an almost pleading, questioning and pathetic voice he simply said, "Sarah?"

There was a moments' silence before Fran replied, "Sorry mate, no Sarah's around here." With that, she slowly pulled off the blonde wig and tossed it down on the floor. All went silent again and the tension in the air was thick. Our spectre was motionless, as if deep in thought. I looked to my side and Stephen looked back at me, wide eyed, with a confused look on his face. I looked to Fran, who just shrugged her shoulders. Had the truth finally sunk in to our troubled soul? Would he realise his error and finally clear off? It seemed the answer to that question was no, which was disappointing given the few moments of calm we'd been enjoying had lulled us into a false sense of security. Our angry ghost spun around on his all but invisible boots and faced me. A look of rage seemed to fill his distorted features and he simply muttered my name, as if he'd decided I was responsible for all his current woes. And with that, his right clenched fist seemed to move in my direction. As before, it didn't make physical contact with me, but some kind of powerful, invisible force pushed me with such power I was sent backwards again, and this time right through the louvre doors! Smashed wood seemed to go everywhere as I crashed to the wardrobe floor in a heap. I was dazed for a few seconds, then I noticed the spectral monster was moving slowly towards me. I heard Fran scream "Uncle!" from behind him, as if she was as lost as to know what to do as I was. I did not know what his intentions were but I didn't really want to find out either. The whole room seemed to run in slow motion and I was bereft of any cunning plan to sort out our predicament.

To my left, Stephen had still been sat on the floor, fingering the pages of his Bible. However, I then became aware he sat himself up abruptly.

"Oh, to hell with it! Enough is enough!" he exclaimed, at which point he threw his Bible squarely in the face of our apparition. The second his Bible was in the air I thought, 'there's no point in doing that! It will just pass through him'. But do you know what? It didn't... I was utterly amazed. That Bible actually hit the spectre right between its vacant dark eyes, making it stop in its tracks. It seemed almost as shocked and surprised as the rest of us, while the Bible itself landed on the floor at his feet. All was silent and all was still, nothing moved and we all just watched, unable to know what to do. I don't know how long it was, probably just a few seconds but it felt like a much greater time elapsed. However, our attention was drawn to a dark smoke which bizarrely seemed to come from Stephen's Bible as it lay on the floor in front of the ghost. It grew thicker and thicker until we noticed the spectre seemed to disintegrate into a dark mist itself, and slowly bit by bit, like sand going through a timer, it filtered towards the smoking Bible. As the moments passed, the spectre's threatening form grew less and less, as it disappeared '*into*' the smouldering book, like a genie disappears into a bottle. Then, completely silently, the top of its body finally went and that was that – it was gone. And two seconds later, all the smoke had disappeared 'into' the Bible as well, culminating in just a quiet hissing sound as it departed.

"What the hell just happened!?" exclaimed Fran.

"Lord above, do you think that thing has gone?" muttered Stephen weakly.

I didn't respond to either of them, being too keen to see the Bible as it lay pathetically on the floor. I picked it up and looked at it curiously. One could certainly say I hadn't seen anything like what we just witnessed, and the same went for the condition of Stephen's' book of God, or what was left of it. For there was a burnt-out round hole completely through it, about the diameter of a tea cup rim. I tried to open what remained of the Bible but couldn't because it was so utterly singed together.

"I guess I won't be using that anymore," Stephen quipped as he put it to his face and peered through the burnt-out hole. However, it fell on deaf ears.   Maybe it was the shock, maybe the fear we'd just experienced finally hitting me, I just don't know, but for some reason I felt angry, and for some reason in my addled old brain, I was angry with Stephen.

"And just what do you think you were doing?" I ranted.

"Sorry?" replied the trainee vicar, somewhat taken aback.

"Perhaps I didn't make myself clear, but we're not in the business of exorcisms."

"Exorcisms! I'm not in that business either Jerry. Look I don't know what happened here just then but it was nothing to do with me!"

"Nothing to do with you! Is this not your Bible? Was it not you that threw it? You must've known what you were doing! It's always been my policy. We don't involve ourselves in ghost removal; it's not in our brief!" I even surprised myself at how pompous I was being...

"Come on Uncle. Stephen was just trying to help. And it's not entirely true that we don't help people remove spirits is it?"

Well that was like a knife in the heart, my own niece siding with the opposition. Oh, the treachery!

"Once or twice I grant you, we've taken someone along to do a clearing ceremony, with, I might add, the full consent of the home owner!" I declared, and quite frankly, I could've stamped my foot like a toddler for good measure.

"It's not as if Jane wanted this thing around anymore," said Fran. "I mean assuming it has gone, I should think she'd be pleased."

There she goes again, my niece being all reasonable.

"I'm just saying he…" and I pointed toward Stephen in a very rude manner, "should not have taken it upon himself to conduct an exorcism! As I just said, we're not in the removals business!"

"Jerry, for the love of God I didn't!" he protested. "I wouldn't know where to start for one thing. I mean, did you see me jumping about the place screaming 'the power of Christ compels you' and throwing the Holy Water around the room? No, you didn't. And that's because I wouldn't have had a clue what I was doing."

There was a momentary quiet as we all took stock. Although I felt the need to keep needling.

"Then how did you and your God book manage that then?" I asked defiantly.

"Jerry, I'm sorry, but I just haven't a clue," he quietly replied. "I've never seen or heard of anything like this. I've had that pocket Bible since I was a kid and at no point did I ever assume it had some kind of ghost busting ability. Or for that matter I'd be throwing it at a violent spirit and it all ending like it did just then!" I could tell in his tone our poor vicar was clearly feeling guilty and full of contrition.

By this point I too was beginning to feel like I'd overdone it, so it didn't help that Fran decided to put the knife in yet again.

"I didn't see you with any plan to sort out our mess! If anything, we, in fact you in particular, given that spirit was heading in your direction, should be grateful that Stephen did something to sort out the complete balls-up that was your own making!" I must say she'd changed her tune. It wasn't that long ago, she was none too keen on our cleric friend, but now all of a sudden, he's a bloody hero.

"I had it completely under control," I snapped.

"Really!?" replied Fran facetiously. "And what was *your* plan then?"

Of course, she had me there, and I just huffed and blustered and couldn't actually think of anything coherent to say, which she seemed to take great satisfaction in.

"Well there you go then," came her self-important closing statement as she folded her arms smugly. I decided a change of subject was the most tactful option and I think the other two were thinking along the same lines. We surveyed the devastation in the room and checked our few pieces of equipment. It was of no great surprise that it had all gone haywire, so the chances of getting any paranormal proof were nil. Everything had been thrown across the room with all Jane's bits and pieces. I counted myself lucky that apart from a few marks, it was all still just about in working order. Any video sound recordings or video evidence? I'll be lucky. That is to say, of course there wasn't.

We began to collect up our stuff when there was a timid tap at the door, whereupon Susie popped her head in. I could see in her facial expression she was very taken aback by the mess and disorder.

"Everything OK?" she asked, somewhat wide eyed as she looked around. "We've been hearing a lot of noise, but didn't like to come in."

"Everything's fine now," I remarked. "And I'm pretty sure Jane and the rest of you won't be having any more problems."

"You mean you've got rid of it?" she asked.

"Yes. I think so. Although it's not our normal procedure," I squirmed, passing a knowing look towards Stephen and Fran. "I think it's gone. In fact, to quote my good friend here," as I patted Stephen on the shoulder, "*to hell with it. And may it be happy there.*"

"We're just going to get our stuff together and be on our way. And speaking for myself, I really need a ciggie," Fran added. I knew what she meant, for my own nicotine need was on high alert.

"Oh OK," said Susie, "need any help?"

"No, we'll be fine," I replied, as I looked around the dishevelled room. "Dear me, what are you young ladies like? Look at the mess you live in."

I could almost feel the burning eyes of rebuke in the back of my head from my two assistants as I said it.

~~~

Finally, I managed to get my aged Rover loaded up with all the gear. It took a while doing it on my own given the very Reverend Stephen Light and my niece thought it appropriate to spend ages tidying up Jane's bedroom. I wouldn't have bothered myself, since technically we didn't make the disaster area but probably not a good idea to have another séance to invite our grumpy spectre back to tell him to clear up his own mess. With my torch I glanced over my electrical equipment as it lay in the car boot. Some of it was a bit scuffed after being supernaturally thrown through the air but thankfully, not completely broken. I slammed the boot lid down and turned towards the accommodation block door to see my assistants emerge from within. Noticing that Stephen had caught Fran by the arm as if he wanted to say something private to her before we went, I thought one ought to look away diplomatically so as not to be seen as snooping. As such, I took out a cigarette and lit it, but squaring my left ear in their direction so I could listen in. If I was going to be talked about I wanted to know what was being said!

"Thanks for squaring things up a bit with your Uncle," said Stephen quietly. No doubt wanting to show his gratitude to Frankie, but not being able to speak properly back in the building with Judy and Susie being in there with them.

"Yeh well, I was just reminding my Uncle of the facts."

"Well I appreciate it. I really am interested in Jerry's work you see."

"It's not just him you know!" Fran snapped.

"Oh yes, I know. Sorry. I'm not doing very well am I tonight? I annoyed your Uncle, now I'm annoying you. It's just that, ever since being a kid, I've been very interested in this sort of thing so I really do want to be on the team. Well, when you'll have me... You don't think after, you know, earlier, I'll never be invited back again?"

"How should I know? You'll have to ask Unc," replied Fran coolly.

"Right, right, ok. I will do then," said Stephen bumbling on. I'd finished my fag and was fed up with ear wigging their conversation so I felt the need to chivvy them on. It was after all, the middle of a chilly winter's night.

"Are you coming Francesca?" I called. Without speaking, Fran walked over with Stephen trailing behind her and they joined me by the motor.

"Sorry again Jerry, you know, about earlier. I really don't know what happened there, I was just trying to help. I panicked I suppose, and I should've left things to you. You're the expert after all, and I'm sure you would've thought of something to sort it all out." As he said this I'm pretty sure I heard a derisory grunt from Frankie, but I ignored her.

That said, Stephen looked glum so I thought I'd better put him out of his misery.

"No apology needed young man. I guess I didn't have a plan, as such, so somebody needed to do something. I'm just amazed by what did happen. I've never seen anything like that before. It just breeds more unanswered questions doesn't it?"

"Yes, if you say so. Apologies, I'm being thick... What do you mean?" he asked.

"You're a man of the cloth. Was it relevant that it was a Bible that did that? Had it been the latest cookery book from yet another 'nobody' TV chef, would it have had the same effect?"

"Now you're going into deep philosophical waters," Stephen grinned.

"Then again, maybe it's you? Are you a secret vampire slayer on the side? By day, a Godly curate, by night, an assassin of the undead? Have I worked out your previously hidden life Stephen?" I asked mischievously.

"I don't think so somehow. I'm not sure I'm that exciting," replied Stephen, somewhat stony faced. Poor bloke hasn't yet worked out when I'm jesting with him. That said, you've got to watch the quiet ones. However, at that point I turned around and noticed Fran was shivering with the cold, although what does she expect if she goes out at night in a short skirt all the time, flashing her long legs to all and sundry.

"Unc, I'm tired, I'm freezing and after wearing someone else's wig, I really want to get home and wash my hair. I'm scared stiff I've got nits now. So can you boys have your make up session tomorrow?"

"Get in the car then child!" I hissed, and she promptly did, rudely not even saying goodbye to Stephen. She's a fickle girl my Fran, friendly sometimes, and other times not. But she's my sister's girl, and I love them both. Thereupon I said a farewell to the suitably contrite Stephen, got in the car and fired up the old V8. Given I had a few bumps and bruises after the evening's events, I'd like to say I needed to get home to the loving bosom of my caring wife. But I can't, not with my spouse. I would have to make do with a bag of frozen peas on my wounds, but somehow, they have more warmth in them than my Cynthia. And the large glass of medicinal brandy would help ease the pain as well.

~~~

I kept in touch with Judy and Susie in the coming weeks. It's always appropriate post-investigation to keep up to date with any developments. I can only assume that whatever the hell happened with that blasted Bible, with its bizarre, perfectly round burnt hole, it somehow got rid of the horrid spirit tormenting Jane. Now don't get me wrong. I'm not big on religion myself, although I have no issue with anyone who follows a God of their own choosing. So, I'm not about to say that if you have a ghost, just throw a Bible at it and everything will be okay. I don't believe that is the case, although at the same time, I have no idea how it worked in this instance. I don't believe Stephen is a secret exorcist. And I don't believe he is a miracle worker unknown to himself. Sure enough, having seen him down at the homeless centre it's clear he is a kind hearted, gentle giant of a man, who just happens to be a member of the God-squad. But a demon, dragon or zombie slayer? No chance. So how that perfect throw of his age-old Bible, hitting our spectre right between the eyes, should make it disappear in plumes of smoke I will never comprehend. Since that night, I have sucked on many a cigarette and downed many a pint of best bitter, pondering on that very question. I've never seen or heard the like of it ever before. And no, Frankie, Stephen and I didn't all dream it.

Nevertheless, both Judy and Susie have since reported to me that they and all the others involved, have noticed a much lighter, easier, happier and less oppressive atmosphere in their part of the NHS staff accommodation block. Now is it all in their minds? A placebo effect just because we did an investigation there and made things a little bit untidy? However, it has to be stated for the record that since the night of our investigation, no one has seen or heard or felt anything more of the menacing giant spirit. But I know what you're thinking. The key thing is whether Jane saw anything more of that spectre, since she was the primary focus of its attention. However, I'm afraid that is difficult to answer as I never got to see or speak to her ever again... You will no doubt recall she went off for two weeks emergency leave. Now I don't know how NHS staff contracts work. So how she managed it one couldn't say, but she never went back... Either to her staff block bedroom or her job at the hospital! Judy and Susie had very little information to give to me on this as for whatever reason, Jane wasn't keen on them having very much detail of her new life. And they were supposed to all be such close friends! Perhaps Jane thought the ghost would interrogate her mates, reveal her location and come after her. Although they did try and convince her they all believed the nasty apparition had gone. Poor Jane. All we know is that she is back in Ireland, working somewhere remote in private service. She didn't come back for her possessions or anything else. Her hospital buddies were quite upset there wasn't any opportunity to say goodbye. Maybe there was even a bit of guilt on the part of the séance initiators. After all, none of this would have happened had it not been for rank amateurs dabbling in things they didn't really understand. You start poking around in the world of the dead and you just don't know what's there. Yes, friendly great Aunt Mabel who died in the blitz might just be trying to get a message of hope or good fortune through. But what about the nasty spirit pretending to be great Aunt Mabel? There are plenty of malicious, malevolent spirits just waiting for the gullible to go inviting them into their lives. Don't open that path of darkness and trouble my friends, or on your own head be it. Judy, Susie and pals never went down that road again, that's for sure. Going forward, they're sticking with tradition for their party nights. Male strippers and alcohol. Now what could possibly go wrong for those ladies with that combination...!?

TALE NUMBER TWO - INSECURE SECURITY AT TUTTWOOD HOUSE

I've never been a fan of Mr Reece Hammond, our local property destroyer. Sorry, I mean property *developer*. Don't let him near your back garden whatever you do. Give the swine five feet of land; he'll put a dozen shoddy houses there. A broad-shouldered, in your face, up his own backside, dodgy dealing, snake in the grass if ever there was one. And those are the nicest things I can say about him.

I sometimes have a lunchtime pint down the 'Jolly Farmer' now and then, if I'm not at the 'proper' job, as it's a nice way to catch up with the local characters or to pore over that day's Daily Telegraph if no one's feeling particularly talkative. The downside with the Jolly Farmer is that bum-wipe Hammond sometimes pops in for a lunchtime beverage if he's passing. Of course, he likes to flaunt his wad of cash by buying the whole pub a drink and for the record, just because I'll sup his beer whenever he comes in - so quite a lot, it doesn't mean I like him. You may already be getting that vibe.

Anyhow, one damp and dreary November Tuesday, I was taking refuge from the world at a corner table down at the afore-mentioned hostelry. Not quite the same these days now a chap can't light a cigarette without going outside to a glorified bus shelter but don't get me started on that one. I hadn't got very far into the broadsheet pages when the easily recognisable thunder of his Range Rover Sport pulled up two inches from the pub door as it usually does. Why he has to park so close to the entrance I will never comprehend, because the longer walk would do him the power of good. An auspicious chance for him to lose some of the flab of his luxuriant diet and before you ask I'm not jealous! Just because he has a big house, villa in Spain, gorgeous wife, deep tan, tons of money and flash motors to boot. Who needs it? Don't answer. And another thing, why do people in his line always drive big 'four-by-fours' or is that a condition of purchase? Do the four-wheel drive dealers up and down the country always ask potential customers "Are you a property developer or house builder? – No...? Sorry, you'll have to buy a Mini".

I seem to have digressed again. Sorry about that but I feel better for getting it off my chest.

As I was saying before my bitter little rant, yours truly was to be found at a corner table in the Jolly Farmer on a wet and dull November day. In fact, the weather was being so perverse, there were at least fifty shades of grey outside. I heard the unmistakable sound of his massive four-by-four pull up very nearly through the pub door and I will admit my first thought was 'oh good, that's handy as my glass is nearly empty'. He has to have a use somehow. And so he thrust his person into the building, by which point the regulars who hadn't already groaned at his arrival promptly did so. Landlord Mike licked his lips as pound signs rolled around his eye sockets because he knew what was coming and sure enough Reece uttered those immortal words "Drinks all round Landlord please!" Well, it would be rude to turn a drink away like that and never let it be said that I, Jeremiah Thorne, would be so discourteous on a November Tuesday. Occasionally one would glance up from my newspaper, so as to gauge the number of minutes before I should get up, collect my drink, thank my benefactor and make my way back to the corner to be purposely out of the way. However, to my surprise and dismay, heavy-weight Hammond picked up two pints from the bar top, carried them over, put both down on the table and sat down and joined me. So there you go, no such thing as a free lunch or in this case, locally brewed Best Bitter. You see, I don't normally have to sit with the man. I just enjoy the free booze.

"Drink there for you Jerry".

"Oh thank you very much Reece, very nice of you," I said graciously, with a feeling of impending doom.

His bulky form leant forward across the table and with complete disrespect for my newspaper, dishevelled the pages and spilt his drink on it as if it wasn't there. "No problem. Actually, I'm glad you're in here today, I was hoping to have a little chat with you."

Here we go, what's he after? I mused.

"Am I right in saying Jerry, you have an interest in say, little oddities? I mean, that's what I've heard but if I've heard wrong I'll leave you in peace."

Now what I should have done was told him that oddities were the last thing on earth I'd want to have anything to do with, promptly followed by the word 'cheerio' but he intrigued me, strangely, although for a second or so, I did worry he was suggesting I have a sexual deviance towards small, cuddly animals. Which, to be clear, I don't.

"What do you mean exactly by 'oddities'?" I moved in closer to him and this time it was me showing a total lack of respect for my Daily Telegraph. Although I immediately moved back an inch or two because his crimson-cheeked fat face set beneath bottle manufactured gingery blonde repulsed me a bit. And no, I'm not being nasty, just factual. Anyway, I've gone off at a tangent again. He looked over his shoulder surreptitiously then looked back at me straight in the eye and said, "things not of this world."

"I have," wondering if I was walking into a practical joke, "made a bit of a study of the paranormal if that's what you mean. If however, you're looking for a medium or clairvoyant, then I am not the man you want and would therefore direct you to the Yellow Pages." I was firm but fair, it's the only way to deal with men like him.

"I don't think I need a medium. I don't believe in all that cobblers. My Janet swears by horoscopes but to me it's all just a scam. You make your own way in this world; I don't care what anyone says about spirit guides and planet movements. You're not into that crap, are you?"

There was a pretty regular flow of his saliva heading in my direction as he spoke but with flabby lips like his, he probably finds it hard to control.

"I'm not a big fan as such but I do believe there are things in this world or worlds that are beyond our comprehension at this time. Is there something specific then?" I wanted to get him talking again but took precautions this time and sat back a bit.

"Jerry mate, you must understand I don't believe in anything like that and particularly not ghosts and the like, but when I start getting annoyances in my business, then I have to exercise the grey matter and decide what's best to do."

Wiping his nose on the back of his hand in the most unattractive manner he then proceeded to elucidate further.

A few weeks ago, I bought a rather splendid, if somewhat run down, Georgian manor house which was being used as offices. Now normally my line would be to turn a building like that into apartments for the up and coming executive, you know what I mean?"

Oh yes, I knew what he meant. Rip out all the nice original detail, tack up some plasterboard to make lots of pokey flats, slap it all in magnolia emulsion and stick an inflated price on each of the little rabbit runs. Still, I nodded acquiescence.

"That said, cash is king, as I'm sure you know in business, and my funds are tied up a bit at the moment. But I thought, well, this old place is dirt cheap, a bloody bargain! They couldn't wait to get shot of it. Therefore, I does a deal, buys it quick and thought I'd let it out again to some other firm. Sort of, 'grand corporate head office' for a business which wants to impress. I get it painted out inside, nice bit of Buttermilk over the walls, new carpet tiles, it looked the bizzo."

The observant amongst you will have noticed he used Buttermilk emulsion not Magnolia, but I wasn't far off, was I?

"So what's the problem Reece? Nobody going for it?" sounding as sympathetic as possible given I couldn't care less about his fiscal turbulence.

"Well, it's a bit of a slow economic time ain't it? And it's a big old property. Maybe I'll need to divide it somehow and get a couple of smaller firms in there. Either that, or wait until I can convert it proper. But regardless of what I do, at the moment it's empty. And I don't like to leave a place like that empty without protection." For one ghastly moment I thought he was going to start talking safe sex.

"So where exactly is this place?"

"Over at Tuttwood. It's Tuttwood House as a matter of fact." I didn't really know the place but it rang a bell. Nevertheless, he then relayed the crux of the matter.

"Thing is," there was another surreptitious look over the shoulder; "my security firm just can't seem to keep anyone there on the nightshift for anything longer than five minutes. They finally got their best guy on the nightshift. 'Fearless' his nickname was. Ought to have sued them under the Trade Description Act. Fearless my backside. He was the worst of them, couldn't even last the whole night. Morning shift guards would turn up each day to take over and were getting used to being told by whoever the night duty watchman was, that they wouldn't be going back to the place. 'Fearless' wasn't even there for the handover! He'd buggered off leaving the place wide open! And this is the service I'm paying for!"

Our Mr Hammond was getting a bit irate whilst relaying his tale and the old boys at the bar kept glancing over to where we were sat, as if they thought it was me who was upsetting him. I gestured him to lower the volume and I will admit, my interest in is dilemma was becoming aroused.

"What exactly was the problem then for Fearless and his fellow valiant cohorts? Surely they weren't scared of the dark?"

My attempt to make light of it was ignored and, in a mocking, sarcastic tone he replied, "they thought it had a bad atmosphere! Can you believe it? What a bunch of hysterical skivers." If there had been a bucket for him to spit into, he would have done so, such was his disgust.

"Interesting though," I said. "That is to say, it affected not just the one guy but several. Several men employed as security guards who are presumably old enough and ugly enough to be comfortable sitting in a large building, at night, on their own. But stick them in this Tuttwood House, and they all turn to jelly." However, Reece was having none of it.

"Suggestion Jerry, merely the power of suggestion. Take the first guy for instance. He's in an old house, it's night time, it creaks a bit with old age and his imagination wanders and he never wants to go back. Word gets out. Then the next guy goes along, he knows the first one got the heebie-jeebies, walks around an old house in the dead of night, he gets the shakes, then so on and so forth".

"You seem like you have made your mind up already and that its all nonsense. So, what do you want me for? Why don't you just get another security firm in?"

He was ahead of me. That's why he was a sickeningly successful business man and I was sitting in country pub with nothing better to do.

"I've tried, word gets around, no one will take the place on. The current firm has managed to get a guy in there by paying him double time. A cost which, I might add, they are passing on to me. But if a gang of tanked up vandals come along, a sixty-five-year-old, stick thin geriatric isn't exactly gonna send them running now is he?"

That was a little ageist I thought. He wasn't talking to any spring chicken after all.

"Well I suppose he can call the police, if nothing else."

"Whoopy-do. And they mosey out half an hour later when they've finished their tea-break – great. No Jerry, what I need is for someone with a known interest in these areas, such as your good self, to pop along one night, have a look over the place, start make reassuring noises to the security firm that there's no killer bogeymen, then everybody's happy and it's job done."

"Reece, if I'm going to look in to this, I want to do it properly. Like I do with any of my investigations, sensibly and seriously. I'm not going out there to fudge some sort of reassurance to a night watchman just on your say so. But for a proper study of the place, well, that's another matter."

"Fine whatever you want," he replied, beaming at me. "They'll be a drink in it for you of course."

"Really, I'm a thirsty man you know. How many drinks exactly?"

With a greasy wink he answered, "Quite a few old son, quite a few."

I booked it in for the following night.

~ ~ ~

George Harrison was belting out one of his classics in rather splendid fashion on the car radio as I pulled up outside my cottage and cranked up the handbrake of 'old reliable', my '75 Rover P6, and I shut off the engine. I was now home after my unexpected little meeting with our slimy local house builder and developer. I wasn't rostered to work so the rest of my day off was my own. so I thought one would take the opportunity to see if there was anything much I could find out about this Tuttwood House place. However, there were more important matters to address, that being an absence of food in my belly. And so I went in to the marital home to be greeted by the not so loving wife Cynthia in the hallway, putting on her raincoat.

"Oh, you're back then," she muttered sourly.

"Hello love of my life and how art thou?"

Odd that when I talk to Cynthia, I find myself drawing a deep intake of breath yet only speaking at the very last point of exhalation. Like I know our conversations are fruitless.

"Well I can tell you've been down to the pub again, I can smell the alcohol from here," she quipped with her usual charm and abhorrence. Her sense of smell was right up there with a highly trained Spaniel. Her ears weren't dissimilar either.

"Are you going out dear?" I enquired.

"Very observant. I did tell you this morning that I would be going to one of my Ashvale Ladies Group meetings this afternoon. I expect I shall probably stay on for supper with Angela. I'll be home about eight, but you'll no doubt be down in that silly 'den' of yours?"

"Maybe. A little project has come up. Is there any lunch on the go?" I bravely asked, not holding out much hope.

"As you were at the pub anyway, why on earth didn't you eat there for goodness sake?"

I do hate it when she starts throwing good sense at me.

"Because my humble budget cannot justify food *and* beer, it's one or the other and I'm afraid beer won."

"I simply despair of you. Well, I haven't had time to do a shop because some of us are busy. I seem to recall there being a pork pie left in the fridge, I don't think it's out of date yet. Goodbye." And with all the speed and force of a mini-hurricane she whirled past me and she was out of the house. Thud. The door furniture shook with a clank as the heavy weight was slammed against its frame.

Consequently, I tottered off to the kitchen to go and hunt my lunch down, which given I only had to walk to the fridge was pretty easy.

One pork pie on a plate and a dollop of brown sauce later, I sat at the kitchen table, mobile phone in hand and gave Fran a call. She must still have been working so I left her a message and no sooner had I put it down when it rang. It was my new friend, the young trainee vicar.

"Hello Stephen. This is a pleasant surprise. How are things in the God Squad?"

"As good as it gets I suppose. I'm calling from my hands-free in the car as I'm only about ten minutes from your place. Was wondering if I could maybe pop in and see how you're doing?" I was always glad of a friendly face, given I don't live with one, so I was most emphatic about allowing him round.

I sneaked in a quick ciggie and sure enough, a shade under ten minutes later there was a knock at the door and it was the new pal of Church of England employment.

"Hi Jerry, I hope I'm not interrupting anything?" said Stephen in his soft, well-spoken voice.

"Of course you're not, I'm off today. I've just nipped upstairs to the study to turn the PC on. Bit of research I wanted to do."

His eyes lit up with interest.

"It wouldn't be of a paranormal nature by any chance?"

"No, looking up some hardcore porn." He looked shocked. "I jest you Stephen. If I looked at porn at my age, I'd go all unnecessary. Of course it's of a paranormal nature." I loved having a fellow observer in my midst. "Well, it might be. There is a slight suggestion of that, but time will tell, I only got to hear about it at lunchtime. I ran into a developer guy I know, just an acquaintance you understand, I'm not his biggest fan. Would you like a cuppa?"

"Yeah. Why not? Thanks."

He went and sat at the kitchen table as I put a brew on, while I told him about Reece Hammond and the issue with the insecure security staff.

"Where is this old house then?" he asked with concentration.

"Some gaff called Tuttwood House, that's why I've put the computer on, see if there's anything on the internet."

I placed a mug of very fine Jeremiah Thorne tea – not too strong and not too weak – down in front of him.

"I know Tuttwood," he replied. "I mean, I wouldn't exactly say it's famously haunted but I've read the odd line on the web about the place. Rumours mostly, nothing major, but local history sites might have more I suppose."

I sat down at the table with him, and suggested he spill the beans but with that my mobile went off again. It was Fran.

"Hello you, you finished work now?" My lunchtime pint or pints, let's not worry which, had put me in a jolly mood.

"Hi Unc, yep I've finished. Had a morning shift and it was busy this lunchtime. Anyway, what did you ring for?" Fran can be a good girl when it suits her and it sounds like she rang back straight after work as I could hear her walking in the background and she sounded in a rush.

"A little project has turned up. Bumps in the night have been upsetting a few security staff. Gives us something to look into anyway. Did you want to pop over and have a chat about it?"

"No, I'll call you back tonight. Think I'll pop into town and have a look round the shops." Not quite sure of the importance of this given she seems to throw away clothes rather than have the bother of washing them.

"Oh that's a shame, where's the devotion to duty nowadays? Stephen's just popped round and he was about to tell me a bit about the place I'd hoped we could have a little investigation at. I don't like going on my todd. Maybe he could come with me." I looked toward Stephen as I said this and he was nodding most emphatically.

"I suppose I could come over then if you give me twenty minutes or so," she replied indifferently.

"Well I don't think you need any more clothes darling. I mean, for crying out loud, you're always shopping, no wonder you don't have any money!"

"A woman always has a need to shop. As a man, allegedly in your case, you just don't understand that."

She had me there. Not the dig about being a man, I meant a woman's need to shop. After all my years, I should've known better than to try to understand the female psyche.

"Fine, well get here when you can then. See you shortly."

I turned to Stephen. "Fran's on her way over, we'll talk shop when she gets here if that's OK."

"No problem. It'll be nice to see her again."

Stephen was clearly a glutton for punishment but there's no accounting for taste.

~ ~ ~

Stephen held back on what turned out to be his disappointingly limited snippets of information about

Tuttwood House until the third of our number joined us.   As such, we had a bit of a search around the world wide web for more details but nothing much more revealed itself about the old manor house we were to probe, other than what Stephen had already told us, bar a few historical snippets. It all helps to build the picture though and so the joint collation of knowledge can be summed up as follows.

The house was built in about eighteen hundred for a local landowner, the sizeable property was of a reasonably high standard in the class stakes but not what you'd call a stately pile and built mainly in locally produced red brick. A couple of forgettable low in rank Royals, by that I mean none of the main squad, more your second cousin twice removed level, stayed there in that century and it was turned into a posh country club by nineteen twenty-six. Not sure what it was used for during the war but its fall from grace continued when in the mid-fifties it became the corporate headquarters for a shipping company. Manicured front gardens gave way to car parking places, landscaped back gardens gave way to unattractive, industrial looking storage units.   Quite the comedown for a building which, so it would seem, was the only genuine historical property in an area otherwise devoid of any class at all, being a relic within a concrete jungle of nineteen sixties and seventies drab business units and rows of terraced houses.

So, if that was the situation with the place in the 'real' world, what was the story in any second dimension which could be marked as the cause of the current, alleged disturbances?

Well in the words of my favourite Glaswegian television cop, 'there's bin a murder'. Or rather there was, about one hundred and fifty years ago. It appears a maid managed to get herself killed. Actually, I shouldn't have put it like that, as it's an unfair assessment of the girl's final minutes, because I'm sure she would've rather continued her job of floor scrubbing and bed pan rinsing, than have been slain in a violent, messy bloodbath. I could be wrong though.

Jealousy you see. Along with money, is the root of all evil and much as I hate to say it, apparently the butler did it. Yes I know, what a cliché, but I can't help history. Seemed the butler fancied the no doubt heavily starched and scratchy linen pants off the girl and he thought it was reciprocated. Rather an assumption by all accounts as she was frequently out back having a tongue sandwich, so to speak, with the footman, who was closer to her own age and setting her heart, along with other parts of her body, aflame.

Here the details start getting sketchy. However, from what the three of us could fathom from the snippets of info and hearsay gleaned from internet forums and small articles in a couple of my old reference books, the story went like this. Middle aged love-struck butler has one too many dry Sherries one evening while the master and mistress are away somewhere, living it up, and decides in a drunken stupor to confront the maid in her attic room quarters about her friendly disposition towards the hunky household footman. Just like a modern-day soap opera. Presumably the poor girl didn't have a sturdy bolt on her door and even if she did that wretch of a 'fortified wine' crazed butler would've probably kicked it down. Heavy sherry consumption is enough to send a chap wild no doubt, but I still prefer draught beer and a whisky chaser. Back to the history lesson, there then followed murder most horrid in that very room. And where is her footman to protect her? No one knows but I should imagine he was taking his sorry backside out of the building at a fair old rate of knots, heartlessly leaving his woman to the face the music herself. So as men go, he's not much better than our executioner.

The body of this poor house maid was found in a nearby village pond the next morning and it would seem, so the story goes, the butler dragged the lifeless blood covered body all the way down the stairs from the attic bedroom, across the gravel drive and down the lane, which no doubt back then was little more than a dirt track. From what I can make out by referring to my modern-day road atlas, that quiet lane which witnessed the disposing of her wretched corpse is now a major A-road, with several thousand vehicles thundering along it each and every day. The village pond, which was supposed to conceal her body has long since been built over and currently has a takeaway kebab house over it – I wonder if that place is haunted? Note to self: Give 'Kev's Kebabs' a call about this and ask them.

Anyhow, it's not a fitting memorial for this girl, whom I have no doubt would have never realised the delights of a kebab in her distant time but is now exposed to them morning, noon and night. Just as well she's dead in that respect. Can't stand kebabs myself, however Fran's been known to have a late-night lay-by kofta, but she's young and therefore slightly crazy.

So that was the tale of Tuttwood as far as we know it, hoping of course that any embellishments to the story, as it was handed down the generations, were kept to a minimum.

"Shall we meet here tomorrow night, about nine o'clock and make our way over there?" Given Fran's social diary I like to get her pencilled in early, as booking often prevents disappointment. I wasn't so sure about Stephen's diary, for as a low rank vicar or curate or whatever he is, I couldn't be sure he wouldn't be praying in a darkened room somewhere or watching DVD highlights from TV's Songs of Praise.

"Fine by me," he chirped.

"Suppose it better be nine," retorted Frankie unenthusiastically. "By the time we get all the gear in your car, drive there, set up, listen to you give out your orders..." What a cheek I thought!

"I don't give out orders, just operational direction. Stop complaining."

"Mind you, if we're going there tomorrow night when are you going to give it a daytime look over?" Fran was quite correct to ask, as I do, wherever possible, like to snoop around an investigation site in the light of day so I can get a feel for the place. Plus, it's a good way to gauge whether we're wasting our time of course.

"Have no fear, oh favourite niece, I will be popping over tomorrow at some point." Of course, I said this, not having given it a second's consideration, but I do try my best not to look stupider than I already do.

"But you'll be exhausted surely? I mean, we'll be up most of the night, won't we?" asked Stephen. And I must say how nice it was to now have someone caring on the team. Must be his calling in life and for a generally unloved old fool like me, a bit of concern from a fellow human being was much appreciated.

"Have no fear Stephen," wishing to reassure his kindness, "there's still life in this old dog."

Frankie exhaled a disparaging guffaw, which with quiet dignity I chose to ignore.

A little while later they made their departures. I watched them leave from the front window. Poor Stephen! I'm not sure what he must think about our Fran. I couldn't help but think how quiet and respectable he is as he gets into his small, sensible Japanese hatchback, throwing a glance towards Fran as she hoicks up her mini skirt and straddles her shocking yellow Moped. My, those two are chalk and cheese, what with her thick tights, heavy boots, funky jacket and graffiti covered designer bag. Him with his polished shoes and tidy hair. What a contrasting trio we make but it takes all sorts to make a world and we have our common interest – proving the existence of the paranormal and it's that work which really matters. To me anyway.

~ ~ ~

I had some time on my hands so I gave Reece Hammond a call to arrange seeing Tuttwood the following day. During our conversation he gave me the home telephone number of the current and only security guard prepared to be on duty at the place over night. Worth a chat I thought, given we'd be meeting him the following evening and he may have been able to increase our knowledge base. The chap's name was Bert Mackie and immediately after finishing my conversation with the detestable Hammond, I gave the guy a call. Turned out he only lived about half an hour or so away from me and he was more than happy to talk about the house at the centre of our investigation. So much so, he said I was welcome to pop over. Given my teatime home life is a relatively empty one, I accepted his kind invite, deciding to strike while the iron was hot. Within ten minutes, my aged Barbour jacket and Bushman's hat were on, a naughty ciggie was between my lips, the three-and a half litre V8 in the car was powered up and I was on my way to chez Mackie.

~ ~ ~

It was a fairly typical council owned estate of nineteen sixties, terraced houses, some original grey roughcast and a few with exterior emulsion of various but somewhat contrasting colour schemes. Scuffed and battered cars were packed in every spare nook and cranny but I did manage to park 'old reliable' behind Bert's motor on his short concrete driveway. His house had one of the tidier front gardens, even if they were all small. It was one of the few which still had a bit of nature in it, with a tiny but neat patch of grass, some shrubs and a couple of pots with winter Pansies. Most of the front areas of the neighbouring houses were taken up with rubbish bins and at a couple of houses the frontage was home to mean looking, high powered sporty motorbikes.

I got out of my car and walked past the extremely floral net curtains of the only front downstairs window and on getting to the door I pressed the bell button, at which point from somewhere within the property, the familiar sound of a battery generated Westminster chime could be heard.

A stout, rosy cheeked woman proceeded to open the door wearing a dress even more floral than the aforementioned net curtains but her welcome was warm and her smile wide and friendly. This, I discovered, was Mrs. Mackie.

"Come in dear, Bert said we'd be having a visitor, he's in the sitting room, just through there dear, go on, go on."

I was ushered in to a small sitting room by the jovial, Birmingham accented Mrs Mackie who followed close behind me. It was small, but clean and cosy, although the few bits of furniture were old, not in an antique way, but dated leftovers from the sixties and seventies. An old gas fire was giving the room a warm glow and clearly Mrs Mackie was a house-proud lady so it would take a long search to find a speck of dust in the place.

"So you're the gent who phoned earlier then?" A skinny man with a neatly combed, slick backed hairstyle in his early sixties arose from a small armchair in the corner of the room and offered out his hand to shake and welcomed me as warmly as his wife.

"I am indeed and thank you very much for allowing me to visit you at such short notice. This must all seem a bit curious to you?"

"Well it came out of the blue I admit. What did you say your name was?"

"Jeremiah Thorne, but please just call me Jerry."

"All right Jerry, I'm Bert, pleased to make your acquaintance. Oh, and this is my Doreen." He gestured towards his wife. I forgot she was standing behind me.

"Sit down dear sit down, can I get you a tea? Go on, have a cup of tea, I'll see if I can find a nice bit of cake too..."

And without waiting for any answer she was out of the room and away. What a charming lady, in a fussing, call me a dear, kind of way.

"So then," started Bert, taking up a tin of tobacco and packet of Rizlas, "what's this all about then? I couldn't quite make out what you was getting at on the phone earlier."

Accordingly, I filled him in on my intended paranormal investigation of Tuttwood House the following evening. His grin seemed to suggest he was a little amused by the whole affair and I wasn't sure whether he was laughing at my hobby, or the problems being faced by Reece Hammond concerning his night shift security staffing. Doreen returned with a tray of tea and I wasn't in the least bit disappointed to see a plate with a colossal slice of what looked like homemade Victoria sponge cake.

"Me and Bert have had our supper early as he's on nights see. So I hope you don't mind eating on your own me dear. Any sugar?"

"Ah just the one Mrs Mackie."

"Call me Doreen dear, we don't stand on any ceremony here. Here you are, and a fork, there you go dear."

As the proud house wife poured three teas in floral, (what else?) china mugs I tucked into my cake. Wow, 'our' Bert is a lucky man, delicious home baking like this every day would send my waistline in a very negative outbound direction.

"I hope it's all right dear, I made it yesterday afternoon so it's not as fresh as I would like to give out to visitors."

"No worries there Doreen, it's absolutely smashing. A real treat. I don't get cakes like this at home." And it was good too. Moist, spongy sponge or as spongy as sponge is supposed to be, yes I know I wouldn't make a food critic... oh, and plenty of strawberry jam too. I could've eaten double but one doesn't want to look a pig.

Bert was taking a deep draw on his roll up. "Don't fuss over him so Doreen. You'll suffocate the poor fella in a minute!"

"Oh pipe down Bert. And I wish you wouldn't smoke in here, 'specially in company."

Bert just rolled his eyes when she wasn't looking and turned toward me. He brought us back to the subject in hand.

"Thing is Jerry, and I hope you don't mind me saying this, but when I'm doing the night shift at the Tuttwood place, I just keep me 'ead down, you know what I mean?"

As he said this, it did happen to cross my mind that if a band of sinful robbers did turn up at wherever Bert was on security duty, no offence to the man, as I'm no Jackie Chan either, I'm just not sure his emaciated, aging frame would be much of a deterrent. Having said that, I suppose if there was any trouble he can dial 999 so maybe I'll just keep my opinions to myself.

"Actually, I'm not sure I do know what you mean."

"Well, I wouldn't say I believe in ghosts and I wouldn't say I don't. I'll admit there is something unpleasant about that place but the thing to do is stay in the hut."

I was about to ask if he meant an all-night *Pizza Hut,* but decided I needed him more than he needed me.

"In the hut? What's that?"

"Well, we have a little security hut by the gate you see. When I'm on shift, I take me old mini TV for company and spend most of the night in there. Every couple of hours — if I haven't nodded off," he chortled, "I have a walk around outside, but I keep it short and sweet, just to say I've done me job and then I go back to the hut and more than likely put the kettle on."

"Aren't you supposed have a walk around inside?" I asked.

"Supposed to yes, but, well, I don't." The smirk of self-approval seemed to disappear from his face at this point so I thought it worth following up.

"Look Bert, I'm not here to check up on yours or anyone else's work. And I'm not about to pass on information from our conversation to Reece Hammond. He's no friend of mine I can assure you."

"He's no friend of mine either. The few times I have seen him I thought he was a complete, well I can't say the word in front of the missus, but it begins with w and has a k somewhere in the middle."

"Oh Bert!" interrupted Doreen. "Honestly! Bit of a top up there dear?"

The lovely Mrs Mackie was waving a teapot in my face and who was I to refuse a refill to my half empty cup?

"Please. Lovely!" I turned back to Bert to pursue the point. "So no offence, but why don't you check the inside of the building?"

He sighed a little but then carried on. "I did once or twice back when I first had to go there. You're supposed to check all the floors and a selection of rooms as you go. Well I did, like I say, but there isn't a nice 'feeling' in the place. More on the top floor see. Horrid up there it is, don't know why. Just is. Having said that, I think it was during my second inside patrol of the night, and I got to the door to leave and I looked back toward the staircase and I was sure... no, I'm just being a silly old sod."

"Come on Bert dear, tell the man," encouraged domesticated Doreen. Somewhat abruptly he fired out his last sentence.

"I thought for a second or so I saw someone watching me from the top of the stairs, only there couldn't have been because I'd just come from there. That's all. I just imagined it. Gave me the willies for a few minutes but then that was that. Anyway, I've not been inside the house since. I keep to the outside only and when I'm not outside I'm in the hut watching rubbish on night time TV."

The lovely Mrs. Mackie seemed to have a look of relief at her husband's safety precautions.

"Gives me the willies too dear, hearing ghostie stories, I can't be doing with all that. Give me an evening in front of the box watching a nice romantic film or the daily soaps and

I'm a happy girl." Mrs Mackie gave a bodily shake to emphasise her point about ghosts or 'ghosties' as she calls them while I couldn't help but think her days of being referred to accurately as a 'girl' were long gone. But her baking is top notch so I won't complain.

"Who else does the nightshift now?"

"Well that's just it. I'm the only one who'll do it. For five nights of the week anyway. The other two have to be done by the security firm manager. He don't like it either but there's no one else and a contract's a contract ain't it?"

"Has he had any problems there?"

Bert laughed with satisfaction.

"There was this one morning when the day shift turned up at six and he was apparently as white as a kite. Reckoned that early on in the night, he was in the hut and glancing out the window thought he saw some bloke dragging a body down the drive, right past him as bold as brass. Anyway, he fired himself up and ran out there to confront the man, only in the space of those few seconds whatever he thought he saw weren't there no more! Scared the crap out of him, it did!"

His boss being in receipt of this upsetting experience was giving Bert some considerable amusement, but it was interesting nonetheless, as I'd only recently read somewhere that a butler had dragged his victims body along the driveway. Was this a ghostly re-enactment? I did have to wonder.

"He still does the night shift though?"

"Ha! he's got to! No-one else is going to do it for him, I told you, a contract's a contract. And the guv'nor don't want the aggro of that Hammond fella going off at him anymore. Four other blokes tried the night shift and not one lasted more than a night, not even Fearless Fred!"

"Oh, I've heard about him," remembering my original conversation with Hammond.

"Yeh, you wouldn't believe it. Nothing normally scares him, if there's a fight outside a pub, if he wasn't in it already, he'd jump in. If there was rioting in the streets he'd be at the front. Built like a brick sh..." Doreen gave him a disapproving look and he adjusted his speech.

"Built like a brick out-house. Skin head and arms like tree trunks and Fred – he didn't even last a whole night! Big fella like him too! We didn't half laugh!"

Bert was chuckling away to himself, but my mind had moved up a gear. The information obtained there was useful but I could do with having a chat with this Fred bloke to find out exactly what the problem was. My host began to roll another fag and grinned to himself.

"Suppose you could say, being the only one who'll work there, I'm a bit of a hero!" He chuckled again, clearly pleased with himself.

"You're a hero in my book Bert and no mistaking. And you Doreen, bake the best cake I've had in ages." She blushed. What an old smoothie I am!

I took my leave of them, not before getting an idea of where I might find Fearless Fred the next day. I'd be seeing Bert again tomorrow night at the investigation but given he doesn't stray far from his tea and television hut, I doubted I'd see that much of him. I started up 'old reliable' and lit one of my own cigarettes as the smell of his roll ups had given me a taste for one. I took a steady drive back home in the company of a *Dean Martins Greatest Hits* cassette, as I digested both the delicious sponge cake and information received. I had much to think over.

~ ~ ~

The following morning, I rolled out of bed at about nine thirty. My wife and I have twin beds and as usual she was gone and her bed was made with its typical military precision. I went to the window, held back the curtain and looked out at what the day was offering. Heavy, grey skies and damp in the air. So, in other words, not a lot of anything nice. I double-backed towards the door and grabbing my old dressing gown en route, made my way downstairs for the morning caffeine shot. As I passed the drawing room, I could see Cynthia in one of the armchairs, dressed smartly as always and reading the days' *Telegraph* with her half-moon spectacles perched on the end of her nose. Most inconsiderate I thought. I shan't have anything to read while I drink my coffee.

"Morning darling!" I said with as much enthusiasm as one could muster towards a woman with whom I wasn't that enamoured, despite being married to her.

"Good morning Jeremiah," she replied in her imperious way, without so much as a glance in my direction. I carried on toward the kitchen and saw half a jug of filter coffee left. Maybe Cynthia wasn't all bad then, at least she knows me well enough to be aware of her husband's morning coffee requirement. I grabbed one of the mugs I was allowed to use, that being one of the thick, plain earthenware ones as opposed to the bone china mugs which were kept for Cynthia and her guests, and I poured myself the first of the morning dosages. Taking a swig of coffee heaven with one arm, I pulled out a breakfast bar stool with the other and sat down. Delving into the pocket of my shabby dressing gown, I grabbed the next item on the agenda, that being filtered cigarettes and a cheap, plastic, shocking yellow lighter. Why do they have to make them in such awful colours? Contentment was just a moment away as I put a cigarette to my lips, lit it and drew back. Yes, now I could think straight. Tonight, was the night of the vigil at Tuttwood and I would've liked to have 'accidentally on purpose' met up with this 'fearless Fred' security man but there was one small problem. I had an eleven till three shift to work at the library. Most inconvenient. However, in the interests of science I would have to take emergency steps and reached for the telephone to phone in sick. I don't like to be dishonest but sometimes a chap has to sacrifice himself. Besides, if I phone early enough, there'll be no one in the office and I can leave a message on the answer phone. It's always so much easier when pulling a sickie to describe the symptoms of one's dreadful bout of pretend sickness and diarrhoea to a tape recording instead of an enquiring supervisor. Much as I hated to let down the library service of our great nation, I had my own vital research to attend to and such valuable hours were very much needed with this short notice investigation. A moment later, the phone call taken care of, the cigarette smoked and the mug replenished, I returned upstairs to get ready. There was work to be done.

~ ~ ~

A couple of hours or so later I was swerving the motor into the car park of a hostelry in the less salubrious part of town. Niece Frankie had joined me as she had the day off from her bar job. She's not the sort of girl who would be completely averse from taking an untrue sickie or duvet day, as I believe they are now known, but today was an official absence. Unlike her uncle... Now Frankie is a hip and trendy girl it has to be said and I have no doubt she's staggered inebriated outside many a boozer in her time but even she raised an eyebrow of disapproval to this place. And that's saying something. My intelligence led me to understand this particular public house, under the name of The Elephant and Castle, was a popular drinking place of our 'Fearless' Freddie whenever he was off duty during opening hours. Talking of which, I thought I may have been a bit premature in our arrival given the place must only have been open a few minutes. Not wishing for us to stick out like a sore thumb by sitting outside the place in the car, we made our way towards the entrance, given our location, treble checking I'd locked the car doors of course. Now, I shouldn't be judgemental about the place just by looking at the immediate area. For all I knew it could've been like *Buckingham Palace* inside. However, on venturing in and taking my first view of both the interior and clientele, all I can say is 'rock on judgementality' because it was bang on. The place was actually quite busy, so I can only assume they must have been queuing up to get in, either that or no one had left the place from the night before!

I certainly stood out like a sore thumb, being the only man there who didn't have a skin head and arms like *Popeye the Sailor*. Frankie stood out by being the only female and I wondered if she regretted her morning decision on what to wear that day, as her skirt was rather short and her body language suggested even she felt a bit too naked. Normally my Fran is very 'body confident'. We may have been in winter but that doesn't stop her flaunting her slim-line figure, albeit with thicker tights on. Everyone stopped what they were doing, which was either swigging lager or playing on one of the many fruit machines and proceeded to look in our direction. It was reminiscent of an old cowboy film when the good guy or bad guy, delete as applicable, walked into the Wild West saloon. In the silence we sauntered toward the bar and I addressed the landlord. Oddly, unlike his patrons, he was skinny and aging, with a grainy face which seemed over exposed given his long chestnut hair was combed back and held in place with copious amounts of some kind of greasy hair product. Or chip fat from the kitchen fryer maybe.

"Good morning," I said.

"Yeah?" he replied. It was evident he was a master of modern customer service.

"I'm looking for a guy called Fred. He works for Culverland Security. I'm told he drinks here." The landlord just looked at me. Didn't say a word. Just stared hard into my face and if I wasn't very much mistaken, I'm sure I could hear the sound of his teeth grinding. It would not be an understatement to say I felt uncomfortable about his silence because I didn't know whether it was because he was deaf or just didn't want to speak to me. Would it have been rude to repeat the question I pondered? Oh, these social conundrums! I'm not sure it particularly helped either, when Frankie chipped in with, "oi, you deaf?" I wouldn't have dared say that.

Then from behind us I heard someone in a menacing gruff voice, ask the question,

"Who wants to know?" Frankie and I turned and a burly fellow had stepped forward. Like all the other men there, except the 'talkative' barman, he looked like a denim wearing bodybuilder. And he was only a dress size bigger.

"I said... who wants to know?" he repeated.

His tone was now aggressive and threatening so I took hold of Frankie's arm as if to reassure her I would protect her. This in itself is laughable as if there was any trouble; she'd more likely be the one to protect me. She has a sharp tongue when she wants and a fiery temper and I rather think she could do some damage with her furry boots following a rapid high-kick. I needed to clear my throat with a wimpy cough before I could speak anything other than gibberish.

"Err, the name's Jeremiah Thorne, but, call me Jerry. I was hoping to speak to Fred of Culverland Security."

"Yeh, I heard. Why?" he snorted back. Frankie, bar the outburst at the Landlord, had been silent but I could see that angry look in her eye. She lunged forward and prodding him on the chest with her finger demanded, "Look pal, either you know him or you don't. Yes or no? Our business is with him, so don't waste our time!"

There was a comical murmuring among the other men in the bar. Presumably the sight of this good-looking but mouthy young woman standing up to this burly thug was the best entertainment they'd had since the last big pay out on one of the slot machines. The heavy brute looked around at his peers with a slick grin, obviously enjoying this tussle and being the centre for their amusement.

"A lot of gob, coming from a pretty lady eh!?" His comment aroused some mild sniggering from the room, as I felt a growing unease. And as unease goes, it was already pretty bad when we first got there.

"Either you're a very nosy twat who thinks he's hard or maybe you're just plain stupid" she added tactlessly. Frankie's response to him caused even greater amusement and I cringed at her usual ability to make a difficult situation even worse. Unfortunately, our antagonist didn't see the funny side of her outburst this time and promptly lunged forward grabbing her by the throat with his right hand, while moving his face an inch from hers with gritted teeth on display like a rabid dog. Now what caring uncle would stand by and see his beloved niece manhandled in this way? Without a second's thought I interceded, initially taking hold of his right arm, momentarily reflecting how worryingly thick, heavy and muscular it felt.

"Let go of her this minute!" I demanded, tugging at his arm with all the force I could muster, which couldn't have been very much because I didn't seem to be making any difference. Unbeknown to me as I did so, Frankie had managed to knee him in the groin area by pulling him close to her with a yank at his shirt front. This would explain why his angry face was becoming even more crimson. Now there's good and bad in most situations I suppose and the good in this one meant that this thug had let go of our Fran's neck. However, the bad news was, that he turned his rage on me and with both of his hands clutching the front of my wax jacket, he promptly lifted me on top of the bar surface. It's all a bit of a blur from this point you understand, with elements of my life flashing before me clouding the memory still further, but there was the distinct sound of smashing glass as presumably my hastened arrival on the bar counter sent glasses and bottles flying. Poor Frankie was recovering from her neck being attacked by holding her throat area and gasping for some oxygen. Meanwhile the bar room spectators jumped up and down like chimps in a zoo, albeit bald headed ones, enjoying every minute of their impromptu entertainment. (I have since found out that fights like this are a daily occurrence at this pub. Nice... Must put something on *TripAdvisor*...) This man, who hadn't introduced himself so I could hardly say we were intimate, had by now pinned me down to the counter but started to repeatedly pull me up and down by the scruff of the neck with the intention of banging my head to a pulp on the wooden bar surface. Thankfully, I have a thick skull. And I did, sort of, still have my bushman's hat on, which cushioned the blows a bit. I couldn't help but wonder, like you do when a skin head assassin happens to be trying to kill you, what the issue was, given all we asked was if anyone knew of a security worker called Fred. As such, I wasn't quite sure how we had managed to rattle his cage quite as much as we had. But I suppose the world in which we now live, is one where it doesn't take much to spark off a war whether that be with just the one person or a whole nation. I blame Twitter. Eventually, my assailant took a moment from his physical exertions to take the opportunity to shout some obscenities in my face which culminated in,

"I'll teach you to mess with me you little runt." (Well, it rhymed with runt).

"Who are you calling little!" I replied, somewhat breathlessly. This seemed to annoy him again and he just roared in my face like a lion with a drug addiction, before sliding my body back a few inches on the bar top like a catapult. He then fired me forward, so to speak, so that I flew along the counter like a bullet, sending even more glasses flying as I went. Thankfully, I don't think it had been cleaned for weeks so the sticky circular lager rings of days passed effectively slowed my progress and stopped my body from flying off the end.

As I'd been busy with trying not to be killed, or damaged beyond repair, I hadn't noticed that behind my jubilant attacker at the other end of the bar, stood the now fully recovered Frankie. She was holding the legs of a wooden bar stool, well I say holding, more accurately I mean aiming, as a few moments later she brought the furniture down on top of this chap with some considerable might. He stood, body spinning a little, in a pool of cheap broken pine furniture. The room had gone silent and the chimpanzee style spectators just looked on motionless. He made a strange sort of noise, his eyes seemed to roll, then with quite a crash, he fell to the floor. Out for the count.

"Bloody hell! You haven't killed him have you?" I asked, jumping down off the countertop in a certain amount of pain and looking rather dishevelled. Fran crouched over him and checked his pulse.

"No. Afraid not, there's life there – but not as we know it."

With that announcement the whole room returned to normal. It was completely surreal. Everyone went back to where they were sat; they picked up their gutter press newspapers, or their drinks, or pushed their small change into the game machines. Like absolutely nothing had happened and they were completely indifferent to the unconscious thug on the floor, almost as if he'd let the 'skin head' side down and was now being ostracised by his peers. In fact, none of them bothered to check on him or anything! He was abandoned in the pile of broken furniture in which he fell!

I gave Fran a reassuring rub of the arm.

"Come on," I said, "think we've outstayed our welcome." We were both more than happy to go but as we turned on our heels the Landlord called us over.

"Oi, you two. Over here."

"Oh, you can speak then!" Fran remarked sarcastically.

I assumed he was going to demand money for the damages, or declare he was going to have the police on to us but instead he nodded to someone entering the place.

"That's your man," he said, with a newfound co-operation.

We turned and saw a burly man in his late thirties coming in the entrance. Like our attacker, this guy had a brooding menace to him and I certainly couldn't imagine him being afraid of the dark or anything at all for that matter. We walked toward him.

"Excuse me mate," Frankie asked with a flirty grin, "Are you Fred from Culverland Security?"

"Yes darlin'. And what can I do for a sexy little thing like you then?" He replied in a gruff but friendly voice.

"I'm Fran, this is my Uncle Jerry."

"Alright mate?" looking at me now in greeting, with an approachable smile. "What can I do for you? If you're after making a booking for security staff, you need to call the office I'm afraid. I just work for them. I don't do freelance, sorry and all that."

"No, no, we were hoping to speak to you about something else," she said.

"Oh yeah?" he responded, enquiringly, looking down at the unconscious thug on the floor at the same time.

"Is he a friend of yours?" asked Fran. "When we asked at the bar for you, he seemed to take great offence, and picked a fight with us for some reason."

Fred laughed. "Ah that's just Psycho Sid's way."

'OK, *that's all right then'* was the sentence which passed through my mind facetiously.

"He loves a good fight, has one most days, usually for no reason, so I wouldn't take it personal, like. I shouldn't bother calling the cop squad either. Sid has a season ticket in the local cells. How'd he get down there though? He doesn't normally lose in a punch up."

"He doesn't normally fight me though does he..?" Frankie beamed back at him.

"I like your style darlin'," he replied, grinning and almost salivating as he looked her up and down.

I began to wonder if they'd forgotten I was there, so feeling left out, I chipped in.

"My niece and I research the paranormal."

"We want to talk to you about Tuttwood House," added Frankie. But at the utterance of this sentence, the smile being sported on Fred's face disappeared as did any colour to his complexion. He just seemed to glaze over.

"Fred?" Frankie and I looked at each other in bewilderment at his continued silence and frozen features. Then presumably because he didn't want to lose face with his mates he seemed to 'come to', flashed his eyes back and fro between us in a slightly panicky, almost pleading sort of way and whispered, "You better come 'round the back." And so, off the three of us went. This intrigued me. The mere mention of Tuttwood House and Fearless Fred became a frightened fella...

~~

There was an area behind the main bar with a small seating area and a couple of drink stained round tables with grotty beer mats which people obviously didn't bother to use, except it seemed, to note down someone's phone number. Or other little poetic messages. For instance, the one near me declared 'Tara [whoever she is] is a tart'. Pure Shakespeare I thought. We all sat down and Fred, who'd brought a pint of lager with him which was poured automatically on his arrival by the Landlord, took a long swig. He thumped the glass down on the table and stared into it as if to draw some confidence from the golden brew within.

"Who told you about me?" he asked apprehensively.

"I think you're pretty well known within the firm," I responded not wishing to give too much away.

"What? Pretty well known as a bloody laughing stock you mean!"

"No, I didn't mean that at all," I replied calmly, not wishing to provoke another pub brawl.

"I am a laughing stock, I know that. I don't need you or anyone else to tell me. 'Fearless Fred' they've always called me, what a joke that is now, boy, how bloody embarrassing. I sometimes think that's the worst part of it, the shame. I've never run from anything, me, nothin'." He paused and shook his head, as if he was feeling disgust, but in himself.

Here was a man struggling with this stain on his character and hard man reputation.

"What's this all about then?" he asked with a deep intake of breath, like a man would when he knows he's going to speak about a subject he'd rather not talk about.

Frankie, who had been briefed about the story on the journey, took over the questioning. Sometimes her frankness cuts to it much better than my way of doing things, in fact I often call her 'frank little Frankie'. I know, I'm sad. Anyway, she was straight in at the jugular.

"How come you didn't last the night at Tuttwood House?" Ouch, I thought. Put the knife straight in, why don't you!

"You haven't really told me what you two are after. You're not from the Press are you?" he protested. I thought I better elucidate for his reassurance.

"Look, my niece Francesca and I have a keen interest in researching real life paranormal activity. I happen to know Reece Hammond who told me about his night staff retention problem at Tuttwood."

"Oh, that git. Friend of his then?"

I wanted to clarify that bit straight away.

"No I'm not! To be fair, my feelings toward him are not dissimilar to yours. Basically tonight, the two of us and an acquaintance of ours will be spending the night there and seeing what we can make of it. Maybe we'll hear something, see something, film something, anything that may prove or not prove the existence of paranormal activity. That's it. That's what we do. Consequently, we're gathering a bit of info beforehand, which we always try to do. Therefore, anything you tell us will not be common knowledge, so you don't need to worry about your pals through there ribbing you in any way. Not on our account I assure you."

"If you want my advice you'll steer well clear of the place mate. And as for spending the night there, you must be mental. I've been in more fights than I care to mention, I've had drunken yobs coming at me with broken bottles when I was a bouncer, I've even taken on fellas with knives. But one thing I ain't gonna do again, is go near that bloody house on the Elsmere Road."

Frankie by now had softened her interview technique as she could see a giant of a man genuinely traumatised before us.

"What did happen then? Did you get hurt or something?" she asked.

"Not physically no. But it played with my mind, you know. Three times since then I've woken up shouting in my sleep at that... that, feeling or presence I felt there. It was like, well, it was like the darkness was watching me, actually suffocating me."

"You mean you were attacked by something?"

"Not as such. Oh I don't know...! Look, the best way I can describe how I felt was that, well, I'll take anyone on yeah? I'll defend myself against anyone. But you can see 'em can't you? But how do you defend yourself against something you can't see, but you just know is there, in the darkness?"

He had me there. The best I could offer him after all my time researching and reading about the supernatural was a shrug of the shoulders. Yes, I know, I didn't impress myself at that moment either. Well, I had been sliding along bar tops and I'm not as young as I used to be, so the shock of our bar brawl had addled my brain.   Thankfully Fran was more with it; presumably the euphoria of smashing furniture on someone's head helped her along a bit.

"Fred, why don't you tell us about the night you worked at Tuttwood?"

The poor man, with tattoos and muscles galore, but he still looked uneasy with the topic and proceeded to wipe some tension from the temples of his hairless head.

"Look I ain't proud of myself, walking out on a job like that.   Made me a bloody laughing stock at work, ya know what I mean?"

"It's OK, we're not here to laugh at you. We just need a bit of background to the place before we spend a night there doing some tests, to see what we can uncover," I said, trying to reassure him.

"Listen mate, if you want my advice you'd steer well clear of it. Something evil there, I'm bloody sure of it."

He took a large swig of lager which left my own beer drinking technique look positively amateurish. Suitably bolstered by drink, he continued.

"I was OK when I got there. Took over from Cyril, the afternoon shift guy and we chatted about this and that in the security hut outside with a coffee. He went off home and I decided to check the place out. It was about quarter past ten and dark, so grabbing me torch I went for a stroll around the building perimeter. There was no moon that night; it was cloudy in fact and windy so it was pitch black and the trees were really moving, if you know what I mean. And what with all the night time animal noises the place was already getting under my skin. I'm normally working at city joints you know. City noises I'm used to. I don't normally do country places, well, it's not really country anymore is it? It's so built up 'round there now. But it's got a big ol' garden still, even if a lot of it is under tarmac. So anyway, I get the keys and open up the main entrance so I can do the indoor rounds. I go in, stand in the hall and then I nearly had a coronary as the bloody front door slammed shut behind me. Just the wind I thought, but when I think back I really wonder."

"You said it was a windy night, so it probably was just that," encouraged Fran.

"Well whatever darlin'... So, I goes and has a look around see? I'm walking around the main hall and two or three times I have to shine the torch up to the top landing as it just felt like someone was watching me and I'm bloody sure I heard footsteps. I went up the stairs to see; I didn't want no burglars on my shift, ta very much. Then I'm practically to the top and me torch starts to flicker. I mean, it was dark enough as it was, so I really didn't need that. I whacked it on my hand like you do, when I was nearly knocked down the stairs by what felt like someone banging against me as they rushed passed. I managed to grab the handrail as I fell and as the torch seemed to come back to life I shone it downstairs, then back along my floor, no-one. No-one there. Well, I know I don't have much hair, but it certainly felt like it was standing on end then, I can tell ya!"

"Why didn't you put the lights on when you went in?"

"I would've, if they were working. But the owner of the place, what's his name – that Hammond bloke, he got most of the circuits turned off in the place so no one can use up too much electric by burning lights all night. Tight git. There's a few sockets left on here and there I think but that's ya lot."

I couldn't help but notice that Fred was becoming more and more anxious as he relayed his story. I thought if he held his pint glass any firmer it would smash in his fingers. After a breather, he continued.

"Anyway, I'm standing at the top of the stairs thinking about what to do next, and then I hears the creaking of a door at the end of the passage. So I shone me torch at it straight away, and there's this door, slowly opening inwards. I thought, right, gotcha, so I steamed down there shouting 'I'll have you, you bloody...' well I won't say the exact words in front you sweetheart..."

I must just clarify at this point, that Fred was referring to Fran when he said 'sweetheart'. I think he was anyway, but we won't go there. He went on as follows.

"I gets to the room and I run in. Empty, not a soul in there, just bits of junk, a crappy old desk lamp, a broken office chair, paper, stuff like that but nothing to hide behind that's for sure. Oh..."

He paused as some forgotten little detail presented itself in his recollection.

"It smelt too. Stank of drink. Not drink like in here, but port I think, that sort of thing. Not really something I'll knock back, but I'm sure it was port. But there was nothing in the room which would've made it smell like that. So anyway, I go back in the corridor and then, bang! There's a crashing sound above somewhere. I runs to the other set of stairs, there's a smaller set to get to the attic rooms and I'm up to the top passageway in a flash. It's like a fridge up there and smelt real damp and mouldy. All the while, I'm assuming I've got an intruder on site, so I make my way along the corridor as quietly as I can, looking in each room as I go and they were all pretty much empty apart from a few bits of old office rubbish here and there. Then I gets to this one room and there was that funny port like smell again, and I wondered if there was an old tramp or something in residence. I go into this little room, shine me torch around and there's nothing whatsoever in there. No one there, just a few scraps of paper on the floor."

He takes a breather and has another significant swig of his lager.

"Anyway, I must have been off guard or something, as out of nowhere, something just swept my feet away from under me and I was on the floor with a wallop, you know. Now, I'm not being funny but I'm no lightweight and to have me legs swiped from under me, *Doc Martins* an' all, took some doing. I didn't half come down hard on my left arm, in fact it's still bruised to buggery but I'm glad I didn't go down on me back."

"You poor love," exclaimed Fran, stroking his arm with compassion. I think she was flirting with him and I was beginning to feel like the protective uncle again. "What did you do then?" she asked.

"I just lay there for a few seconds trying to work out what the hell just occurred. But then I started to feel really breathless, well, suffocated across my whole face, like something was completely covering it, trying to kill me, yet there was nothin' there. There wasn't much light as I'd dropped the torch on the floor beside me but it was still on. Yet I couldn't see no-one, I was fighting back as best I could but against what I don't know because I couldn't see nothing. I really started to feel like I was going, I mean, I was really struggling for air by now, but somehow, and I don't know how, I managed to claw my way out of that room, and into the corridor. I instantly felt better and took in some deep breaths and had a good fill of the lungs, but I didn't hang about I tell ya. I didn't stop to look around, I just grabbed the torch 'cos it was bloody dark in there and got out. Didn't even look back."

"Nothing else happened after that?" I asked.

"I think that was quite enough for one night mate!" he responded somewhat curtly. "Given I was doing a runner, I thought I better shut the front door behind me, but I tell ya I still didn't look back. As if that offered some kind of protection! I took me sorry ass to the motor, and I was gone mate. And I ain't never going back. No way."

"I appreciate you talking to us. And don't worry, our discussion will remain completely confidential," I told him.

"Good, it better!" he replied firmly, "if any of the lads heard about this I'd never live it down. Anyway, no offence mate, I've told you all I can remember so do you mind if we end this conversation? I've got an empty glass and the pool table is calling, you know what I mean? Apart from anything else, it's something I'd like to forget about." Frankie and I rose from our chairs.

"Thanks for your help," she told him.

"Hey darlin, you don't fancy a quick game do ya?"

I might as well have not been there given his boldness at trying it on with my niece.

"No thanks, we've got to go," she said. "Maybe another time," she added with a flirty grin.

"Arh, come on darlin, I think you and I could play well together. Anyway, it'll do my fragile nerves the world of good seeing someone with as fit an ass as yours bending over the table."

Once again, I'm pretty sure it wasn't me he was talking to, although my own ass isn't completely unpleasant, I assure you. However, thankfully Fran made polite excuses to avoid staying. We crossed to the bar and bought Fred a pint of lager for his trouble and went, stepping over bits of broken furniture as we crossed the floor, although interestingly, there was no sign of our friend from earlier. He was presumably sulking in a corner somewhere, rubbing lager on his wounds no doubt.

I'd arranged to have half an hour with Reece Hammond at Tuttwood House, in that we could get a look at the place in daylight, so we couldn't hang around here. If me and Frankie were to be spending that very night there, we needed to get back to our respective homes and grab a few hours shut eye during the afternoon. Thus we got into 'old reliable', roared up the rumbling V8 and headed over to Tuttwood, debating our meeting in the pub on the way.

"You know, I suppose he could have just been imagining all his experiences...?" I said somewhat meditatively, drawing in on my cigarette. Although Fran was not impressed by that particular line of thought, she wasn't completely convinced by the guy either, despite her sympathetic soundbites to him earlier.

"I don't know. He's not the sort to go making stuff like that up, particularly as he doesn't want anyone to know because of his so-called hard man image." She responded, drawing in on her cigarette, stolen as usual from my packet. "But take that bit where he said he was on the floor suffocating, what's to say he wasn't having some kind of fit? He may have a medical condition he's unaware of."

"I can't see that myself," I said. "If they've got their warm and cosy security hut, I guess it's just as likely he didn't want to venture out of it on a windy, cold November night and simply stayed in the warm, fell asleep and dreamt the bloody lot. He probably never even set foot in the house."

"Even if he did dream it, he believed what he saw. I mean, he may drink in dodgy boozers that even I wouldn't be seen in, but I think he was being pretty straight with us nonetheless."

"Actually, to be fair, I think I agree," I concurred, "I guess he wouldn't do a runner if he'd just had a bad dream." I swerved into a petrol station as an unplanned detour. "Listen, it's lunch time and if we're to get to Tuttwood before Hammond departs, we haven't got time for anything more substantial. Plus, we've got to find time for an afternoon nap later. Do you want anything in particular to eat?"

"Yes, I'll have an anything," she responded sarcastically.

"Well you'll get what your given then," and off I popped to the petrol shop for high fat, high calorie sustenance supplies and some fizzy gut rot. When we're on a case, there's not always the luxury of a gourmet business lunch.

~ ~ ~

The entrance to Tuttwood House had lost any grandeur it might have had when it was a private residence. The gates and adjoining wall were completely adorned by advertising signage for Hammond Properties, offering the place for office letting. We pulled in and made our way along the gravel drive, driving past the little wooden security hut we'd previously heard about, which housed the duty security guard who barely looked up from reading his red-top newspaper as we drove by. Reece Hammond was there, sat in his aggressive looking four by four vehicle, whilst looking over some papers and talking on his mobile. Behind his car stood the majestic Tuttwood House in all its red-brick glory. Well I say glory, I mean faded glory. It obviously had a charm in its day, not being a mammoth property but still of a substantial size for any long past local dignitary. There was a touch too much ivy growing over one side of the place for my liking, and the white sash windows would have benefited from another coat of gloss, but I'm sure that any remedial work for maintenance was kept within very tight budgetary constraints by new owner Hammond. As we got out of the car, I soaked up the outside atmosphere. Although not far off a main road, it was still fairly quiet given the level of traffic passing by but maybe that noise was disguised by the gush and hiss of the surrounding, ancient trees as a pretty potent breeze shook the branches. Funny though, I didn't remember it being particularly windy earlier.

Reece had obviously finished on his call, which I gauged from the fact he'd thrown his mobile phone down on his passenger seat in a bit of a rage. He flung open his driver's door and jumped out with the exclamation, "Bloody timewasters!"

"Bad news Reece?" I asked, not really caring a damn.

"I had a meet here with some guy from an IT recruitment outfit. They were looking for office space in this neck of the woods and they were interested in having half the house, which would've suited me nicely, as half a building let, is better than none. Anyway, the git didn't turn up so I just called him and he said they'd found somewhere with a better location. I didn't thank him, needless to say, for not cancelling our meeting and stated in no uncertain terms I was a busy man who didn't like his time wasted by inconsiderate idiots. So, there you have it – anyhow, how you doing Jerry?"

"Better than you by the sounds of it. By the way, this is my niece Frankie, she helps me sometimes on my little investigations." Fran stepped forward and greeted him, at which she received a nod and smile and not a lot else from him. Which was surprising because normally chaps are all over her, being, as she is, a very pretty young lady.

"Come on then, I'll give you a quick look around the place, but I haven't got all day." He ushered us to go with him and off he stomped clearly an impatient man who would've rather have been somewhere else. As he walked with the two of us trailing behind like poodles, he gestured toward my '75 Rover P6.

"Isn't it time you traded in that old wreck and got yourself a decent car. You want to get with it." Not slowing his pace at all as he talked.

I burned with indignity and Fran looked at me with a raised eyebrow as if to say 'what a charming man'. I remained polite although what I really wanted to do was punch him on the nose and urinate in his fuel tank.

"The car gets me about Reece so it does just fine." He made no comeback at all, as if he had no interest in anyone else's opinion and his view was final.

He threw open the big heavy oak front door of the old domicile and we walked through to the hallway. There was very little in it apart from an old, cheap office style reception desk and chair to one side, sat on black and white tiled flooring. Fran was being quite efficient and had started to take readings with a couple of bits of equipment she had on her.

"What's she got there?" asked Reece looking at her in puzzlement.

"It's an EMF meter. Fran's measuring fluctuations in electromagnetic fields."

"Is she really?" he replied in a mildly derisive tone.

"Yes," I continued, as being a bit slow on the update, I hadn't – quite – realised at that point he wasn't remotely bothered. "Basically, we're doing a few baseline checks to see what the energy variables are now......... Actually, you're not really interested, are you?"

"No, not in the slightest Jerry. But do whatever floats your boat," and he promptly walked on to continue the tour, which was somewhat rushed to say the least. Lots of rooms which could all be lots of offices, tarted up with lots of magnolia emulsion, so that any period detail that may have existed in the place had been veiled under an ocean of cream paint and no doubt a fair bit of plasterboard.

Fran was being quite industrious and jotting down EMF readings for as many rooms as she could, given how quickly Hammond was taking us around the place. Every EMF reading was showing as zero though, which may have been explained by the lack of electricity running through the building and there seemed few other possible sources of interference. The temperature throughout seemed constant as well, that being chilly everywhere, but it was November in an unheated house so no real surprises. After a little while, I could see that by the time we reached the second floor, i.e. the attic rooms, Reece was getting a bit impatient and clearly wanted to be going off to ruin someone else's day somewhere.

"Look how much more did you want to see Jerry, I need to be getting on. I've got three planning meetings to attend this afternoon and a pile of paperwork to sift through. I can't hang around this white elephant for much longer."

At first, I thought he was referring to me, but then I realised he meant the house.

"Let's just have a look in this room," as by my reckoning we'd reached the room where fearless Fred had nearly breathed his last.

"Isn't this the room where the murder of the housemaid took place?" asked Frankie. Reece looked surprised.

"And how did you know it was in here young lady?"

"Oh, call it female intuition," she replied with the cute little smug grin she always uses to deflate arguments or trouble.

"Very perceptive. And yes, it was. Not that that sort of thing bothers me, it was bloody years ago after all. As far as I'm concerned, it's an office to be let, like the rest of the place. Mind you, the decorators were a bit funny about being in here," he muttered dismissively.

"Oh yes? Why?" I asked. My interest was piqued by his throwaway statement.

"Just like the security guards, bunch of easily spooked losers. Would only work in here in pairs, because they *'didn't like the atmosphere'*. I mean, what the bloody hell is that all about? Grown men!! Can you believe it? It feels fine to me, like any other room in the place."

He wasn't wrong; I had to give him that. It was no warmer or colder than the rest of the place and on discussion with Fran later, neither of us felt edgy or uncomfortable in the room, as I do think the two of us are normally quite sensitive to the 'paranormal wavelength', as I like to call it. Just for a second though, I did wonder if I got a whiff of Port... OK, it might've been damp.

In the end though, this was the last room we had a daytime viewing of, as I could tell we were outstaying our welcome somewhat. You didn't need to be a bit sensitive on any wavelength to pick that up and so the three of us departed Tuttwood House and gathered by Hammond's imposing Range Rover.

"Right, well there you go Jerry. Nothing spooky inside there to justify all my security staffing problems, don't you agree?"

"We've only had a half hour, day time tour Reece. Let's just see what we find when we stopover later. Paranormal events tend to be more active during the night so it may be a different story then," I protested.

"Oh come on! I know you do these little investigations as you call it, but you're not trying to tell me there's anything to it? I assumed it was just a bit of a lark on your part." He has quite a thunderous demeanour when he's got the arse with you.

"I wouldn't waste my time with it if I didn't believe there are things we can't explain," I added.

"Let's get one thing straight. I called upon your services Jerry, so that you can do whatever it is you do, then report back to me and anyone else who cares to listen, that there's nothing whatsoever for my security people to be getting their knickers in a twist about. That's what I expect you to tell me tomorrow morning. No ridiculous flights of fancy to veer off on to, simply your semi-professional verdict that Tuttwood House isn't remotely haunted. That's the deal – OK?" He directed this order like some kind of second world war Nazi Commandant.

"I don't quite recall our arrangement being like that..." I remonstrated, but he butted in.

"I'm afraid your memory is therefore playing tricks on you then, old-timer. Spend the night here if you want, you can get the keys from that one guard who does the night shift and do what you have to do. But you know what I expect you to say at the end of it!"

"Then there's no point in us even being here," I retorted grumpily. But he didn't listen, he'd already climbed into the driver's seat of his car, shut the door and started the engine. As he moved it into gear, he opened his window.

"I'll hear from you in the morning then." And with that closing proclamation he roared off in his flash motor, leaving Fran and I looking on.

"What a lovely bloke you've got us doing business with," said Frankie sarcastically.

"Do *you* think we should just not bother?" I asked her.

"But we've put all this effort in! You pulled a sickie from work. Your vicar mate is having a night off from praying to come with us. I think we may as well just do it. And be damned!" She had a point I suppose, although I hoped we wouldn't be 'damned', as she put it.

"Oh, come on, let's go get some shut eye before tonight," I replied. As per usual, that man had given me the bloody hump.

~ ~ ~

I got home and went around the back of our house to use the door to the kitchen as I thought it would be a good idea to pack up some food and drink supplies for the night ahead. Energy foods are best, nothing too stodgy or I'll fall asleep on the job, so to speak and most important of all, caffeine and sugar filled drinks and decent black coffee. No messing about!

Cynthia appeared with her usual frosted face.

"It's only you then. I thought we had burglars when I heard all this noise. I take it you're out again tonight on one of your odd little nocturnal activities?"

I just didn't have the energy to argue with her.

"Yes, that's what I'll be doing dearest."

"Messing about with all that vile occult stuff, I can hardly hold my head up in church some Sundays."

"There's nothing remotely occult about what I do, you know where my interests lay."

"Well if messing about in graveyards trying to see the dead isn't occult I don't know what is."

"I don't need to see the dead, I live with you dearest love, and there's not a lot of difference."

The tea-towel she was busy wiping a perfectly clean worktop with, was thrown with great disapprobation at the mug stand and off she went, slamming the door behind her. What a day! Maybe I should've just cancelled the evening as the whole business seemed like trouble from the start but I just couldn't deal with the last-minute aggravation. I got the food stuffs together, went down to my garden den to leave it with my ghost investigation equipment and I crashed on the camp bed. Before long I was asleep....

And what a disturbed sleep it was, having had a swirl of the recent events blowing my mind, so much so I had a headache brewing. I sat up rubbing my skull, still dozy, thinking about my bizarre dreams of Tuttwood, images of Reece Hammond dressed as a butler trying to kill Frankie, Stephen was there driving Hammonds big car back and forth into a tree stump. Then Cynthia appeared in my confused land of nod, we were back in the kitchen and I seemed to be trapped in the fridge while she stood holding its door open laughing at me like some kind of demented demon, the whole image spinning & gyrating before me. That's enough of that I thought, as those recollections were not helping my head pain. I then realised it had started to rain heavily, and it beat hard on the roof of my make-shift summer house office. That was all I needed I mused, having to load the car in this weather with all the expensive equipment, and not least soaking us all to the bone, before sitting in an unheated old house for most of the night in November, but I suppose that goes with the territory. I dug out some medicinal aspirin, lit a medicinal fag, downed some medicinal coffee, which I think was Colombian this time, and started to get myself ready, albeit with a heavy heart.

~ ~ ~

After driving through heavy rain and picking up Fran en-route, we arrived at Tuttwood House and I nosed the motor up against the front of Stephen's car, who being the sort of efficient fellow he is, had probably arrived a long time before us and was sitting patiently in his car, praying I shouldn't wonder. Probably felt he ought to check in with the guv'nor upstairs. I was first out of the Rover and being pre-occupied with trying to put up a small umbrella that I keep under the driver's seat in case of weather emergencies, I hadn't noticed that standing close behind me was a dark figure. Consequently, as I turned and caught sight of what stood within a few inches of me I nearly jumped out of my skin and let rip a couple of obscenities which would hardly meet with the approval of the membership of my Cynthia's women's guild, should I ever be in their company – which I won't, thank God. The tall dark figure seemed to join my temporary fright but soon regained its composure, as did I when it uttered,

"Hello again, did I give you a fright?"

It was Bert the security guard. I'd forgotten all about him in my rush to get to Tuttwood in the atrocious downpour that was all about us. He must've been sat down in his security hut as we drove in but given I didn't even think to look in that direction I would've easily have missed him. Over the top of his uniform he was wearing a long black rain coat with a hood, dripping with rain water, that partially covered his face and as the only light shining in the complete darkness of this cloud covered night was the one inside my car, it wasn't surprising this barely lit dark spectacle gave me quite a scare.

"There, is that better?" He put his torch on.

"Hi Bert, yes thanks, a bit more light is certainly useful. How are you doing?"

"Ah not so bad, apart from this weather. What a night! Can't see any ghosts wanting to stir on a night like this, can you?"

I chuckled. "No, shouldn't think so. I don't suppose Reece switched any electric on in the house tonight did he?"

"Nah, that Hammond bloke is as tight as a camel's arse in a sandstorm." He reached inside his pocket and produced a large bunch of keys. "I'll open the place up for you and help you get your stuff in."

Within a couple of minutes, as the torrential rain had made us all work faster, the four of us had managed to get in all we needed from the cars and Stephen had switched on a rather good battery-operated lantern so at least we had some all over glow, as well as a couple of torches on the go. As I put the last, most important bag, being the one with the food and drink in, down on the floor I realised I hadn't given Bert a proper introduction to Stephen and my Frankie. I turned to find he was already in the open doorway, his face looking quite grey against the black of his storm coat and the fluorescent illumination of the battery lantern.

"Are you off already? Didn't you want to join us for a coffee Bert? I was going to introduce you to..."

"No, I won't trouble you all no further. I'm happy enough in the hut but be sure to come and get me if you find any burglars!" he replied, with a sort of nervous chuckle.

"And what if we find any ghosts?" asked Fran sarcastically.

"Well if you find anything like that, I 'spect you'll be driving out pretty fast anyway," and with one last little uneasy look upstairs, he was pulling up his hood and off he went into the night's bad weather. Stephen closed the door behind him.

"Ah well, and then there were three..." he quipped.

"Never mind about ol' Bert," I said, "let's sort ourselves out and have a cuppa."

And so we got to it. Myself and Frankie set up what equipment we could given there was no power for anything. Thankfully, I have a camcorder which works on a rechargeable battery which we put on the first-floor corridor and a couple of 'passive infra-red' movement detectors, one of which went in the hall area and the other along the corridor near the digital video recorder. Stephen was in charge of setting candles up around the place, although we concentrated our work on the hall, and a downstairs room which would've been the drawing room in days past when it was a house. Other areas included the first-floor corridor, a room at the end of this corridor and of course, the 'murder room' on the second floor. We also had candles in the kitchen area, as that was to be our base camp, or in other words, where we sat for coffee and a snack, or three. Which was where we met up with Stephen twenty minutes later as he entered with his torch and sporting a broad smile.

"I take it from that happy face all is fine and dandy and you weren't plagued by any troubling spirit?" I enquired.

"No not at all, it's quite fun really."

"I'm too tired for it to be fun," responded Fran, at least that's what I thought she said given the yawn was so prolonged and noisy as she spoke. "Wake me up when it's time to go."

"Jerry, I hope you don't mind but I've left a small crucifix to act as a trigger object on a table in the big room off the hall," said Stephen showing a decent serving of initiative. For the purposes of clarity, a trigger object being an item left on a piece of blank paper and checked periodically to see if some entity or other has moved it.

"Good stuff. I hadn't got round to putting one out so that's a job off the list," I replied gratefully. "We'll have a check on that in a couple of hours."

"Can you hear that rat?" Fran said, swinging her torch to the corner of the kitchen, where a big and tatty kitchen unit towered almost to the top of the high-ceilinged room. "Under that cupboard!"

Fran has a dislike of rats but in an old place like this there's probably hundreds of the little sods and it wouldn't surprise me if it was only the sound of these verminous creatures in the walls which was scaring the insecure security guards. It'll make the odious Hammond's day I suppose, if that's what I tell him is all that's wrong with the place.

"It's probably just sheltering from this dreadful weather Frankie," reassured Stephen, but she still looked uneasy.

"I need one of those biscuits, it'll take my mind off it," and so she dived into the bag on the kitchen table and the three of us sat down to start a little briefing on the night's proceedings, with our thermos cups of coffee.

"Oh, there's another thermometer in here," she said, holding it in one hand as a double chocolate chip cookie was in her other.

"Bother," I retorted, "I meant to put that by the camcorder."

"I'll run it up if you like," offered Stephen.

"You've only just sat down lad, your coffee will be cold, we'll do it later." I sounded a rather slack, unprofessional investigator then, I have to say, but Stephen being polite and enthusiastic, protested, saying he'd only be a minute. So off he went to run the spare thermometer up to the first-floor corridor and like the experienced old timers that Fran and I were, although old isn't the right word to describe her, she and I remained sitting with our coffee, whilst enjoying another chocolate biscuit. Energy food you see. Very important. Then it gives us an excuse to have another smoke.

Stephen was a bit longer than expected, and when he did return he looked a little perplexed and a bit less excitable.

"You all right?" I asked.

"Yeh, think so, although there was something a little odd." Fran and I sat up a bit, with a mixture of apprehension for our new friend and concern that we might have missed out on something.

"What's happened?" she demanded.

"It's probably nothing." There was a thoughtful pause and he continued. "It's just that as I put the thermometer down next to the video recorder, I thought I could hear a woman sobbing. At first I thought it was you Fran, but then I realised it sounded more like it was coming from upstairs. You know, up on the second floor..." We were all quiet for a moment pondering a response as the rain lashed down against the old sash windows. Then I broke the thoughtful silence and spoke.

"Did you go and look?"

Stephen looked a little guilty.

"I walked slowly to the next staircase, trying to listen as hard as I could, and I was sure I could still hear crying but it's so hard to tell with all the noise of that rain outside. Anyway, when I got to the stairs any sound had stopped. If there was any in the first place, of course."

"You should've gone up," I muttered, a little peeved.

"Yes, I suppose I ought to have done," he replied apologetically. "Truth be told, I think I got a bit spooked, pardon the pun, being on my own."

"Like you would've gone up on your own, I don't think!" chastised Fran in my direction, "you wouldn't have gone unless I was there to hold your hand!"

"Whatever you say missy!" I retorted indignantly, affronted that my manly pride was being questioned by this impertinent wild-child niece of mine.

Stephen looked a bit wounded that he had let the side down but like the soft cuddly teddy bear I probably am, I thrust the packet of biscuits in his direction and told him to sit down and drink his coffee before it got any colder.

~ ~ ~

Some little time later we'd split up and were in different parts of the house but keeping in contact if any drama arose by using our walkie-talkies. Unfortunately, nothing really happening so I think the situation can be best described as one of complete radio silence. I was in the lion's den as it were, by situating myself in the 'murder room' on the top floor. Stephen was in the room at the end of the first-floor corridor and darling Francesca was patrolling the ground floor, no doubt regularly going back to the kitchen and helping herself to another biscuit on the sly. On that basis, I knew I should've stayed down there but it was too late, I was where I was and what a cold, grim little room it was too. Clearly when Tuttwood was the grand local house in times of old, this was only a servant's room but in its more modern times I would guess it must have been a store for office supplies. The emulsion painted walls were very scuffed and scraped and there were many empty screw holes where subsequently removed shelving and racking had presumably once been making the best of the available space for files and paperclip storage. I had bored of sitting in the corner of the room on the freezing floor looking silently into space, as a single candle afforded me the only cheery glow and visual aid. I got up and crossed to the single, small window and looked out at the night. The rain spattered hard against the glass, one pane of which had a nasty crack. The wind seemed to have got up as well and it blew occasional blasts of its frustration against the building, causing the sash window frames to rock against each other. I thought of Bert in his security hut, wrapped up warm, lounging in a comfy chair, no doubt with a daily paper strewn over him and probably the floor too, as he'd most likely fallen asleep while reading it. My little reverie was disturbed by the click from the walkie-talkie coming into life and this sudden noise gave me quite a start.   It was Fran.

"Hey you guys, thought I just saw something," she whispered.

"What?" I asked

"I was just walking down the passage from the kitchen and turning into the hall, when I heard a movement, and thought 'oh no, it's another bloody rat,' so I had a look around with the torch. And then just a second ago, I'm sure I saw some sort of mist, only quite thin mind, but like a little swirl, and it seemed to move up the staircase. Then I couldn't see it anymore."

"Actually, you two," chipped in Stephen, "have either of you just passed the room I'm in?"

We both responded in the negative.

"Right," he said followed by a long pause. "Because I could have sworn I heard a few footsteps along the corridor and they seemed to stop the other side of my door for a couple of seconds before moving off."

"Bloody hell!" I uttered. Perhaps the game was afoot after all. "Maybe we've got something on the video recorder then. Have you gone out to see if there's anything outside your door, or in the passageway?"

"No not yet," he replied, sounding uneasy.

"Well, go on then!" I urged him, "Nothing's happening up here so I'll come down and join you."

So, with my somewhat unreasonable demand, Stephen did slowly emerge from the end room and made his way along the corridor to the top of the staircase. By this point I, rather unfortunately as it seems, wasn't yet there to rendezvous with him as the next thing I heard was quite clearly, the sound and screams of someone falling down stairs. I quickened my pace and on reaching the top of the staircase shone my torch below, where the light fell on Frankie kneeling at the side of a motionless Stephen. 'Oh crap!' I thought, as I made my way down to see what had happened, while Frankie leaned over him doing the best Florence Nightingale impression she could muster.

"Stephen! Are you OK? Are you hurt?" she questioned frantically. Thankfully, he wasn't dead or anything dreadful like that as he tried to sit up, making the understandable odd groan of pain and discomfort as he did so.

"I've felt better," he said squirming with a shot of pain as he adjusted himself again. "Just as well all my years of rugby playing have toughened me up a bit, although a muddy field is a bit softer than bouncing on and off that banister."

"You play rugby?" asked Fran.

"Yes, a bit now and then, although not so much these days," he replied, surprised by her questioning.

"So... you're quite muscley in there then?" prodding at his thick winter coat, which isn't the thing to do to a man who's just had his ribcage assaulted by a wooden staircase.

"Oh, you are too," she said in surprise. "I never thought a trainee vicar would be quite so toned."

"Frankie, this is hardly the time to be asking about his bodily facilities! In case you've forgotten, he's just fallen down a flight of stairs! And stop squeezing the poor boy, for goodness sake!   It's   probably   blasphemy   given   his profession."

I turned to the patient. "What on earth happened!?"

"Someone pushed me! I know it sounds stupid but I just took a second or two at the top there, and as clear as I could touch either of you, I felt two hands push me really hard!"

"Don't look at me!" I protested. Not that anyone was looking at me, well certainly not my two companions, but I felt sure something was upstairs looking down at us; in fact, I felt the bristles on the back of my neck tingle. To be honest, and I can't be sure given the noise of the heavy rain outside, but I wondered if I heard a faint mocking laugh from up in the darkness. As such, I shone my torch in that general direction but it revealed nothing, so I turned my attention back to the team, neither of whom seemed to have heard anything themselves from above, so maybe I was imagining it.

We helped Stephen to his feet and made our way back to the kitchen for a break and a chat about how things were going. Therefore, a few moments later we were once again sat around the kitchen table breaking open the rations, and in the case of Fran and I, reaching for a restorative gasper.

"It's a bit early in the night to be going home, but you are sure you're up to staying here Stephen?" I thought I'd better check, as the last thing I needed were Men of God passing out with mild concussion all over the place. Goodness, if I was to go driving past Bert shouting we were on our way to Accident and Emergency, it wouldn't do the rumour reduction strategy among the security guards much good, which would doubtless send Reece Hammond into an absolute fury.

"I'm fine really, but I will just have a couple of Paracetamol. Got a bit of a headache coming on."

"You definitely need to sit this one out," responded Fran, who showing genuine concern, bless her heart, immediately reached in the bag for the painkillers to soothe our wounded soldier. Man-down, as I think they say in American military circles.

"I think Fran's right, perhaps you should stay in here..." I said.

"With the rats," she added cheerlessly.

"I was about to say, stay in here, rest and we'll keep coming back to check on you," I continued, trying to brush over her tactlessness.

"Oh no, I'm not crying off. I'd feel like a wimp, there's really nothing that wrong with me."

"You've just fallen down some stairs and now you're getting a headache! I don't want to take any chances, in fact if you're still like this when we do leave, you can let Frankie drive you home, so long as you don't mind her driving your car."

"No that's fine."

"You really are brave then, given her driving style is Grand Prix to say the least. She even, very nearly, has a driver's licence."

"Eh?" A look of concern crossed his face, which is probably normal among respectable law-abiding chaps like our curate pal.

"Don't listen to him, I have a provisional licence, you've got a full one, don't worry. If we got stopped by plod we can just say the L-plates have fallen off. I'm sure there are lots of people having driving lessons in the middle of the night."

"Right..." said Stephen meekly, clearly not wishing to offend Fran but deep down worrying he'll be sent downwards at the Pearly Gates.

So we convinced Stephen to stay put and half an hour later myself and Fran went off for a look around the house, this time deciding not to split up given the earlier disaster. We started by having a look around the first-floor rooms but I have to say, it wasn't a pleasant experience for either of us.

"There's not a nice atmosphere here Unc!"

"No, it's a cliché I know, but I really feel like we're being watched. I just want to keep looking over my shoulder all the time. And all that bloody rain outside, and the damp inside, is getting into my bones. In fact, I've got chills and they're very much multiplying."

"You're getting old," she said, amusing herself.

"I quite like Stephen, he's a decent sort of fellow don't you think?" I said, trying to change the subject to ease the anxiety our environment was causing us.

"Yeh, he's a nice guy. But then, so he should be, given his job."

"Your mother would like it if that was the sort of man you took home."

"If that was the sort of guy I took home, Mum would faint instantly with the shock and I would probably die of boredom."

"How do you know? Anyhow, you only think like that because you've spent so many years going out with yobs. The problem is, you've become programmed to go for that type." I surprised myself with that remark, because it actually sounded intelligent and that I knew what I was talking about. Unfortunately, Fran didn't share my elation.

"Whatever. If you like him that much, why don't you chat him up? Anything's got to be better than living with Auntie Cynthia."

"I can certainly concur with that last comment; do you know what she..." I stopped mid-sentence, as there was a loud thud overhead!

I switched on my torch instantly and shone it straight at Fran. "Was that you?" I whispered.

"How could it bloody well be me you idiot, I'm standing right next to you! And get that bloody light out of my face!"

"Just checking." My heart was pumping fast and in the deathly silence, bar the constant driving rain, I was sure I could hear my own blood pumping round all the veins in my chubby body. I grabbed the walkie-talkie.

"Stephen, are you still in the kitchen?" I asked, releasing the trigger.

"Of course. I'm sat here watching the 'Dance of the Rats' by candlelight just as you left me. Why?"

"Oh nothing. Over and out." I moved closer to Frankie. "Are we going up there to have a look?"

"Suppose so," she responded, far from boundless with enthusiasm. "We wouldn't be proper paranormal investigators if we just ran in the opposite direction every time we heard a funny noise."

"True. And it was probably only the creaking of an old house in bad weather. Like a sash window banging in the wind."

"Exactly," she concurred.

"Off you go then," I said.

"You sod off, if we're going, we're going together." I suppose that was the fair course of action, and so we made our way out of the once grand bedroom or as it was more recently, grubby office conversion and across the creaking floor.

"You see, all the noise these old floorboards make, there's bound to be a simple explanation for what we heard." When Fran said this, I'm not sure if she was trying to convince me or herself.

"Surely floorboards only make noise if there's someone walking over them?" I suggested.

"OK... well, maybe it's the wind then! Come on, we're supposed to be looking for the rational explanation all the time, aren't we? Get a grip Unc!"

We slowly crept up the less grand, smaller staircase that led to the second-floor attic rooms. I shone my torch along the long corridor that lay ahead of us.

"Ladies first."

"Go on then," retorted Fran angrily, pushing me forward, but I had locked my legs because I needed to stop and the reason I needed to stop was because I needed to think.

"What's the matter? Have you seen something? You've got that look, like a light bulb's gone off in your head again."

"I was just working it out and you know which room was above us don't you?"

"Don't tell me, the one where a young woman got brutally murdered. What a surprise!" she said with her usual sarcasm. "In that case, you're definitely going first," she quipped, pushing me forward with some gusto.

"All right, all right!"

We slowly edged along the passageway and reached the front of the murder room. We stood armed only with the torches for light, as the couple of candles which were left up here seemed to have gone out. Maybe a draught had blown them out, although maybe not. Either way, it was unnerving and very inconvenient.

"Ready?" I asked considerately.

"Just get on with it," she responded inconsiderately. I reached for the door handle.

"I could have sworn I'd left this door open earlier," I said as I tried to turn the door knob, but it simply didn't move...

"What's the matter with it?" Fran squeaked impatiently.

"I don't know, it was all right earlier. Help me push." And so we did, but that damn door didn't budge.

"Are you sure this is the right one?"

"Of course, I'm sure! Third one along, I was only up here a little while ago so I should know!" I barked, getting somewhat pipped.

"I'm only checking, you're not getting any younger so I just wanted to make sure that old memory of yours isn't playing up again. Did you accidentally lock it?"

"How can I? I don't have a key! And I'm not that bloody old either." I decided to assert my authority. "Now on the count of three, we ram it together. Shoulders as boulders. OK?"

"Suppose".

"Fine. One, two...."

I looked at Fran and she looked back at me as we took in a deep intake of the musty air and braced ourselves.

"Three!"

Before I had hardly got the word out, that door flung open, yet neither one of us had touched it and how we managed to stay on our feet as we both careered in to that room I don't know. However, within a second of being there I think it's fair to say we both leapt out of our skin anyway, as the dark outline of a man stood before us in front of that little, cracked sash window. All I can remember from that sight, before the pair of us turned on our tails and ran back out of that room at top speed was that the only distinguishable feature on the towering figure waiting for us, were two glowing yellow eyes. And curiously, that's all Fran can remember of it too.

As I understand it in modern day parlance, the descriptive phrase to use is that we 'legged it'. Yes, not very professional and I know that as a semi-pro ghost researcher, what I should have done was to stop and try and communicate with the entity. But such was its malignant and despicable demeanour that neither Fran nor I could stay in the room longer than the two seconds we managed, nor did we feel comfortable or courageous enough to go back and have another look. Within a short space of time we had got back to the kitchen, Fran first, who immediately went behind the door and promptly closed it within a second of me tearing through the opening just behind her. The bang no doubt must've echoed throughout the whole house and a very alarmed Stephen was most anxious to hear what had happened to make us return in such a dishevelled and anxious state.

"Hang on Stephen," Fran said to him, holding up a hand as if having to deal with him was too much, too soon, as her priorities lay in rummaging through her handbag, producing her packet of cigarettes, issuing a gasper in my direction before lighting us both up. We drew back on our smokes and as I looked across at my niece she was unnerved enough to have shaky hands. And mine weren't that much better.

"OK, we're now available to speak," she added, so he fully understood nicotine needs came before explaining our high-speed entrance.

Finally, we told him of the unpleasant occurrence on the second floor but not before I had wedged a chair under the door handle in some false hope that such an action might keep a malevolent ghost at bay. Although given that such an entity could probably materialise wherever it liked, was a complete waste of time and energy, but like a placebo tablet, it made us feel better at the time.

~ ~ ~

We didn't do very much after that. Fran is a very resolute and strong sort of girl and I'm not a timid field mouse either, yet we both seemed to lose our nerve after our unpleasant experience. And what had happened to Stephen didn't exactly help. Maybe I wasn't in the right frame of mind in the first place, what with lack of sleep and the weather, but that's the joy of hindsight. Stephen was eager to go upstairs but we wouldn't let him go on his own, particularly after his 'fall' and him being damaged goods and all. Neither myself or Fran were brave enough to escort him, in fact we were both quite keen just to go, so the three of us, whilst keeping together, collected up the equipment. Incidentally, I wasn't confident of anything showing up on the recorders and just for the record, the 'trigger object' Stephen set up was unmoved.

It was still raining as we opened up the front door with our belongings piled together in the hall way beside us, but it wasn't as heavy as earlier and I for one was glad to feel the fresh air of freedom. As we loaded up the cars Fran reminded Stephen of the offer to drive him home.

"No really, I just have a few bruises, nothing more than what I'd get during a game of Rugby. I really don't need anyone to drive. Besides, how would you get home?"

"Suppose I could walk," she responded, probably knowing it was a silly idea.

"In the middle of the night! I don't think so!" protested the gallant curate.

"Compared to being in this place, walking the streets in the middle of the night would be a doddle," she replied dismissively.

I noticed the approach of Bert in his long dark rain protection outfit, so turned to my companions and gestured them to pipe down. I didn't want Bert going back and saying anything to his colleagues about our activities. Even if I told him about our Tuttwood experiences, he'd probably think we were making it up and to be honest, I wouldn't blame him. Did myself and Fran really see anything? The power of suggestion interfering with our minds? That is to say, a dark room, noisy weather, being aware of the unpleasant history... I just don't know but running away like a pair of twats was not very scientific of us.

"Hello. You're off earlier than I thought you would be. Everything all right?" asked the cheery man of security fame.

"Yes, thanks Bert, everything's fine. Not much going on here I have to say, so we thought we may as well just have an early night."

"If you can call three o'clock in the morning an early night," added Frankie.

"Well, I didn't think you'd discover anything. I said to my Doreen on the way out tonight, I said they're wasting their time! Still, if you enjoyed yourself that's the main thing."

"Yeh well, not sure about enjoyment, given the weather and lack of anything to report, I think we'd all have preferred to stay in our beds," I lied.

As I was saying this, Stephen was getting in his car and let out a little groan of pain.

"Is he all right?" asked Bert.

"Fine," I said, "He plays a lot of ecclesiastical Rugby and occasionally does himself a mischief with his Holy orders."

Bert looked perplexed "Eh?"

"Doesn't matter. Take care of yourself Bert." So I shook off the umbrella, jumped in the motor and we departed, both cars driving off at a speed which suggested to any onlooker that we couldn't get away quick enough, rudely leaving Bert alone to shut the house up behind us.

~ ~ ~

By the time I'd dropped Fran home, got back myself and unloaded the car, it was nigh on half past four in the morning, so I didn't appreciate the irritating jingle of my mobile phone going off at barely a few minutes past eight. How silly of me to leave the blasted thing on and how even more silly of me to leave it next to my pillow so it nearly blew my head off. Then came the agony of trying to decide in my half sleep whether to throw it at the wall or actually answer the damn contraption, but I ended up answering it.

"Morning Jerry, it's Reece. How did you get on last night then?"

The last thing I needed was his thunderous voice booming down the phone at me.

"Oh Reece, umm yes, fine," I responded as best I could, hardly able to remember who I was, let alone what I was doing last evening.

"Good stuff, well, make sure you're down The Jolly Farmer at lunchtime, say one o'clock, I'll get you that drink I owe you and we can talk. See you later then."

I just about managed to respond with a grunt (which in itself took rather a lot of effort) before he rung off. He must've known I would be in bed but that's the mark of the man, deliberately being a git for his own amusement. Anyway, I was supposed to be at work that afternoon, and I don't like a lunchtime session before going off to my library slot. I could always phone in sick again, I *thought,* I mean I'm not well after all. OK I'm just tired, but it's the same difference. I flung my head back down on the pillow, but it was no good, exhausted as I was, my body was not letting me go back to sleep. The little grey cells were churning over the night's events. What should I say to Reece and when would I have time to look over the sound and film recordings we made? Not that I was holding out much hope of anything showing up. An overactive mind in combination with the overly happy singing birds outside and Cynthia listening at high volume to the Today programme on Radio Four downstairs, made slumber impossible and so I got up for much needed caffeine and nicotine. I arrived at the kitchen to the homely smell of scrambled eggs and toast, which clearly Cynthia had cooked herself for breakfast and turning to the window I saw winter sunshine streaming in through the glass. What a contrast to the night I mused, as my beloved wife, note the sarcasm, entered the room.

"Thank you for all the crashing and banging in the night Jeremiah. Some of us were trying to sleep. You see, that's what normal, reasonable people do at night time. And then of course, there are odd people like you."

With that, she banged an empty mug down on the kitchen top and flounced out of the room.

"Morning dear!" I called after her, which was followed by the slamming of the drawing room door. I could see this was going to be a marvellous day. It had started off bad and seemed to be going downhill fast.

~ ~ ~

Despite a pounding, lack of sleep related headache, I spent a little time going through our recordings of that night's Tuttwood vigil and there was absolutely nothing to show for it. When we packed things up, we'd already seen our 'trigger object' was rooted to the spot and hadn't been moved by some kindly ethereal agent and so may as well have been super-glued to the surface. I'd scanned through the videos, but nothing, paying particular effort at the point when Stephen thought he heard footsteps outside the room he was in on his own, but certainly nothing showed up on film – as per normal. Consequently, with no immediate evidence, I knew I would have to be careful what I said to Reece at our lunchtime meeting.

I got to the pub a bit early and although what I really needed was a large whisky, I knew that given how the day was going, I'd be over the alcohol limit and three yards down the road there'd be blue flashing lights filling my rear window. As such, I played it safe and much to Landlord Mike's astonishment, I got myself a filter coffee. I went over and sat at my usual corner table, wishing that I could light a ciggie without having to stand outside but we can't, so I just sat quietly waiting for Reece's arrival. All the usual gang were at the bar talking about the usual things we all moan about. Politics, country life, the price Mike charges for beer and they occasionally looked my way as if inviting me to join the debate but I wasn't in the mood. I felt rough anyway, but the meeting with Reece was turning my stomach, although I'm not sure why I was getting myself so worked up, but for some reason I was. And then, bang on time, I heard the easily recognisable sound of his big, in your face and up your backside four by four, pulling up as normal, practically half way through the entrance door of the pub.

The door opened and in he came, his flabby bits twitching in his too tight clothing.

"Afternoon all. Get the drinks in Mike, whatever anyone's having!" He shouted his order in his customary imperious manner and headed in my direction. "Jerry my boy, how are you?"

"Not too bad Reece thank you. How's business?" I tried to sound like I gave a toss, but I really couldn't care less.

"Ah well, it has its up and downs, but I reckon you're about to give me some good news eh? Therefore, today, I'm a happy man! So what about last night, bored out of your brain I bet? And what about all that bloody rain? I hear some of my golf course was flooded. I don't suppose you play golf, do you? Anyway, what happened?"

I definitely felt like I was squirming a bit and couldn't quite get my tongue around the challenge of replying to him.

"Come on Jerry spit it out. What's the matter with you? Too much coffee and not enough beer by the look of you. All you need to tell me is that the place isn't haunted and I can get that stamp of approval with the security company and start moving forward with the place. Sorted."

"Well that's just it Reece, I'm not entirely convinced there isn't something going on there!" I chipped in meekly.

"What!?" It's amazing how just one word can sound threatening if it comes out of the right person's mouth.

"Look Reece, I don't have proof, as nothing showed up on camera. That is, as far as I can see from my initial scan through as I was rather rushing this morning, but I'm pretty sure there is some kind of evil entity there."

"This has got to be a wind up?" he thundered.

"No," came my rather mild reply.

"In all my years of business, I have never heard anything so ridiculous. In fact, this whole situation is ridiculous! I can't believe all the bother I've had with this place, it's just another renovation project like any other I've done, a hundred times before, yet this bloody heap has been nothing but trouble! I thought you of all people Jerry, would add some sense and clarity to all of this and I must say what a disappointment you've turned out to be!"

"Sorry," I uttered meekly.. "Please just hear me out though. I know all this must sound odd and I really wish I had some fool-proof evidence for you to see but all I can offer you is my word. There is definitely something there; I saw it with my own eyes."

"Oh you have got to be joking! Saw what with your own eyes?" demanded Reece.

I was really struggling with my vocabulary that day and I wouldn't even convince myself, let alone a stroppy sceptic like Hammond.

"I don't quite know what to say to you. There were certainly odd things going on..." I did sound a rather pathetic weakling, perhaps due to my lack of slumber.

"Odd things!" interrupted Reece in a mocking, demeaning tone. "What is that supposed to mean? I suppose you were the worse for wear with drink eh?"

"I was no such thing! One thing I can be clear of, is that Fran and I without question, saw a dark, human outline in that second-floor bedroom. And I would think it's pretty damn likely it was the spirit of the man who murdered the maid all those years ago!" I argued back defiantly now because he was giving me the needle.

A nasty and almost scary expression then came over his face and his response was now in a cold and quiet tone which was even more intimidating than him shouting at me.

"Jerry. Obviously, you didn't quite understand our arrangement. All you had to do was spend an evening there and make it clear to all and sundry that you found nothing remotely paranormal about the place..."

This time I did the interrupting.

"But that wasn't necessarily the case. I simply can't lie about it, I can't be sure it's not haunted and regardless of what you want me to say, two of us saw something and that's aside from all the other odd stuff which was going on in the night., such as one of us being pushed down the stairs for instance, let alone all the events which other people have reported!"

"You think you saw something Jerry, that's it. Now just you listen to me. You don't say anything to anyone about this, you understand?" A finger from his otherwise clenched fist was being pointed very close to my face.

"Yes," I said suitably scalded.

"Good, because if I find out that any of this cock and bull nonsense you're spouting has got out, particularly to any of my staff, I'll sue the pants off you. Comprende?"

"Yes," suitably scalded again.

"I'm glad we understand each other. And to put this matter to bed once and for all and so as to confirm my own sanity, I'll spend tonight there myself because there must be some scam going on and I'm damn sure I'm gonna get to the bottom of it!"

"I'm not so sure that's a good idea Reece..."

He rose from the chair opposite me but he hadn't quite finished his tirade.

"Shut up Jerry, I'm sick of hearing your nonsense now!"

The cheek of the man! But still he continued.

"I must say, you've disappointed me. I'd expected better from you and yet clearly, you're as big a nutter as the rest of them. Whether this is some kind of bizarre conspiracy I don't know. Whether you're all in the employ of one of my competitors and you're just trying to wind me up or do my business some damage, I don't know that either. One thing I'm sure of, you and the rest of those losers, had better keep out of my way!"

As he said that, he'd leaned forward to such a degree I had thought he was going to grab me by the scruff of the neck and shake me like a cruet. However, he stomped off and departed the pub, slamming the door behind him.

"Hey, who's paying for all these drinks!?" Mike cried out, looking toward him with a look of fiscal panic over his face. But by then, Reece was practically in his car and down the road while all the regulars who were supping the unpaid for drinks, were doing so as fast as they good in case Mike tried to get them back. I saw my pint on the bar top and I guess Mike saw me eyeing it up, because with great speed he whipped it off and put it under the counter to sell on. Shame, I could've done with it. I got up to leave, as I wasn't feeling all that sociable now and made for the pub door. Landlord Mike called across to me.

"What have you done to upset him?"

"Guess I didn't polish his ego enough," and I left without further discussion.

~ ~ ~

I telephoned Frankie in the afternoon as I needed someone to talk to for moral support and I needed to cry on the shoulder of a kind and considerate person. In the absence of someone like this though, it had to be my Fran I called... I certainly needed some sympathy given my irate state over the earlier encounter with Reece Hammond.

"That guy is such a twat," she said. "You should have given him what for, I'm bloody sure I would've done."

And I'm sure she would, as she is far more assertive than I am at such things and wouldn't think twice about slapping him around his chubby fat face.

"But where would that get us? And as for that conspiracy theory of his, goodness me, why on earth would we be working for his competitors? He's losing the plot I think, too much money and power. Ha! And he has the audacity to call me a nutter! I think he's losing it himself or lost it completely. Far too much rich food and laying under a sun bed, it's all gone to his head and frazzled his brain."

I yawned as my lack of sleep was getting the better of me.

"Shouldn't you go and have a nap Uncle?"

"I'm a bit too worked up and annoyed to go to sleep. Perhaps I'll go out to the den and write up some case notes on last night."

"You shouldn't keep going out there to work, not at this time of year! It's far too cold, no wonder you're always ill."

"I am not always ill!" protesting against this exaggerated accusation.

"Mind you, all the drink and fags probably don't help you," she retorted.

"I like that! Coming from you of all people! Talk about the pot calling the kettle black!" There she was again, accusing me of exactly the same sort of sins she got up to. "Anyhow, as for working in the den, I just prefer being out there sometimes. Your Auntie Cynthia has a habit of creating an atmosphere so thick you can cut it, which sweeps through every room in the house. Besides, I'll put the little heater on if I need to."

So that's how I passed the next few hours. I sat in the den, my Barbour jacket done up to the neck and my bushman's hat still on, noting all our experiences of the previous evening, trying to leave no stone unturned. Well, for about fifteen minutes that is, before the lure of my camp bed and the cosiness generated by the electric fire induced the desire for a pleasant and refreshing teatime nap. And much needed it was too.

Even though my afternoon nap gave me a slight recharge of my batteries, by proper bedtime, I was still absolutely knackered. Every bone in my body seemed to be aching with fatigue, yet despite this, I simply couldn't settle when in my own bed back at the house. I was turning, thumping the pillow, counting sheep and finally getting myself wrapped up so badly in the bedcover, it was like being in a clinch with a boa constrictor. I felt guilty and concerned about that blasted Hammond bloke being at that house, at night and alone. Why should I care? I had no reason to, so why should I feel guilty? I didn't ask him to go and spend the night at Tuttwood, it was his own pig ignorance that made him do something so stupid. The clock was ticking, Cynthia was snoring and the night moved on at such a rapid pace. Something I have never understood about such bouts of insomnia, is how quickly the night passes even though one doesn't get to sleep. It's so infuriating because the night flies by and there is no benefit to the mind, body and soul whatsoever. In fact, this was a classic example on this point, because in what seemed like no time at all, I could hear the grandfather clock downstairs sounding its chime for the midnight hour. I unravelled myself from the bedspread, and sat at the end of my bed, rubbing my stressed-out face and wondering what on earth I should do, given I was absolutely wide awake with a mind turning like a spinning top. I even wondered if I should drive over to Tuttwood House to see if Reece was all right. What a preposterous idea! He probably wouldn't even waste his time going there, he was clearly mouthing off at me in the pub, trying to look like the big man. Knowing him, he'd probably spent the evening relaxing in his home jacuzzi with a glass of champagne in one hand and his full-figured sexy wife in the other, while by now, he was probably fast asleep between satin sheets, wrapped around the afore mentioned lady and snoring almost as loudly as Cynthia was. So under no circumstances should I have felt compelled to worry my pretty little head about the man, given he is a brute and cad of the first order who is plenty able enough to look after himself – as indeed looking after number one is a well-known policy of his.

Then, why oh why, was I dressed and starting up the aged Rover not fifteen minutes later? Clearly, the main answer is that I'm an idiot and a mug, but I have to say I was utterly troubled and had such an uneasy feeling that I simply had to drive to Tuttwood to see if Reece was actually there. I would swear Bert to secrecy over my visit, as I didn't want it to get back to Reece given his threats to sue me, (and he would too) but also because I didn't want to look a complete fool, or even more so than I usually do.

I drove erratically due to my fatigue but also because I was driving too fast, as such was my impatience to get there and I was really pushing the V8 revs high into their throaty best. Smoking a fag whilst driving doesn't help matters either but at least it was helping to keep me awake. It was a colder night than before as the rain of the previous evening had cleared up and the skies were beginning to become clearer and the cold air from the open window was refreshing to my heavy, tired eyes.

The quiet night time roads and brisk pace meant that I was at Tuttwood in what seemed double quick time and I pulled in through the rusting metal gates at such a speed the old motor lurched disagreeably to the side. I immediately realised I would need to slow down otherwise security Bert would, not unreasonably, wonder what on earth I was doing, so I toned down my excesses and drove more sedately down to his little wooden hut. The night seemed very dark considering the clouds were much less prevalent, but there was a cheery glow from within and I was heartened to see him acknowledge my arrival with a cheery but somewhat surprised face.

"Well, well, what on earth are you doing here at this time? No offence but I thought we'd seen the last of you," he said chuckling to himself as he emerged from his warm hidey hole and stood alongside my driver's window, clutching his sturdy torch in his woolly fingerless gloves.

"Oh, thanks Bert!"

"No, I'm only messing about. But I wasn't expecting to see you again, least of all at this time of night. Do you want a cuppa? I've just boiled the kettle for a brew; help keep the chill out like." He immediately gestured to go off and make that second cup but my business was more pressing.

"Not just at the mo thanks, maybe a bit later. I was actually wondering if Reece was here, I know it sounds a daft thing to ask but..."

"Oh yeah, misery guts is here," he interjected, "can't think what he's still doing, stuck in that house at this hour, all seems a bit odd to me. And now you too. Is there summat going on?"

I thought I better be careful about how I answered this, I didn't want to get in any more trouble and although Bert is a well-meaning sort, I could well imagine him having his wooden spoon out and telling his work colleagues everything I say with added bells on.

"No, nothing going on, I was just passing by and thought I'd pop in and give the place another quick going over, that's all." Even I was unimpressed by how lame my excuse was.

"Just passing! It's one o'clock in the morning! Are you havin' me on!?" he exclaimed incredulously.

Someone pass a shovel as I felt the need to dig an even bigger hole for myself.

"Well I've just come from a party you see and it was only down the road from here. So, I thought I'd pop in."

"You're a bit scruffy for a party, aren't you?" He said, looking down at my old clothes, hastily thrown on as I flew out of the front door. Although I was still moderately indignant at being described as scruffy I must say, even though to be fair, I wasn't quite up there with the best from *Vogue* magazine.

"Yes, I suppose you'd say I'm just a casual kind of guy Bert," which was all I could muster in response, keen as I was to get back to the point. "Anyway, I'll pop up to the house and see how Reece is getting on with his work," I added, trying to disguise any urgency.

"Why? What's he doing up there in the middle of the night?"

Bert was beginning to annoy me now, because all his questions were quick witted and intelligent, and my answers were wetter than the beautiful Lake Windermere. I decided my best bet was to ignore the question completely and get on with what I was there to do, so I shifted the car into 'drive' hoping he would take the hint.

"It's getting late, I'll just go up and say hello to him, then I'll be on my way."

However, before I could take my foot off the brake, Bert was trotting around the front of the car.

"Hold on," he said, "I'll come up with you." Before I knew it, he was getting in the car and making himself comfortable. "It'll look good since the boss man is here if I come along and make it seem like I'm doing the job proper!"

"Yes, but you've just made yourself a cup of tea," I protested.

"Oh don't you worry about that, soon get another one later. Comfy this old car of yours isn't it? Nice soft seats. Are we going then or what?"

Clearly, there was little I could say or do to change his mind however inconvenient and potentially embarrassing his presence might be. Visions of Reece Hammond standing in the hallway of the big house, watching me pull up outside with Bert in tow, and promptly flying in to a fury at me were running through my mind. I seriously wished I hadn't come to Tuttwood after all. I could've been at home in a warm, comfortable bed, albeit crazed with temporary insomnia. Thoughts of Hammond litigation were in my head, with him suing me for what few pennies I had.

We approached the building and it was in darkness, almost menacingly so. In fact, remembering my own experiences of the night before, my stomach turned upside down and I suddenly felt more than a little uneasy. Hammond was not the sort of guy to sit in complete darkness, but it was more than that. I was simply unable to put my finger on it, but something felt very wrong.

"I wonder where he's hiding himself then?" quipped my companion, who was clearly not troubled by the view before us and was no doubt enjoying this little change in his usual night time routine. Although, he wasn't privy to the same knowledge as me, I almost wish I wasn't either, given how troubled my innards were feeling, which I was pretty sure wasn't down to any digestive issue either, despite the fact my intestines had started to wobble like a jelly in honour of my current awkward situation.

I shut down the car engine, and we got out. Bert went straight to Hammonds monster Range Rover, muttering something under his breath about Reece probably being asleep on the back seat. However, this line of enquiry proved negative.

"Well he ain't in here," he said, shining his torch into every conceivable corner of the vehicle's interior. "Oh 'ello!".

His made this little exclamation, because on trying the car doors, he wasn't expecting to be able to open them.

"Fancy leaving an expensive motor like this unlocked!" he said in a chastising tone.

"Perhaps he has every confidence in your abilities to stop any car thieves on the way out," I replied, trying not to sound too sarcastic.

"I wouldn't waste my time for that bloke," he replied, snorting derision. "You better go inside the house and have a look Jerry." I noted the team effort we started off with had now turned into a solo mission, in my court, but I suppose this was what I had expected to do when I left home anyway. It's just that I'd started to take some comfort in having Bert for company.

I looked toward the building and any charm it may have had in daylight hours had certainly left it. The silence was eerie and the winter coldness was beginning to cut into my soul, whilst the darkness all around us was intimidating and thick.

"Didn't you want to come in with me?" I asked my companion with hope.

"Not especially," was his singular reply.

"But I didn't think to bring my torch with me," I uttered beseechingly.

"OK, I'll come to the door with you and if the arsehole doesn't show up when we call him, I'll let you borrow mine to go inside." How generous of him I thought facetiously, and we made our way toward the big heavy front door.

"He's left that open as well!" commented Bert in a disapproving tone. "He wouldn't make much of a security guard."

I didn't reply as such was my overriding feeling of doom. Things were just too quiet, just too dark, why on earth did Reece have to make a point, like the pig-headed ignoramus he is? But for that matter, I asked myself yet again, why was I even bothered? I could've been in a nice warm bed. I stood by the ajar door, listening, and took a deep breath. Maybe I was fussing over nothing and I started to imagine the surly developer curled up in a sleeping bag, probably an expensive, fancy one at that, in deep slumber and dreaming of his money. This gave me the courage and indignant indifference to go on and I pushed open the door which squealed slightly but which seemed all the louder in the silence.

"Shouldn't we knock first?" asked Bert.

"It's a bit late now," I responded, "just shine your torch inside."

This he did, waving the damn thing in all directions so given the frenetic visuals, I decided to call out to see if there would be any response. After just a few seconds Bert pointed something out.

"Look! What's that dark mound over there?" and with that he directed his torchlight to something which looked very out of place in the large entrance hall.

"Looks like a pile of tablecloths or curtains," he added. I squinted my old eyes in the hope it would help my focus.

"Well, unless there are shoes attached to those tablecloths, I'm pretty sure that's Reece!" I went rushing in but Bert remained by the door, shining the torch at what I had now clearly identified as Hammond lying on the floor. He was on his side, and not being a first aider, I had no idea if I should roll him over toward the torch beam, but I never gave it a thought and did so anyway. I suppose I assumed there was a chance he was just asleep. There seemed to be treacle like substance attached to his hair which I could hear as I moved him, but the light was so bad I couldn't tell. By now, the complete lack of any movement from the body meant I was sure Reece wasn't just in the land of nod. My eye caught sight of what I thought was his torch broken in bits just a couple of feet away.

"Hey Bert, shine that light of yours on this," I demanded. It turned out not to be a torch but Reece's battery-operated lantern, which I hastily reassembled as it was only the batteries and casing which had distributed themselves somehow and a crack in the side seemed of no importance. A few moments later I had more light to cast on the situation and was better able to look over the scene. The sticky substance was not as I had imagined in my naivety treacle, but thick stodgy blood which was all over his skull.

"Oh, bloody hell!" I whispered, then increased my volume as I called to Bert to ring for an ambulance.

"I've got a phone down in the hut," he called back.

"No just go my car! My mobile's in the glove box. You better get the police out as well." And with that he rushed off.

I turned back to Reece just as he uttered a vile snort of discomfort as if he was coming around from a temporary concussion.

"It's all right Reece, there's an ambulance on its way. Just hang on in there," I gushed, rather pathetically.

He looked back at me and stared hard in my eyes, with a face so white and wretched it will fill me with horror for all my days.

"It was him," he whispered with what looked like some strenuous and painful effort.

"Who Reece? What do you mean?"

But with that, he coughed and the few muscles that had briefly activated in his body, dropped and there was silence. He was dead!

I was dumbstruck. A wave of shock rained down my body and I suddenly felt physically sick. For a second or so I couldn't even catch my breath as the range of emotions from disbelief to guilt filled my heart and mind. Was I responsible for his death? Could I have prevented this?

I looked back to the front door from my dimly lit confines to see if Bert had returned but there was still no sign. How on earth did this atrocity happen? I instinctively looked above me and we were exactly underneath the balustrade of the first-floor corridor. Could he have fallen? I turned around and looked toward the staircase, which was hardly visible in the light of the broken lantern. At the top and to my complete horror, I observed two evil yellow eyes looking back at me. They were only there for a couple of seconds and then they were gone but they didn't just disappear, it was almost as if a head was turning away from me yet I couldn't really see any bodily outline. I was too shocked, too dumbstruck, to utter any word or exclamation after it. Of course, I should have leapt up to pursue this strange spectre but it was as if my whole body was seized. My daze was then awoken by Bert's return.

"They're on their way!" he cried, still remaining by the doorway and venturing no further.

"Bert. He's dead. He's bloody well dead!" I blurted.

"Bugger me sideways!" came Bert's enigmatic response, presumably from the shock of this news, and not, I hope, an invitation.

~ ~ ~

It's been some months since the incident at Tuttwood House, but the memories of the whole affair are so ghastly I haven't really been able to bring myself to finalise my account of the terrible business.

Within a short time of Bert calling the emergency services, an ambulance was on the scene, but of course there was nothing they could do for Reece. About five minutes later, two bored night shift police officers turned up who obviously underestimated the seriousness of this particular call-out.

The younger one was quite green and I mean that literally as within seconds of seeing the blood and brain cocktail the poor wretch Hammond was lying in, this youthful officer of the law was running to the door and throwing up. His colleague, a more seasoned individual, took a firmer line and was straight onto his control office and not fifteen minutes later the count of police saloons outside with flashing blue lights had increased to three. Within the hour, this was followed by two serious looking men in suits, by that I mean detectives, who were probably all the more severe for being called to such a vile incident in the middle of the night.

Then of course I was in the difficult position of having to explain my presence and to bring up the subject matter of the paranormal at the scene of a suspicious death. That of course, went down like a lead balloon, which in some perverse kind of way, is probably how Reece met his end. I wasn't allowed to leave the scene until five in the morning after much questioning by the austere dark suited CID chaps and with hindsight I am grateful that Bert came with me to the house that night, because if I had discovered the body on my own I think I would've been on shaky ground vis-à-vis the police investigation. I do genuinely wonder if I would've ended up being charged with murder or something. Thank goodness fate sent me company. But it just goes to show that in the ghost hunting business, never go solo. Mainly for safety, but also for an alibi...

Needless to say, by the time I got home I was on my knees with exhaustion and it didn't help having a call before ten in the morning from our Frankie. She, in response to my tale of the night before was surprisingly reticent, but I don't think she was sorry the world is now without this particular property developer, judging by the names she was calling him. I gave her my stern uncle rebuking voice and reminded her to refrain from speaking ill of the dead. Particularly given my own feeling of guilt of the whole affair, but ultimately, I knew where she was coming from.

The police investigation went on some time but I believe it was inconclusive. There was no real evidence to suggest murder or any belief it was suicide either. An 'unfortunate accident' was the last description I heard on the grapevine. What nonsense though, as if Reece would've fallen over the handrail! There is no doubt in my mind that somehow, I know not how, but for certain the evil spirit residing in that second-floor bedroom had some part in his death. Maybe a forceful push in Reece's direction, a bit like it must've done to Stephen at the top of the stairs. Not that I can prove it and I have no urge to go back there to try and do so. And I certainly didn't make that suggestion to the investigating police officers in case they thought I was gaga.

As for Tuttwood House, it is still empty and I am sure Bert is still one of the few security guards who will do the night time cover, sat in his little hut drinking tea and eating his wife's delicious home cooked cakes. Reece's business was sold on pretty quickly by the grieving widow, so who owns the company now, and indeed Tuttwood House, I have no idea.

As for the aforementioned Mrs. Hammond, her grief was pretty short-lived. In her married life she was hardly on the bread line as it was, but with the insurance pay out and the sale of the company with its vast property portfolio, she became more minted than a *Polo*. A mere handful of weeks passed by before a new man was shipped in to the old marital home and although she was quite a bit younger than her departed husband, her new chap is very much a toy boy to her. I couldn't possibly comment as to whether it is true love but the young man in question, an esteemed gent by the name of Kevin, was a mobile car valeter. For the last couple of years, he was apparently a regular caller at the Hammond abode, cleaning and polishing her luxurious Jaguar convertible. Rumour has it, the car wasn't the only thing he would be buffing up, but there you go, not for me to comment. However, I can only hope their relocation to a new life in Cannes on the Côte d'Azur is all that they could wish for. And I have no doubt Mrs. Hammond has the cleanest sports car on the Riviera.

TALE NUMBER THREE - THE STUMPY, GRUMPY CELLAR SCOT

Using the parlance of all Great Britain's footfall fanatics, my wife Cynthia is in the premier division of unpleasantness. However, she is not top of the league. She is beaten by her sister Agnes who would no doubt receive the *Premier League Trophy* for unpleasantness, should such a thing exist.

Agnes does not like me, even less so than Cynthia in fact, however I take some comfort from the fact the feeling is mutual. That said however, this doesn't make it any easier when I'm required to accompany my wife on one of our biannual weekend stays to the Agnes house of horrors. Although the only horrific thing in their house is actually my sister-in-law herself, but she does a pretty good job of it.

There was a slight change to the routine on this last trip however, insofar as they have moved to a new house. Agnes' husband Stuart has done rather well for himself in life and retired relatively early, if the grand old age of fifty-five is still classed as particularly early nowadays. He was a very senior director at a well-known, historic and reputable Scottish bank before finally taking the statutory farewell carriage clock and no doubt, further share options and exit bonus. As such, for many years they resided in a very impressive and grand townhouse in the centre of the beautiful city of

Edinburgh, but on retirement, they decided that being so close to the action of such a busy and vibrant metropolis was not the way to ease into the declining years. So, they took the plunge and made the bold and dynamic move to another very impressive and grand townhouse in the slightly leafier fringes of Edinburgh. I rather thought that going to all the bother, disruption and expense of moving about two miles from one prestigious old house to another one which is very much of the same ilk, seemed a bit overdramatic but given how well off they are financially, I suppose such concerns are of no consequence.

As such, we were due for a visit to them, although this trip was an extra special one as it was the first time we'd seen the new property and no doubt Agnes would wish to show off every last inch. It was not going to be quick, easy and painless for me, but I had to be brave and it's not as if the experience isn't one I'm familiar with. I was well versed unfortunately in this twice-yearly agony.

As usual for our trip up to the north, we let the train take the strain as the ad used to say, Cynthia nursing the pricey ceramic housewarming gift she'd bought them, with me lugging the bags around as usual, whilst being constantly reminded by my wife I'm not holding the bags properly or indeed not moving fast enough. Cynthia has a rather military stride, very much in time to the old hymn 'Onwards Christian Soldiers' but more of a wound-up acid house version, with added caffeine.

Stuart and Agnes met us at Edinburgh station and there was much hugging and kissing between the two sisters while

I had the formal but convivial handshake greeting from my brother in law. Agnes just looked at me with the normal repulsion and simply acknowledged my presence by saying "Jeremiah" at me while looking me up and down to see if I'd improved with age, which I'm guessing by her facial expression, I hadn't. At which point we were duly whisked away to their lavish abode in the comfort of Stuart's equally lavish, burgundy Daimler saloon, complete with all its luxury appointments and personalised number plate and in good time we were pulling up outside their new home.

Externally, it looked pretty much the same as the last one, in that it was also a four-storey townhouse in the dark sand and grey stone which is emblematic of the buildings in this part of Scotland. The traditional front door was even painted the same sage green as the last house and the similarities continued once we were inside. The drawing room, with its attractive polished wood floor, white walls and beige upholstery was very much in the same mellow decorative style as was in the old house. Again, and most contrastingly, they had copied their dining room décor over as well, with its curious mix of high, holly green walls with terracotta curtains. I had always found this clash a bit off-putting at meal times, although I was quite a fan of their long, mahogany ten place antique dining table. And their Chippendale chairs are of such high quality I believe they have even had a group of male strippers named after them, but that might just be a wicked rumour.

We were given the guest bedroom which they call the 'Lemon Room' and being intelligent people, you have probably already guessed the colour scheme is yellow. However, I cannot deny it was very opulent and as someone who doesn't care much for being in the same bed as my wife, I was comforted somewhat by the fact it was one of those extra wide King beds, so there was to be a mutually appreciated abyss between our two bodies.

We had plenty of time to have a wash and brush up, in fact Cynthia probably even trimmed her moustache – oh that's nasty, I shouldn't say such things, I apologise - before joining our hosts downstairs for dinner, beginning with sherry (oh I'd rather have a Scotch!) in the drawing room before moving to the bizarrely decorated dining room. I always enjoy the food there because without a doubt they do live well and the one good thing I can say about Agnes, note there is only the one thing, she can cook pretty damn well. However, the rest of our time there is amazingly boring. The sisters talk and talk and talk about nothing of any great interest to me, and whilst myself and Stuart bob along with pleasant enough small talk, we don't really bond as such. He is of a much higher social class league than my humble self, as indeed I'm frequently reminded by Cynthia, and I rather feel I'm looked upon by the three of them as some kind of odd curiosity which has to be tolerated but not embraced. I'm old enough and ugly enough not to be too phased by it now, but I do regret the wasted time on these visits. Edinburgh has such a fascinating array of paranormal tales and legends which I could be investigating in my time up here, but instead we always have to spend Saturday daytime trailing around department stores looking at overpriced home furnishings punctuated by coffee bar lattes, so the ladies can discuss and review their purchases. And why can't we visit when the annual festival is taking place? I'll tell you why, because that would be fun, which is not a word in the vocabulary of the company I have to keep while in the historic Scottish capital, as they are all far too high-brow for such amusements.

I'm not sure about any particularly recent sightings of the well-known Edinburgh ghost legends, such as the tunnel drummer at the castle, the phantom coach tearing along the Royal Mile or indeed the occasional appearances of Lord Darnley at Holyrood but I bet a city of such history and provenance has a tale to tell. Of course, the famous stories are all well and good, but the not so famous, off the beaten track tales, I would very much enjoy looking into whilst I am up there. But I know my place, and it is to walk behind my betters carrying shopping bags, admiring any attractive architecture if outside or any attractive department store ladies if inside. These little musings pass the time until the next meal break, fag break or loo stop. Yes, I know how to have a good time.

Agnes culinary skills were most successful on the Friday evening, starting as we did with a most splendid Scottish smoked salmon roulade, followed by venison fillet with neeps and whisky sauce. At last I got some whisky, just a shame it wasn't in a glass. The iced parfait of some sort of tropical fruit orgy was also quite passable and the whole meal, as usual, was quite a treat compared to the thrown together mishmash I have to do for myself at home, as Cynthia infrequently cooks anything for me these days, citing the reason she never knows when I'm in or not.

At least the repast made up for the conversation, which was basically a catch up on the trappings of the comfortable life that Stuart and Agnes enjoy, which doesn't bother me, Stuart earned the money so fair enough, it's just that when we hear these tales, Cynthia normally responds with derogatory comparisons against myself.

"Yes, Jeremiah still just does his little part time job at the library and of course that silly hobby of his...." Or, "yes, he still drives around in that ancient Rover; why we can't have a sensible, modern car I just don't know." Or, "Jeremiah still smokes like a chimney you know," and turning to me, which is rather gracious of her as they normally act like I'm not there, "you will remember to go outside to smoke won't you? I don't want you intoxicating Agnes' lovely furnishings..."

And you've heard the expression, 'good cop, bad cop'? Well, here we play 'good hubbie, bad hubbie.

"I'm trying to convince Stuart to write his autobiography, as a little project for him in his retirement," fawned Agnes.

"What a lovely idea!" chipped in my wife, genuinely excited for them.

"Well, I don't know about that, ladies, I think I'll have a bit of a rest for a few months first. Maybe, if I get bored, I'll have a go at it," gushed Stuart with hollow modesty.

"Oh darling, but it would be such a good read. How you got to the top of the banking profession, an internationally respected finance figure, a business expert with many skills to lead and instruct those willing to learn from you..." our hostess continued to plead.

I wondered about writing an autobiography and I could tell the world about how I stack and rack books at the library, it might even be enough to change the face of the western world. I stopped my bitter musings as Stuart continued.

"Agnes dear, I will give it some thought. At the moment I'm looking forward to a bit of golf and maybe a few more weekend shoots each winter. Are you a golfing man Jerry?"

"Me!? No, not my scene, and I don't think I'd suit the pullovers." Then before I could go any further, Cynthia took over.

"I'm afraid Jeremiah is not into sport of any kind. Too much effort for him."

"Yes, but the muscles on my drinking arm are second to none," I retorted sarcastically, which unsurprisingly resulted in a scowl of disapproval over Cynthia's face, and a sympathetic glance from Agnes to her sister for having to live with me. Although I rather think I noticed a little grin from Stuart who was probably secretly admiring my bravery and rebellion.

"I love my golf; in fact, I'm a member of the Royal Troon Club in Ayrshire. It's not that long a drive from home, but Agnes and I are looking at getting a small apartment in the area, so we don't have a late drive back here after one of the club dinners. I expect in the warmer weather, I might end up spending more time over in Ayrshire golfing, than being at home here."

I resisted the temptation to say 'bully for you' as my wife was so busy clapping her hands with glee and excitement at this news, I wouldn't have wanted to spoil the atmosphere.

After we'd had some coffee with delicious home-made chocolate mints, the ladies declared they wanted to move through to the sitting room for more catching up. I personally, given my contented and full belly, would have been quite happy to have gone outside (as requested) to smoke an end of day ciggie and retire for the night. Normally on these visits, myself and Stuart would follow the ladies and just sit with them, nodding and saying 'yes dear' to our respective partners at the right places like little lap dogs. However, rather unusually, Stuart invited me to his study as we were leaving the dining room and then, making polite excuses to the women folk, he led me through to a room just along from the hallway.

Although we'd had a bit of a tour of the house earlier, shortly after our arrival, this was one of the rooms we had not seen. He had described it as his study, but it was a bit more than that, and I fell in love with the room immediately, indeed I was quite jealous that I didn't have such a room for myself at home. Although, I like my garden den, my little centre of paranormal investigations thinly disguised as an old summer house, Stuart's study was more of an in-house gentleman's club.

The lower half of the walls were of white gloss wainscoting, while the rest of the walls were painted in a dark, rich aubergine colour. His 'study' area, by that I mean the part which had an old leather topped pedestal mahogany desk and captain's chair, was by the arched, but curtainless windows. However, the rest of the room was furnished with traditional chesterfield leather chairs and a sofa, whilst a stunning antique bureau bookcase almost lined an entire wall it was so grand. It was topped, almost at ceiling level, by four marble busts of respectable looking chaps of a previous time. Don't ask me who they were though. A large, ornate gilt mirror topped the mantelpiece as an open fire smouldered beneath, albeit without much life in it.

"Come and sit by the fire Jerry," he said, reaching down to it with a poker and giving it a prod, before throwing a couple of logs on top. "Let's see if we can get a bit of flame in here, take the chill off. I should have popped through and stoked it up during dinner, but my memory isn't what it was. I expect you feel that too nowadays, eh?"

"Now and then," I replied, not wishing to admit to any bodily antiquity. "Lovely room this Stuart."

"Aye my little haven. A place where a man can be a man."

I wasn't quite sure what he meant by that and was beginning to wonder if he was trying to seduce me. I know they say a change is as good as a rest and I'm an open-minded sort of a fellow, but he really isn't my type thank you.

"Let me get you a snifter," he said moving toward a small drink's cabinet, whereby he produced two cut crystal brandy balloons and proceeded to pour generous portions. I noted the elegant bottle was marked XO, so it was some good gear and certainly beyond my budget at home. He then walked over to one of the cupboards in the bureau and produced a small humidor. He opened the lid in front of me like a subservient waiter, revealing a row of neat and impressive tubes of Havana cigars.

"My wife has the same low opinion of smokers as yours, but she doesn't mind if I have the occasional after dinner cigar once or twice a week, so long as I only do so in my room here. Would you care to have a chew on one dear boy?" Well, it would be rude not to I thought.

"Thank you, I think I can be tempted and it will make a nice change," I replied graciously.

"Excellent. You'll need the cutter. Here you go."

In a moment or two, we were both comfortably sat each side of a now more vigorous fire, with our excellent cognac in one hand and a fat, expensive cigar in the other.

"Jerry," started Stuart followed by a long pause, as we both stared into the flickering flames.

"Yes?" I replied, eager to hear what he had to say, given I don't normally get invited for a drink by him on our visits. In fact, this was the first time ever.

"I know Agnes & Cynthia don't really have any time for your specialist interest, you know, ghosts and ghouls and that sort of thing and to be honest, it's not something I'd ever given a second thought to. That is to say, I always thought if it was something that interested you, then so be it. Each to their own. But if someone was to stop me in the street and ask me outright if I believed in anything paranormal then I would probably tell them that such things, in one's humble opinion, were complete nonsense. I'm just that sort of fellow you see, being in banking all those years I suppose. With money everything is either black or white, everything must make sense to the last penny. Do you see what I'm getting at?"

"Yes, I do," I replied. "You don't believe in the supernatural and I respect your opinion. I'm guessing though, there is more to this conversation than you merely denouncing the paranormal, as if for the formal record.. No disrespect, but I've been making these little visits to your home now for years and this is the first time I've enjoyed Cognac and a cigar with you. So I suppose there's a 'but' on its way?" He may have been a clever-dick banker, but I wasn't born yesterday.

"You're more perceptive than you look but yes, you could say that, aye. And I must ask you to forgive me for my lack of hospitality in the past and the fact my inviting you for guidance and advice now is quite so obvious."

"You want advice from me?" I asked somewhat surprised.

"Please. At least I want to tell you about a couple of odd little occurrences which happened recently. Although to be frank, I'm not sure if I should be telling you or a psychiatrist, which is part of the problem. I rather wonder if in fact, I'm actually going mad or senile. Or maybe perhaps I'm just struggling to get used to this whole business of being retired and it's having an effect on my mental state. Of course, I haven't seen my doctor about this, not sure why, I just feel so damn uncomfortable about doing so in case they cart me off to the funny farm."

The man was clearly troubled by something and so I put my sympathetic face on.

"Well if I can help in anyway, of course I will. Has something happened then?"

"Indeed. Well at least I think so, assuming it's not all in my mind."

"I'm sure it's not, so tell me." And so, after taking a puff on his cigar, he got to the nub of it.

"One night, about a month ago, I was having trouble sleeping. We'd had another week of decorators being in the house, but that was the last day of them being here, thank the Lord. What with all the paint fumes and disruption, I was in quite an excitable mood given they'd finished, so we could start getting some normality back in our lives. As a result, I was tossing and turning in bed because my mind couldn't switch off from thinking about what needed to be done next in the house, taking some more furniture out of storage, running through where things were to be placed and so on. Well, I didn't want to disturb Agnes and it was pointless me staying in bed, so I got up and went down to the kitchen to make a cup of hot milk or a malty drink of some kind.

"And so, about fifteen minutes later, I was sitting at the kitchen table nursing my mug. I was a bit annoyed that I was up and still awake at one in the morning but tried not to think of too much as I was hoping to let my mind switch itself off. And to my shock the damnedest thing happened!"

He looked me straight in the eyes as he said this, as if to emphasise his earnestness.

"Go on," I said encouragingly, taking another nip of the high-quality brandy.

"The kitchen door opened, and I looked across, assuming it would be Agnes coming downstairs to see where I was, and to my complete surprise, there before me entered the most ugly, short, fat little man I ever did see! I was so astonished I was simply unable to utter a word. He had a big ginger beard and bald head and the queerest looking clothes. He strutted across the kitchen, not making a sound or even giving me a second look, went over to the cellar door, opened it, went in, and that was that. Well I just sat there, speechless and completely frozen to the spot, not supernaturally, I just mean with the shock. As I said earlier, I didn't believe in ghosts and still didn't, even after that strange occurrence, but I couldn't believe it to be real either. I know I should've got up and gone straight after the blighter. But I didn't. When I was finally able to move myself, I simply rushed to the cellar door, jammed a chair top under the handle and ran upstairs to bed, where I passed a most unpleasant night, not sleeping a wink."

I mulled over what he had told me for a second or so, and then asked for some clarification.

"What happened in the morning? I mean, if it was a real person they would still be in the cellar the following morning, wouldn't they? I assume there's only one way in or out?"

"Yes, it's the only door to get down there. The next day I came down to the kitchen, with Agnes, in complete trepidation, wondering if I'd caught a burglar and needing to call the police. But then I assumed that somehow, I'd dreamt about the whole business, even though it all felt so real and I thought maybe I'd been wrong, maybe I was asleep and simply dreamed about this odd little man. Maybe the effect of the paint fumes and all that. But my heart sunk when she opened the kitchen door and there was the chair I'd left under the cellar door handle.

"What on earth is that doing there!" she exclaimed, at which point and without moving the chair, I told her what had happened the night before. She looked at me incredulously, and I could tell in her eyes she'd just thought I'd had a bit too much to drink the night before.

"If you think there is someone down in the cellar, why haven't you called the police?" Agnes demanded.

"I didn't want to look a fool if there wasn't anyone there," I told her.

"But you were just insisting someone did go down there!" she rebuked, "but if so, how did they get in? The locks were changed when we moved in darling, the alarm was on, and we've just passed the front door and that hasn't been disturbed."

"I've no idea!" I cried, "but I know what I saw!" Of course, that didn't cut any ice with the old girl, you know what she's like, and so she moved the chair away from the handle, opened the door and turned the light on.

"What are you doing? You're surely not going down there are you!?"

"Well of course I am Stuart! I'm sure I don't know what's the matter with you!" And with that she shouted down the stairs.

"Hello?" she screamed. But there was silence.

"Right, well, this won't do," she announced and promptly went marching down the staircase to the depths of our basement.

"I don't think you should be doing that Aggie!" I urged. "At least, arm yourself dear!"

"Oh, don't be preposterous!" she barked. "I want to know what's going on." One could hardly let her go down on her own, so I grabbed a wooden spoon off the counter as it was the only substantial thing to hand, and went after her. Then of course, we got to the cellar, which hadn't got much in it, just some old junk here and there we can't decide what to do with, but there was nobody there.

"Well?" she said, reprovingly, "not a soul here!"

"Quite," I replied timidly. Then she looked at me, standing before her in my dressing gown brandishing a wooden spoon, and started to laugh.

"Oh, you can be quite a daft-pot darling, let's get you some tea, and you can read the morning paper and maybe go back to bed and catch up on a bit of sleep. You've worked yourself up into quite a silly little frenzy, haven't you?" She said all this with concern, albeit slightly patronisingly.

"And that, Jerry, was all that was said on the matter between us, as I didn't want to pursue it with her in case she sent for the men with straight-jackets. You know how strong-willed she is."

"It's an interesting account Stuart; I suppose it could've been your imagination playing tricks on you. The effects of being in a house filled with paint fumes or something like that. But I'm no doctor."

He looked back at me as I said this with a very serious expression and leaned forward.

"Ah, but that's not the end of it. There's more!"

"Really?" I exclaimed, tactfully waving my near empty brandy goblet in his line of vision.

"Ah, I see your glass is almost empty. We'd better have a top up."

"Oh, I hadn't noticed," I lied, at which point he arose from his Chesterfield leather chair and topped up our glasses with the very fine Cognac.

"That's kind thank you. So what else has happened?" I enquired, my concentration returning now that I had a replenished drink.

"Well the whole matter was running through my mind for the following few days. I kept thinking about what I should've perhaps done. I think for my own sanity I wanted to see if this strange event would happen again, so I thought long and hard about what I should do. Then I realised that given it was a Friday night I saw this strange apparition, if indeed it was one, and if indeed I did see something, perhaps I should sit up on the next Friday evening to see if it would happen again. So, I gathered up all my courage and then exactly a week later, I waited until Agnes was asleep, then went down to the kitchen to wait. This time I sat at the table with a mug of good strong coffee and I must admit the adrenaline was pumping around my veins at frenetic speed. And then, sure enough at a minute or so after one in the morning, the kitchen door slowly and silently opened and in walked the same creepy little man! This time as he waddled toward the cellar door, I noticed he had a small hump on his back and his dirty face had more than his fair share of warts on it. I was about to speak to him, demanding to know who or indeed, what he was, when unlike last time, he actually turned and looked straight at me! The chill that went down my spine I cannot tell you! Any courage I thought I had to try and speak to it was knocked right out of me... And as you can see I don't have much hair now my declining years have set in, but I tell you the few I have left stood on end. The first time in my life I've actually felt such a sensation. But he didn't just look at me, he angrily shook his fist at me, and then as before, casually opened the cellar door, went in and closed the door behind him. Damn cheek! I arose from my chair, all fear gone from me now, being replaced by burning rage, and I promptly stomped across the kitchen, heavy metal torch in hand, to the door he'd just disappeared behind. I flung it open, turned on the lights and marched down the staircase holding my torch more like a weapon than its actual purpose in life. Only when I got to the cellar he was not to be seen. I searched all around it, in every nook and cranny but there was simply no one there. I stood silently for a moment or two listening, but all was peace, although I think all told, this was a bit of a mistake as the lack of any sound simply unnerved me and my bravery then gave way to fright. As such, I ran back up the stairs, firmly closing the door behind me and came straight to this room, poured myself a stiff drink and spent the remainder of the night curled up on that settee there. And that Jerry, was about three weeks ago and I have not probed the matter further, although the whole bizarre business hasn't been out of my mind in all this time. Do you think I'm mad?"

"Yes, I do. Completely cuckoo I'm afraid."

"What!? Really!?"

"Only joking."

I set out to reassure him, because I truly didn't believe it was his imagination.

"No, I don't think you're mad at all. And I think you've been quite brave all things considered. There's many a man who would've moved out of the house the morning after the first sighting."

"I don't, well, didn't believe in ghosts, but I am beginning to wonder, as I simply cannot think of any rational explanation for those two events."

"It certainly sounds like an apparition, maybe some sort of recurring ghost, assuming it returns every Friday, but who's to say it doesn't make the same trip every night? Perhaps it has, for years and years."

"That would follow I suppose," Stuart replied. "I'm afraid I cannot answer for sure, as like I said, both times I saw the thing, it was a Friday. Or technically, early Saturday."

"There must be some reason for its trip to the cellar, unfinished business of some kind, or something he wants. But it does sound like he's grounded here."

"Grounded?" asked Stuart.

"As in, there's something keeping him to this house, but by the sounds of it, it's of his own doing. That is to say, he doesn't *want* to leave it. I don't think it's a residual haunting, not after he effectively interacted with you like he did. That certainly can't be put down to an imprint on time," I suggested.

"I don't really follow any of that Jerry, but one thing I am sure of is that as the legal owner of this house, I am not prepared to be sharing it with anyone or anything, be it of this time or not. On that basis, what on earth should I do? Get an exorcism? I'm not Catholic, but do I need to get a priest in? Do they do it on a pay as you go basis?"

The poor man sounded desperate and I can understand why. It's not nice having ugly short ghosts shaking their fists at you in the small hours, on top of living with a woman like Agnes and so I immediately resolved to help the poor man out.

"Well," I said firmly, "relevant or not, today is a Friday, for another fifteen minutes anyway, so what about the two of us spending the night actually *in* the cellar? Rather than in the kitchen, let's come at him from another angle and see if anything happens the other side of the door."

"Spend the night in the cellar?! Tonight! Goodness my dear chap, you don't mess around do you? That all sounds a bit drastic!" he cried.

"It's what I'd do," I responded, trying to sound heroic and brave.

"And you don't fancy doing it on your own then?"

Something was telling me he wasn't up for the challenge.

"Not especially. And as you say, it's your house so surely you want to defend it and get to the bottom of this mystery?" I had him there.

"Aye, it may be my house, but if the lavatory was blocked, it doesn't mean I'd want to shove my own arm down it!"

This is the problem with dealing with people of Stuart's wealth, position and status in life. They just aren't used to getting their hands dirty and always get someone else to do their chores.

"There is another course of action you could take," I suggested.

"Really? What?"

The Cognac was making my speech a bit free and easy.

"Get Agnes to sit up in the kitchen. One look at her and this unknown entity will run a mile." Of course, I felt bad for saying that as soon as it came out my mouth.

"Do you mind, that's my wife you're besmirching."

"I apologise. That was unnecessary," I replied, lowering my face in contrition.

"Although, I don't wonder why you would say that. She doesn't give you an easy time, does she? I'm afraid my Aggie is a dreadful snob and you just don't appeal to her sensitivities."

"I don't appeal much to her sister's either and I'm married to her..."

However, time was marching on I wanted to get back to the matter in hand. "So, did you want to have a go at my suggestion? I don't mean spending the whole night in the cellar, but if perhaps we were to rendezvous at quarter to one and sit down there for a couple of hours to see what happens?"

"I suppose so Jerry, but how will we explain our disappearance to the ladies?"

Here he was, an experienced captain of the finance industry, and I still have to think of everything.

"Just say you can't sleep and you're going downstairs for some cocoa."

"But if you say that too, they're bound to say something to one another in the morning and they will undoubtedly think it rather odd."

Maybe he had a point and his captain of industry status was sound.

"OK, OK, I'll say I've got an upset stomach and I need to spend a couple of hours sat on a toilet. Anyway, it won't matter; Cynthia couldn't care less where I am."

And so, the arrangements were set in place. We were to rendezvous at a quarter to one in the kitchen and make our way to the depths of their cellar. My word, good Cognac makes me a brave boy!

~ ~ ~

As it was, the ladies had retired for the night by the time us chaps ventured to our bedrooms. When I walked in to the guest bedroom, Cynthia had left the lamp on by my side of the bed. She was already under the covers, facing away from me but awake.

"Gosh, I can smell you from here," was her opening gambit.

"Well Stuart had a cigar too, in fact he was the one offering them up."

"Just make sure you clean your teeth and have a wash. I won't be able to sleep if I'm subjected to the stench of tobacco and alcohol you're giving off."

I just rolled my eyes and went off to the bathroom with my wash bag. By the time I got back, Mrs. Happy Cheeks was asleep, or I assume she was, given she was making noises like a farm animal giving birth. It was now only half an hour until my meeting in the kitchen, so it was hardly worth my trying to get to sleep, although it did cross my mind that Stuart might not show up or nod off and sleep through our appointment. I would be very annoyed if that was the case and I was beginning to get a bit tetchy about it, even though I didn't know for sure he would chicken out. I glanced at my alarm clock. It was half past midnight and given the snoring coming from the other side of the bed was beginning to send my blood pressure into orbit, I decided to don my dressing gown and sneak down to the kitchen earlier than the appointed hour...

To my surprise, Stuart was already in there with the kettle on, and like me wrapped up in a dressing gown, but with the added protection of thick field socks, woollen hat and a fleecy body warmer.

"Hello! You're early too then. Thought I'd better get us a hot drink on the go, as it's damn cold in that cellar. Is that all you're wearing?" he asked.

"Yes, I didn't really think," I replied. Once again, he'd proved why his brain power had made him a big cheese in industry and mine hadn't.

"You'll get cold," he continued. This wasn't a great comfort to me, especially as I didn't want to chance going back up to my bedroom and possibly waking up Cynthia.

"Did you have to make excuses to Agnes when you left?"

"No, although I don't think the ladies went upstairs much before us, Aggie does tend to fall asleep as soon as her head hits the pillow. So, the coast is clear for now. Tea?"

"Please."

"There's some old garden loungers down there, under a dust sheet somewhere, thought we could sit on those. I presume there's not some code of conduct that says we have to stand is there?"

"No that's fine. Got any candles we can take down?" My enquiry led to a look of surprise.

"Candles? Can't we just have the lights on? There is electricity down there you know."

"I just think that we've more chance of seeing something if we're not lit up like Christmas trees. Spirits and the like, assuming this is what you have here, can be a bit shy and candlelight won't be so suspicious."

The seriousness of what we were about to do seemed to become apparent on his face.

"Right-o. I'll grab a couple of candlesticks from the dinner table. Will that do?"

"Yep, they'll do. You finish the tea and I'll go and get them."

And so, a few minutes later, we made our way down the dusty stairway to the cellar and dug out the garden chairs he spoke of. We positioned them in a corner, next to a big pile of tea chests, left a candle by us and put the other two in opposite corners. This didn't exactly give us much light, but the discreet glow was helpful and slightly comforting nonetheless. We finally sat down at ten to one, nursing our hot tea mugs and surveying our situation.

"Jerry, I'm sat in my cellar, during a Scottish winter, in the middle of the night, in my bedclothes. Am I just having a bizarre dream, or have I gone completely round the bend?" asked Stuart.

To the ordinary person on the street our actions could indeed be construed as a little peculiar, and I am sure these sorts of activities to a man like my companion, who is more used to sitting around a boardroom table, than in a plastic garden chair in a cold basement, probably feel a bit alien. Although, as a semi-pro or amateur ghost investigator like myself, this sort of conduct is normal, although I tend to wear more than pyjamas and a dressing gown, but this was quite a last minute, spur of the moment job. I wasn't sure if we were to expect anything or not, maybe Stuart was mad and I was freezing myself to the core for nothing, but I would've regretted not following up on his little story.

"I'm sure you're not mad. You were sane enough to put socks on at any rate. This is a normal sort of activity on a ghost watch, although if we were doing this properly we'd have cameras and recorders and suchlike on the go, but we'll just have to make do with our eyes. Therefore, we should just sit here, nice and quiet, keeping our eyes peeled."

"Roger Wilco," said my companion with duty and gusto. And so we sat there in the cold and the damp and the dim lighting. It was imperative to stay alert and concentrate on the matter in hand.

Which is why it was somewhat disappointing that we both seemed to fall asleep in practically no time at all. How very unprofessional I know, but not really surprising with a good meal inside the belly, good brandy, not to mention the wine over dinner, coupled with the late night and I have to say rather comfortable old garden furniture, given it was rejected and soon to be disposed of.

I wouldn't exactly say I was sleeping soundly mind you; I was asleep but all the while aware of the coldness and my shivering. Then I was aware of another sensation, a somewhat putrid smell... I wasn't sure if it was part of a dream, as this cadaverous odour was so vile and fetid, that visions of rot or for that matter, rotting rodent corpses seemed to be circling my subconscious. I could feel myself rapidly moving my head from side to side, as if I was trying to avoid the origin of the foul stench, and in doing so was becoming more and more awake. And then that's exactly what I did do, although I wasn't entirely sure if I was awake initially as the first view which filled my sight was that of an extremely ugly, dirty, wart covered face about one inch away from my own! I particularly recall there was no white in its eyes; they were more a tobacco yellow colour and he had a deep orange beard which too seemed dirty, while the ghastly smell was that of its breath covering my face and filling my nostrils! This image made me wake properly with quite a start, in fact I yelped like a scalded dog, sending the thankfully empty china tea mug, which had been resting in my crotch as I slept, flying up in the air and then crashing down into several pieces on the stone floor. Needless to say, my commotion had also immediately woken Stuart from his dozing, and we both witnessed the strange little man who must've been standing alongside my chair, and for whatever reason staring into my face. Not that this bizarre creature hung around, because as the two of us sat up in our chairs, the ginger headed visitor was on his toes and promptly darted off across the cellar with an almost comical trot within a matter of seconds and as he got fifteen or so feet away from us, simply vaporised into thin air, as if there was some kind of ethereal doorway there. It seemed to leave a strange, light mist behind it as this happened, which gradually dispersed into the atmosphere and then we were left in silence, until one of us was able to get their mouth in gear.

"That was him Jerry! By Jove it was him!" exclaimed Stuart. "Did you see him? Did you!?"

"Yes, I saw him, and I certainly smelt him!" I replied, pulling a face as the disgusting odour was still lingering in my nostrils.

"Thank goodness. Now you've seen it too, I know I haven't gone mad."

"No, you're not mad. But I wish I had my equipment with me, it would've been great to have picked that up on film. I wonder who on earth he is? Have you no ideas?"

"None whatsoever, but he's not welcome here whoever, or whatever he is. Can we go upstairs now? I'm absolutely freezing even though I'm the one with extra clothes on. Besides which, I just spilt some cold tea in my lap, so it feels like I've wet myself."

I concurred with his suggestion to go back up, as my aging legs had goose bumps on, not to mention a few other bits and pieces, and so we extinguished the candles, before making a hasty dash back upstairs to the kitchen.

"I'm glad we're out of there. I won't be rushing to go back to the cellar, unless it's daytime and it's with somebody else. Do you want another drink?" Stuart asked.

"No thanks, I'm tired. Time I was off to my bed."

"Bed! My mind's racing, I won't sleep, not after that strange business. In one way, I'm so elated that I wasn't imagining this, I'm almost too overjoyed to sleep!"

Being a seasoned ghost hunter, I'm more able to cope with the aftermath of an unusual occurrence on an investigation and as such I wasn't quite as all over the place as my brother-in-law. Besides which, my fatigue was getting the better of me now and even being in the same bed as Cynthia was better than not being in one at all.

"I'm pleased you're happier about the situation. Don't stay up too late. Goodnight." My retreat to the door was intercepted however.

"But Jerry, we can't just leave it there. What do I do about it? Should I tell Aggie? Do I need to get someone in? You know, like I said before, an exorcist or something?"

"Well you don't want to share your house with it do you? So maybe you should. At least now you have a witness to it being genuine. However, I wouldn't mind having a bit of further investigation into it. The trouble with that, is how we deal with our wives. I don't think either would be very sympathetic to the idea and I think if you told Agnes about tonight, she'd organise a one-way trip for us both to the funny farm."

"Indeed," replied Stuart knowingly, looking down in thought. "I know!" he exclaimed excitedly, "Aggie goes to a school reunion at some point next month, I can't remember when exactly, but it's down in Norfolk so she'll be away for two or three days. Oh of course, your Cynthia's going too isn't she?"

"Yes, now you come to mention it, there are faint and somewhat distant bells ringing in the back of my mind. I seem to recall a certain excitement when she said she'd be out of my way for a couple of days."

"There you are then. Why not make a visit up here when they're both at that? Then they don't need to know anything about it and it can be our little secret."

"I suppose so. I'm sure I can get the time off work. Perhaps I could see if our Frankie could come up too. You remember Francesca, my sister's little girl? Although she's not so little now mind."

"Aye I remember her from some family do or such like. But that was years ago, she was only a child then. She can come up as well if you want, I remember you saying once before that she's into this sort of thing too. She can be trusted to keep this business quiet, can she?"

"Frankie can be a mouthy little oik when she wants to be, but she can be trusted."

"This all sounds excellent," he said, almost a little excitedly.

"Good. I shouldn't think we'll be able to talk about it much in the morning, so you'll have to give me a call on my mobile at some point to firm things up. In the meantime, don't get it exorcised!"

And so we left it there, as I went off to bed and left him to be excited in the kitchen on his own. I can't be doing with excitable bankers in the middle of the night.

~ ~ ~

The rest of our weekend up there rattled along on its usual tracks, in that Saturday was spent walking about the city in and out of glitzy shops. Then we had another splendid dinner that evening courtesy of the culinary skills of Agnes and departed for home after a full Scottish cooked breakfast on the Sunday morning. Oddly, during the rest of our time in Edinburgh, Stuart uttered not a single word more to me on the Friday night phenomenon; it was almost as if nothing had happened, yet I just put it down to his keenness for discretion and said nothing either.

It was nearly a week later before the irritating jingle of my mobile phone went off one afternoon whilst I was sitting in my garden den. Knowing his Gestapo like wife, she probably watches his movements like a hawk and so clearly this was the first opportunity Stuart had had to arrange our little clandestine assembly and indeed he was most apologetic about the delay. However, the investigation was duly arranged for when both our wives were away for a long weekend at their school reunion three weeks later.

"Have you seen the little ginger oddity since?" I asked him.

"No, but I haven't looked him out either. Mind you Jerry, I couldn't care less if I didn't see it ever again. And just as soon as you've done your bit up here, whatever it is you want to do, I shall be making enquiries as to how to get rid of it once and for all!"

That was fair enough. I mean, some people can live with their resident ghosts and some people can't, and this one did have rather bad breath.

~~~

About a week before the off, I met up with Frankie in town at an internet café which we occasionally frequent. Given we both have our own computers, it seems a bit of a waste of money, but it gets me away from the house and they do serve a nice café latte. There were the usual varied types of person huddled in front of PC monitors and today there was quite a selection. A huge fat chap with long dark hair who looked like a mature student was furiously pounding away at the keyboard, probably writing a highly complex thesis, (or copying one from the internet). Then there were a couple of teenage boys sharing a machine together and I don't even want to think about what they might've been looking up, but whatever it was, it certainly made them snigger a lot. Conversely, there was a little white-haired old lady, of diminutive proportions, merrily surfing the net looking for exotic holiday offers from what I could see over her shoulder. Good on her say I, for seizing on modern technology with such gusto. I guess I'm a nosey sort of person, making judgements about all these people, goodness only knows what they think about me. Given how Frankie dresses sometimes, much as I hate to say this about my beloved niece, I suppose to some she looks like a call-girl out with a dirty old man, but never mind, I don't know these other people so what should I care?

"Want another latte?" I said.

"Yeh go on then."

"I like the look of those sticky buns, think I might have one. Can I get you one as well?" I offered generously.

"We're supposed to be researching this ghost at your brother-in-law's!" she protested.

"Humpf! We're not exactly getting very far are we? So we may as well treat ourselves!"

"Have your bun then, but don't get me one. I don't want to go up to a size ten."

"Heaven forbid," I remarked back to her. "Though I could do with a sugar rush," and turning around to my favourite of the café girls, I ordered another couple of Latte's and an iced bun.

I was downcast at our unsuccessful research. I mean, you can't just type 'odd little ginger' into an internet search engine and get all the answers. Although it did suggest a couple of surprising celebrities.

"There obviously isn't anything on the web about this bizarre ginger creature. It was a bit of a long shot anyway. We've looked up the history of the area, the street, the buildings, important historical figures of the vicinity, hauntings around the city, in fact, the lot... I think we'll have to resign ourselves to the fact that this is one of the many unknown spectres of the world and just see if we can get a glimpse of it when we go up there next weekend. Maybe even try and interact with it."

"Assuming you and Uncle Stuart actually even saw it last time, given you'd both been knocking back the booze," she replied sarcastically, which almost sounded like the sort of comment my wife would make.

Before I was able to snipe back at her with the level of contempt she deserved, my phone rang and it was our friend and colleague, the young and respectable Rev. Light.

"Hello Stephen!"

"Hi Jerry. Just phoning to check we're still on for next weekend?"

"Absolutely my little religious friend." I assumed he didn't take offence when I made these tactless observations but then again, you can't say anything to anybody these days without someone wanting to sue you.

"Great, we haven't been on an investigation for a little while now, it'll be nice to see you both again."

"Thank you. Funnily enough, we were just having a look on the internet to see if we could find anything out about this strange apparition. Or more specifically who he was in 'life', so to speak, but not surprisingly, we haven't got anywhere."

"Well, that was my other reason for phoning. I was on my *Facebook* yesterday..."

"You have Facebook!" rudely interrupting him.

"Yes, why do you say it like that?"

"You've never mentioned it I suppose. Or more to the point, I just wouldn't imagine a man of the cloth going in for all that hyperspace networking larky. Do you and all the other trainee vicars compete for who has the most online friends?"

"No not really, I wouldn't say anyone I know was that obsessed with it," he replied slightly indignantly. So, my next ill-advised one-liner didn't help and I said it before thinking.

"Do you have Jesus as one of your friends?"

He responded, in a composed, parent like way, "Now Jerry, we all have a friend in Jesus."

I had to hand it to him. That was a good comeback.

"Yes, well, you were saying about Facebook?" I replied, being very much put in my place.

"I was only going to say that an old uni friend of mine got in touch and what's coincidental is that we both did our degrees at Edinburgh, which incidentally is another reason why I'm looking forward to going back up there, as I haven't been since we finished. Anyway, he settled there and got a job at the university, I presume it was in the History and

Classics department as that was his subject. I thought if you didn't mind, I might see if he could use his local knowledge and try and find out a bit about this house, or get an idea of who this apparition might've been."

"I think that's a brilliant idea, because it's not as if we've had any success with any other avenue. So long as he's discreet. We don't want Agnes knowing we're poking around. But it's worth a shot isn't it?" I replied.

"OK, I'll give him a call. I expect the story will give him a laugh if nothing else, but he might be able to come up with something. I'll see you both next weekend at the airport then!"

And off he went to no doubt do good things in the community, while I stuffed my face with an iced bun. We all have our calling in life.

~ ~ ~

It wasn't the smoothest of internal flights up to Scotland and the blustery weather was mainly to blame for that. Plus, the plane wasn't particularly quiet, neither were some of our fellow passengers and it didn't help that Frankie had her music device pounding trashy modern tunes in her ears, sending that awful tinny second-hand sound around her vicinity. However, the main thing is that we got there in one piece and were dutifully picked up by Stuart in his elegant motor car. He clearly thought us to be an unusual trio from the way he eyed us curiously but was polite enough to not actually say so. He and Fran hadn't seen each other in years and he was no doubt a little taken aback by how she has blossomed in to such an attractive, albeit brazen young lady.

It was mid-afternoon by the time we trailed up the main staircase of their grand old townhouse to the guest room that was to be our base camp for the next couple of days. It wasn't the same room as I had with Cynthia on my last visit, in that it was less opulent in furnishings but was larger, and so more appropriate to accommodate the camp bed for the third of our number.

"Here we are," announced our host as we entered the room, "there's a bathroom just opposite. I managed to borrow a camp bed off of the chap next door. He won't say anything to Agnes as they can't stand each other, so I can be assured of his discretion. We'd only been living here five minutes before she decided to take issue with him about the street permit parking system. He has two largish cars outside his place, yet he lives on his own and hardly ever uses either. Consequently, she started on him pretty early in our neighbourly relationship. You know the sort of thing... About there not always being room outside the house for our car, etc. etc, but anyway you don't want to know about all that. Will you be OK with just the double and the camp-bed?" he asked, "As I don't want to use more than one room while Aggies away, as it's more for me to sort out when you go. She's got a keen eye as you know Jerry and I wouldn't want her to notice it's been used."

"We'll be fine, don't worry. I expect we'll give up on the investigation at about three or so in the morning, that's about the normal, so it's just somewhere to get a few hours kip before a late breakfast."

"Who's sleeping where?" asked Frankie.

I surveyed the surroundings as I hadn't given it any thought.

"Well I suppose us two chaps ought to take the double, I don't think either of us wants to share a bed with you Fran."

She tossed her overnight bag down onto the camp-bed and turned to Stephen, and I could see by the glint in her eye she was in one of her naughty, mischievous moods.

"Surely you don't mind sharing a bed with me?" she said to him in a forged sultry tone and proceeded to stroke between the opening at the front of his shirt with the end of her finger.

"I...err, I mean...well..." or words to that effect as I recall, uttered by Stephen in a polite but flustered manner. She continued to tease the poor chap.

"Although, when I'm in bed," and paused as she spoke to move closer to his ear, "I do like to be naked!"

I'm sure as she said that last bit she deliberately blew hot breath on his cheek and straight laced, shy, man of the cloth Stephen turned a pretty shade of crimson, opening and shutting his mouth like a fish as if trying to say something but not finding the words. I had to rescue him.

"Do behave Francesca! You know well and good you'll be in the camp-bed, apart from anything else, the sight of you at three in the morning is enough to make anyone hide under the bedcovers."

"Charming!" she retorted.

"The joy of family life eh?" chuckled Stuart, nervously I thought, as if he was wondering what kind of people he'd let into his magnificent house... I suppose they do say you can choose your friends but you can't choose your family.

"That's one way of putting it. Can we tempt you to join us later?" I asked our host.

"What? When you're down in the cellar? Oh, I'm not too sure about that Jerry. I rather think I'm of the opinion that if I never saw that weird ginger dwarf again, it would be quite soon enough."

"It's up to you of course; I just thought it would've been of interest to you, as it's your house and all. Anyway, there's no guarantee we'll see that apparition again, in fact it might just be a waste of everybody's time. But as I always say, it's like it goes in that song. '*You can take a horse to the water, but you can't make it drink.*'"

"He does, he always says that..." muttered Fran derisively.

"Really," came his vague reply. He had no idea what I was talking about, as I'm sure his musical tastes wouldn't include that particular tune.

"I suppose if you *really* need me....?" His offer was strained and limp so I didn't want to worry the man.

"Its fine, we can manage. We've brought a bit of our equipment with us, although coming by plane means there's only so much we could bring. Mind you, as we're only investigating the one area we should be all right with just the one video camera. It's not like we have the whole house to monitor."

"Did you not want to monitor the kitchen then?" asked Stephen.

"Oh sod it. I forgot about there." That was a good start; I'm not big on event planning. I expect ex-banker Stuart spent most of his life in summits and conferences organising major business initiatives, but I'm more of a man of action. Well, of a sort anyhow, in a flabby, too many pork pies kind of way. Still, our host then offered to buy us all dinner after we had settled in, so we could work out our strategy over a good meal. No doubt, Stuart, being the erudite man he is, would be taking us somewhere decent – oh I do hope Fran finds a longer skirt for such an occasion – and so we stopped for a toilet, tea and fag break, and got on with our daytime 'baseline' readings. That is to say, we went to the kitchen and cellar and measured any current levels of electrical interference, temperature, moisture, noted any sources of noise and took lots of digital photographs of the scene for the file. Nothing out of the normal to report at this early stage.

It was a bit of a disappointment when Stuart drove us a couple of miles into the city and pulled up outside a pub carvery. Not only that, it was still classed as the 'early bird diner' timeslot, so the canny Scot was somewhat elated about only having to spend five pounds per head for what turned out to be a somewhat lame, roast dinner main course followed by a small bowl of ice cream for each of us. Still, a free supper shouldn't be frowned upon, although I bet he'd never dare try and feed Agnes on a £5 pub carvery.

We were back at the house by nine o'clock but decided to wait until eleven before officially starting our investigation.

Within a very short time of being back, Stuart said his goodnights to us, a mug of hot milk in one hand and a half full brandy balloon in the other, and swiftly departed to his bedroom. I got the distinct impression he couldn't wait to get away and leave us to it. Plus, I was a bit put out that I wasn't included in the brandy quota.

Subsequently, we relaxed for a bit, double checked our equipment and put on any extra clothes as required. As time was getting on, the heating had long since clicked off and the temperature was dropping in the old place. A little after eleven o'clock the three of us moved into our respective positions, although officially Stuart saw the ginger apparition at one o'clock in the morning on both occasions, we ought to be ready before in case there was an earlier visitation. Therefore, Stephen was assigned the corridor which leads to the kitchen door, I decided I would remain in the kitchen and sent Frankie on cellar duty. Although needless to say, she took a bit of convincing and there was still debate on the subject at the top of the cellar staircase when it was time for her to go down there.

"I still don't see why I should have to go in the cellar, we didn't even vote on it."

"Oh come on Frankie, you've got youth on your side. Fancy expecting your aged uncle to go and sit in a freezing cold basement," I argued.

"You could've got Stephen to go down there!"

"Yes, but you are more experienced. Stephen is still learning the ropes as it were; I need someone with your professionalism and knowledge to be at what is likely to be the most important location on this investigation, just in case this phantom does make an appearance."

She just looked at me for a few seconds with knowing eyes and said,

"You're just bullshitting me now aren't you?"

"Yes I am," I replied with honest bluntness.

"I thought so."

"Bye then."

She managed one last glare at me before walking down to the dimly lit recesses of the cellar.

"It's like a fridge down here," she shouted on reaching the bottom.

"Those 3 or 4 candles are lit aren't they?" I asked with a smirk.

"Yes, they're making it very slightly less pitch black down here – why?"

"Well they'll soon start warming it up for you!"

I closed the door before Fran replied in full, insofar as I heard her say 'no they...' but managed to shut off the sound before the undoubted expletive which followed, before the word 'won't'.

I went and sat down at the kitchen table, where I'd left my mug of coffee and decided it would be a good idea to check our communications via the walkie-talkies.

"OK team, everything in position?"

Stephen was first to respond. "Everything fine out here. I can clearly see the corridor ahead of me and the kitchen door. Having that standard lamp on in the next room let's just enough light through without it being too bright."

"Good stuff!" I responded, in my team motivation voice. My own lighting arrangements consisted of a desk lamp, not surprisingly of the banker's lamp design, borrowed from Stuart, which was sitting on the kitchen table next to me, so I too could have some subtle illumination. I also had the video camera set up and rather usefully, at the angle it was set up, the field of vision covered both the kitchen and cellar doors. I decided I better check in with my darling niece.

"Everything all right with you Frankie?"

No response.

"Frankie?"

"What!?" She responded in a very vitriolic tone.

"Everything OK?" I asked.

"Yeh, I'm great thanks. I love sitting in a freezing, dark cellar late at night."

"That's all right then. I did say to take a hot drink with you! Did you want to pop up and get one?"

"No! I'm curled up and if I dare to move, I feel even colder," she whinged. I decided, probably unwisely, on a wooden spoon moment.

"Just keep thinking about all the heat those candles are giving off!" I said, which she duly responded to.

"Be grateful I'm not coming back up there as I'd be bringing one of those candles with me and shoving it up..."

Unfortunately, she wasn't able to finish her sentence because I rather meanly, shut down radio operations at the crucial moment. What cheeky youths they are nowadays! Mouths like gutters!

~ ~ ~

In the next couple of hours nothing much happened. I radioed through to Frankie a couple of times to see how she was doing and, on each occasion, I woke her up as she'd nodded off. Stephen however, was very alert and on the ball. He was camped out at the end of the corridor opposite the kitchen entrance, under a travel rug, but occasionally getting up to have a wander around the ground floor to circulate his blood flow and have a general check around. I was getting sleepy myself, having flicked through all the available magazines in Stuart and Cynthia's kitchen. By this point, my head was fairly maxed out on home décor articles, recipe ideas and creative gardening themes, as these were the only topics covered by their literature selection.

I was aware, on the worktop opposite me, there was one of Agnes's rather splendid looking homemade Dundee cakes and I got up, found a knife and was about to cut myself a hefty slice when there came a crackle of life from the walkie talkie. It was Stephen.

"Jerry? Are you receiving me?"

Stephen was very professional in his radio vernacular. I rushed back to the table to grab my handset and as I did so glanced toward the clock, which was showing it was now just after one o'clock. The allure of the cake had made me lose track of time.

"Stephen, what's happening?"

"The EMF meter has just gone into overdrive; the needle has shot right up to the red. And just as you answered I felt an icy blast of air... oh, what's this...?"

He went silent.

"Stephen?" His abrupt silence sent all my senses to full alert.

"There's like a mist... an outline... seems to be gradually moving toward....Jerry! It's going to the kitchen door!"

"Right, I'll, err, hang on!" I was at a loss what to say but on reflection it wasn't a time for conversation anyhow. I dived down behind the kitchen table, for what little shielding that afforded me, crouched as low as my chubby frame could muster and kept my eyes firmly toward the door. Sure enough, a few seconds later in the night time silence, I could hear the subtle sound of the door handle turning and my heart was racing as I listened to this activity – was it just Stephen? Was it Stuart coming downstairs to see how we were doing? Of course, after the recent communication from my fellow ghost hunter outside in the corridor I knew what the answer would be. A few moments later there was the quiet creak from the hinges as the door slowly opened, however there before me, from my floor level viewpoint under the table, was not the mist which Stephen spoke of.

What I saw, were two squat little legs entering the room, which turned back toward the door to slowly and softly close it behind them. I couldn't see the top half of its body, but I was struck by how dirty and decayed the trousers and the old-fashioned buckled boots were of this entity before me, almost as if it had literally just emerged from a grave after decades of slumber to make this clandestine visit. It walked the short distance across the kitchen floor to the cellar entrance and on reaching it, simply opened the door and calmly went through, closing the door behind it.

I couldn't risk calling down to Fran on the radio but, assuming she hadn't nodded off again, she would've heard the exchange between myself and Stephen a few moments earlier.

I waited for a bit before emerging from under the table, at first mentally chastising myself for hiding, but then I took comfort on the basis that if I had been seen by this strange creature, he may not have continued his trip to the cellar and potentially we wouldn't have discovered what he did down there. Of course, if Frankie wasn't on the ball, or had fallen asleep again, we still wouldn't be any the wiser.

I crept closer to the cellar entrance, bending slightly double as if to try and hear what was happening within, although still being a foot or so away, I can't imagine what levels of success I would've had with that. Being in this odd stooping position, concentrating on any sounds from below, and therefore looking toward the floor, I hadn't noticed Stephen surreptitiously entering the kitchen domain, and so as the door creaked it gave me quite a start.

"Sorry!" he whispered. "What's happening?"

"Pretty sure it was the funny little oddball I saw before. It went through there just as expected," I explained in hushed tones, gesturing toward the closed cellar door.

Stephen tiptoed nearer to me and joined me in a stooping position, as if the lower ear level would improve audibility. Funny how these things must be contagious.

A couple of minutes passed and my senses were still on full alert, certainly it almost felt like I could hear the fuzz in my ears. However, Stephen and I both looked at each other when suddenly we could clearly hear the sound of heavy footsteps coming up the narrow staircase within, resulting in neither of us quite knowing if we should stay where we were or if we should dart off to the corners of the room. As it was, neither of us could decide quick enough and we just seemed to vibrate a bit in our shoes with indecision, without actually going anywhere. The door flung open and out stepped Frankie, stopping abruptly in her tracks as she found the two of us just the other side of the door.

"What's the matter with you two? You look like you've seen a ghost!" she quipped.

"We have!" I exclaimed. "Didn't you see it? It went downstairs."

"Oh yeah," she replied, nonchalantly. "Ugly little critter isn't he? I need a cuppa, its bloody freezing down there. Oh look, they've got *cup-a-soup*, wicked; I'll have one of them!" And she promptly grabbed one of the powdered soup sachets before flipping the kettle switch on.

"Frankie, you can't keep us in suspense like this, what did you see?" asked Stephen, with a lot more patience than I would've mustered. Fran leaned back against the kitchen worktop as she relayed her narrative.

"So, after hearing Stephen on the radio, I concealed myself a bit more behind whatever old junk they have covered up down there. Then peering out from the side, I saw this repulsive little bloke, who must've only been about four feet high and well dirty, come trotting down the stairs. He made straight for the middle of the cellar, completely oblivious to the fact it wasn't pitch dark like normal, not that there was much light from those candles. Oh, by the way, I haven't blown them out yet, is that OK?"

"Never mind about that now! You were saying he went for the middle of the cellar, so did he actually do anything?" I enquired somewhat peevishly, while Frankie stirred the hot water into the powdered concoction in her mug.

"Like I say, he darted over to the middle of the cellar floor, pretty much threw himself down on his knees and started dusting away at the ground, you know, with his fingers. Then he started blowing at the dust, real hard, but it was like he had no air in him to blow. So, after a few seconds of that, his face went really angry looking and he clenched his fists, then he shook them in the air, like in a rage, then just fizzled out. Gone. One second, he's there, then he wasn't, there was just a mist for a moment or so, then nothing. I waited for a minute, to see if anything else would happen, which it didn't, then came back up here because I was freezing my tits off. Oh, that reminds me, I need a wee."

"Lovely! I don't especially see the link between cold bosoms and the need to urinate but thanks for the bladder update," I said, as she put her cup down and darted off to the lavatory.

"What do you make of that?" asked Stephen.

"I think she should've gone earlier," I replied.

"No, not about Frankie needing the loo, about what she said this phantom is up to in the cellar."

"Ah I get you. It's not so much what he's up to, it's more what he can't do that I think is its problem."

"I'm guessing by that you're thinking the same as me, in that there's something under the floor?"

As he spoke I'd taken a swig from Frankie's instant soup drink, which I wish I hadn't done, both from the point of view of taste and its temperature which burnt my tongue.

"Yep, sure do. We've got to get under that floor!"

"So, shall we ask Stuart in the morning?" replied Stephen, obviously keen to be polite and seek the householder's permission.

"Blimey no! We can't wait until morning; we need to look into this now!"

"Won't he mind us messing about with the floor though? As I recall from when we were down there this afternoon, it was tiled in stone wasn't it? Your brother in law won't want us messing it up, will he?"

"Of course, he won't. That's why we won't tell him. Just because it's his house, he shouldn't be standing in the way of our important scientific research, should he? Now grab your torch and follow me."

Just too decent and proper for his own good was Stephen, I mused to myself just as Frankie re-entered the kitchen, who to be honest, was at the other end of the scale when it comes to that sort of thing.

"Grab your drink, we're all going downstairs," I informed her as she joined us.

"Oh great, down in the fridge again," she whinged.

"No one said life was easy, darling niece. Come on!" And I led the three of us down to the cold, damp candlelit cellar.

~ ~ ~

"Whereabouts did the little fella head for?" I asked Fran as we reached the bottom of the stairs.

"Over here," she replied, leading Stephen and I to a section of floor just off the centre of the basement, unburdened by any layer of Stuart and Agnes's unwanted household items. "There you go, it was right here."

The three of us circled around the area of floor which Frankie had highlighted and shone our torches on the spot for a better view.

"Must be something down there I reckon," offered Frankie.

"Yes, we'd already come to that conclusion, but the question is how do we find out?" I responded, while pondering the conundrum.

Stephen by now was on his knees, not to pray as his profession might suggest, but he was blowing the dust around and brushing at the dirty surface with his hands.

"You're having a lot more success at that than the ghost was," Frankie told him, "but I suppose you're still alive, which probably helps."

"Well, I hope I am. And indeed, will be for a while yet, if the good Lord lets it be so."

For a fairly young man, he did talk old-fashioned sometimes and I noted Fran had that mischievous look in her eyes.

"Actually Stephen, you look quite sexy on your knees, working up a sweat..."

"Frankie, don't distract the poor man while he's hard at work." I thought I better save Stephen from his blushes and then joined him at floor level. "Are things looking any clearer?" I asked.

"As we were saying earlier, the whole floor area is made up of these old flagstones. They look pretty well cemented in, so you're not going to get one of these up in a hurry," he said despondently.

I shone my torch on an area where there was a gap in the mortar.

"We could try levering the stone up with that hole. Get your fingers under it," I suggested, somewhat underestimating the task. Stephen just looked back at me and I suspect if he wasn't a trainee man of the cloth, he would've retorted something along the lines of 'are you taking the p..wee-wee?' but he is too polite. Fran isn't.

"You're joking, aren't you?" she exclaimed, "he'll pull his fingernails off!"

"What we need is something we can jam in there," said I.

"Here, try this!" Fran dived over to where she had been hiding from our little ginger apparition earlier as she'd remembered seeing a couple of old gardening bits, namely a trowel and hand fork.

First, we wedged in the fork and it bent the prongs. Then we tried the trowel, which just snapped at the handle.

"I hope they didn't want to use those again," said Stephen looking guilty.

"There's never a pickaxe around when you want one!" I said in frustration, going off, torch in hand, to see what I could find under the various dust covers. "There's got to be something we could use down here."

After a lot of huffing and puffing with irritation I managed to find an old metal wrench and a block of wood which we could use for leverage. I used the remains of the trowel to make a bit of a gap under the flagstone, then wedged the spanner in the hole, and laid the centre of it on the piece of wood.

"You are sure Stuart won't mind us doing this?" asked Stephen.

"It's practically two o'clock in the morning, I shouldn't think he'll care less," I retorted peevishly.

"No, I mean tomorrow, or whenever he comes down here and sees what we've done."

"Look", I said, "we're just going to gently lift up this stone, and when we're done, we'll put it back in place, brush some dust over it and no one needs to know anything about it. Neither of them will notice a thing, I promise you."

"OK", Stephen replied, but looking uneasy, while the silent Frankie just wrapped her arms around herself because of the cold.

I knew it would take quite a bit of oomph to raise this big heavy flagstone, so with foot hovering above the end of the wrench, I counted to three and stamped hard on the old metal tool. Imagine my surprise when the stone flipped out of its hole like a hot knife through butter, held itself for half a second on its vertical axis, before crashing down on its other side and shattering into a hundred pieces.

"Jerry, I think they will notice that," Stephen coolly remarked, as both he and Frankie looked on open mouthed.

"To be fair, that wasn't supposed to happen," I replied feebly. "Anyway, let's not worry about that now, let's just see if there's anything under here."

Fran shook her head in disapproval. "Honestly, when you get the bit between your teeth, you're like a bull in a china shop." I chose to ignore the slur.

So the three of us knelt around the gap in the flooring, and Frankie held a torch above us so Stephen and I could scrape away the dirt and sand that was beneath the slab. Frankie had only a few days previous gone to a salon and had her usual garish, trendy, but somewhat tawdry, false nails fitted, so there was no way she'd be doing any of the dirty work.

"I don't think there's anything down here," Stephen remarked as we'd burrowed down a good inch and a half.

"How disappointing, I can't believe we...." But I stopped mid-sentence, for I could feel my fingers touch something. "Oh, hang on, what's this?"

Stephen and I, with much alacrity, brushed away the concealing dirt with our hands which to our surprise revealed old discoloured bones.

"No way! There's a body buried down here! Gross!" exclaimed Frankie with an excited grin on her face.

"It's not human thank heavens," Stephen replied, "it's too small," and we continued to reveal what had lain in the dirt for a good many years.

A minute or two later its species was becoming clearer.

"I do believe it's a small dog," I uttered. "I wonder if it was the beloved pet of the little ginger bloke and he's coming to mourn at its makeshift grave."

"If you saw his facial expression, you wouldn't think he was in mourning, he looked really angry and frustrated to me," Fran said.

"Angry at his dogs passing then."

"Seems a bit unlikely if you want my opinion," she muttered unconvinced. Thankfully an open-minded Stephen gave me a bit of backing.

"Pets do become like a family member I suppose. I remember when I was a little boy and our family dog died, a Labrador called Shaney. I was mortified. Probably cried for weeks. So did my mum for that matter, we all absolutely loved her. When we buried her at the bottom of the garden, we made a little wooden cross with her name on it and we always said hello whenever we passed her grave for years afterwards."

"There you go then, maybe it's just that simple," I said, straightening my posture because of the now aching back muscles. "We'll report as such to Stuart in the morning."

"He'll probably want us to try and do something to get rid of this spirit though," argued Frankie.

"We're not in that business Fran," I replied sternly, "if he wants an exorcism he'll have to slip the local priest a few quid to come round here shouting 'the power of Christ compels you' and all that jazz. No offence Stephen."

"None taken. What are we going to do here now? Did you want to uncover any more of its remains?"

"I don't see the point in digging it up anymore, I already feel like some kind of grave robber, let it rest in peace. Come on, let's get it covered up again," and we immediately began scooping the dirt over the bones.

"Hurry it up you two, I'm freezing my tits off here," Frankie once again so eloquently stated. Clearly, the thought of Frankie's breast area was enough to send Stephen into a frenzy and he managed to double the pace, whereas I on the other hand, couldn't have cared less about how cold that part or any other part of her body was.

When we'd packed the dirt back in, Stephen asked what we were to do about the slab, of which I could muster no sensible suggestion. Consequently, we just put the large chunks back in place, dumped one of the old unused garden chairs over the top and hoped for the best. And if that old bag Agnes ever ventured down there it was Stuart's problem, not mine.

"Come on, we're done here now, let's go back upstairs and wash our hands. Those of us who actually got theirs dirty that is..." I said pointedly, looking toward my niece, "and I suppose we should think about getting to bed."

Frankie was all for getting out of the freezing cellar and joyfully led the way.

"Come on Stevie-boy, you can help me undress!" exclaimed Frankie before a mischievous giggle. I'm sure Stephen had turned a dark crimson, but the lack of light made it impossible to tell for sure.

"Don't taunt the lad Frankie; we're not all quite as wanton as you, thank you very much. And don't worry, I'll blow out the candles then…" But my sarcasm was lost on them.

~ ~ ~

There was a tap at the bedroom door which woke me. It took me a little time to work out where I was, initially being somewhat taken aback to find myself in a bed with Stephen. Thankfully he wasn't wearing his clerical dog collar, which helped make it slightly less weird. But as a second tap was initiated at the door, I glanced at my surroundings, then saw Frankie dead to the world in the camp bed, a stray shapely young leg hanging out the side, and I then remembered I was at my Edinburgh in-laws.

"Come in," I uttered feebly and Stuart entered with three mugs of tea on a tray.

"Morning," he said quietly, noticing that Fran was still asleep and gently snoring. "Ten o'clock call as requested."

"Goodness, is it that time already?" yawned Stephen, sitting up in bed and stretching, which showed off his stocky muscular arms. Presumably all thanks to his rugby playing for team God.

"Afraid so," replied Stuart handing us both a refreshing brew, leaving Frankie's by her bed and trying not to look at the comely exposed leg. "I know you won't feel much like talking yet, but I'm dying to know. Did you see anything?"

"Yes, we saw your little fat ginger friend all right. Unsightly little blighter that he is."

"Oh. Well. Suppose that's good. I mean, at least you didn't have a wasted journey," Stuart replied.

I thought he looked almost a bit sorry about this news update, as if it was further unwanted proof of its existence.

"We'll check over our video recordings this morning, see if we've got anything on film. You never know."

"Aye, that'll be favourite," he said, again somewhat aloof and troubled.

"It seemed very interested in an area of the floor down there..." Stephen offered up helpfully, but I stopped him in his tracks by discreetly kicking him under the covers when our host wasn't looking, as I thought back to the issue with the flagstone.

"Oh?" enquired Stuart.

"We can chat about things later," I said promptly, changing the direction of the conversation as tactfully as I could muster, "time we were getting up, lots to do today."

"Well I'll leave you to do your ablutions then and I'll get some breakfast on the go. Make a nice big pan of porridge, that'll get you going."

"Lovely," I replied, thinking that what would really get me going, was a nice big plate of sausage, egg and bacon, but you can't win them all I suppose. Just then Frankie issued a snort as if waking up, so I told Stuart to give her a little boot to help the process along. He politely declined and left the room, whereas I'm not so polite and promptly got up and gave her a kick.

"What!" she whinged, like a lazy adolescent.

"Time to get up you idle mare, there's a mug of tea here. We need to get a move on." She just grunted and turned over.

Half an hour later, we were all sat at the kitchen table with a bowl of Stuart's porridge in front of us, Stephen and I looking fairly alert and awake, but Fran was there in body but not spirit, her eyes half closed and her body leaning slightly as if she was propped up by an imaginary pillow.

"Unusual flavour to this porridge Stuart. Is it.... Oh, its salt isn't it?"

"Aye, that's the one true Scottish method. Is it OK?" Seeing Stephen's facial expression and guessing his opinion was the same as mine, I decided I had to be cruel to be kind.

"Sorry, afraid us no good English generally prefer a good few spoons of sugar in our morning oats. Any chance of a few rounds of toast instead?" To be fair, he took it on the chin.

"Oh OK, that's fine," and, albeit a little dejected over this wound to his culinary skills, sliced up a particularly fine-looking loaf of bread. So, in the following twenty minutes or so, I related the events of the night, including the dog bones, but omitting the regrettable damage to the floor of his cellar.

"It's certainly a queer old business Jerry, I must say. My house being haunted by some strange, dwarf like character mourning his pet. I simply can't get my brain around it."

"It's only a theory mind, about his mourning his dead dog. We can't say for sure."

At this Stuart was rummaging in a drawer of the big old kitchen dresser and produced a piece of paper.

"I'm not sure if this would be any use to you, but it's the address of the old lady we bought this house from. She's in a care home now, but it came to me last night in bed that maybe she will have some information for you. Anyway, there you go, just a thought," and he handed me the note. "What's your plan of action now?"

"I've got an old uni friend who might have some info for us so we're meeting up with him for a late lunch," said Stephen with great enthusiasm.

"And this might be handy," I replied, looking at the address that Stuart had just given me, "if we could make a fleeting visit to this Henrietta Booth-Rogers on the way, see if she can add anything to the mix."

"Aye, it's not far out of the city," interjected Stuart, "I'll give you a lift."

"OK, we'll give her a call. Did you want to start going over the film Stephen, just in case we picked something up?"

"Course, no problem, I'll start now," he replied, with lots of energy and enthusiasm, which I love to see in my team members.

"It's just that I, and I suspect Frankie also, have got something else pretty urgent we need to get on with."

"You mean you're both going outside for a fag," retorted Stephen dryly.

"Oh about time!" sparked up Frankie, finally coming to life and moving with much speed in the direction of their back door. "You'll have to lend me another one of yours Unc, I've left mine upstairs."

"What a surprise," I muttered, grabbing my hot black coffee and heading outside to join my favourite niece for the much needed first gasper of the day.

~ ~ ~

Needless to say, the video film had picked up practically nothing of the previous night's apparition. You could argue there was the slight mist which Stephen had seen, but hardly the concrete proof I live to provide for the history books. As always, I'd been cheated of my five minutes of fame by the spirit world but it was an experience I'd been getting used to over my years of paranormal research. Therefore, it was a case of remembering the motto 'onward and upward', and with this in mind I was reclining in comfort on the back seat of Stuarts luxurious Daimler v12, Fran at my side and Stephen in the front, as the vehicle swept elegantly up the gravel drive of the privately managed retirement home where Henrietta Booth-Rogers was a resident. Stuart, who had kindly called her and arranged this last-minute meeting had opted to stay in the car with the Saturday newspaper, so it was just the three of us going inside.

The house was quite grand, painted white with black shutters surrounding all the windows. The interior was also rather plush, with lots of clean and polished antique effect furniture and thick, soft carpeting.

"Bet it costs a few quid to see out your days in a place like this," murmured Fran.

I just grunted in agreement as I admired the beautiful oil paintings in the atmospheric lobby and tried to work out if it was indeed roast lamb I could smell wafting through the building which was presumably today's luncheon. It was making me hungry after my relatively scant and uninspiring breakfast.

A prim, smart lady greeted us and took us through to a very large heated conservatory which overlooked a well-tended large garden and was stocked with a sizable amount of quality wicker furniture. There was a very elderly smartly dressed gentleman in one corner fast asleep, head back, mouth wide open, whose big moustache gave the impression he was probably an army Brigadier in his work life. Across from there was an aged lady, busy rearranging a flower display and almost high on the experience, muttering away as if talking to the flowers. I said hello as we passed but she didn't seem to register us.

Finally, at the far corner, the prim lady who led the way, introduced us to Mrs. Booth-Rogers, a tiny, delicately framed lady, who despite having a thick blanket over her knees, was most elegantly dressed, her lapel decorated with a delightful old broach, which indicated wealth and class.

She nodded toward the lady fussing over the flowers, saying "you mustn't take any notice of old Dorothy there, batty as a coot. There's one or two like that here, but still, given the average age of us all, you can't expect everything to be working anymore, least of all the mind. Poor thing has been rearranging those flowers over and over again for the last three hours." She smiled warmly, adding, "Would you care for a sherry any of you? It's nearly lunchtime you see, and I like to have one before we eat."

The three of us declined, sherry isn't exactly my bag and I certainly couldn't imagine Frankie necking a line of *Tio Pepe*. Not sure about Stephen, with all that communion wine I would've thought it was right up his street. However, the lady who showed us in was duly dispatched to tend to Henrietta's alcohol needs and we got down to business.

"I understand you want to talk to me about my old house Mr. Thorne?"

"Indeed. And it's very good of you to see us at such short notice."

"Quite all right. However, your brother in law told me on the telephone you want to know a bit about its history, which is not really something I know a lot about I'm afraid." I decided to come clean.

"Not exactly that," I said reservedly. "We do a bit of research into the paranormal you see and..."

"Ah I do see," she interrupted with a downcast look. I thought, here we go, she'll be sending for security now because she thinks we're nutters, however I was entirely surprised by her response.

"You want to talk about the ghost then?"

"So, you do know about it?"

"Of course. A most unfortunate part of an otherwise delightful property. I trust you're not here on the basis of serving some kind of litigation against me for not disclosing the resident ghost when I sold the place?"

"Oh no, not at all!" I reassured, almost a tad hurt that I look like someone who would do such a thing.

"Forgive me for asking, but we have rather become a 'compensation culture' these days. However, as you can imagine, it wasn't something I thought appropriate to bring up with the selling agents."

"You have my word; we just wondered if there is anything you can tell us about this ghost."

"That's fine then." She paused as another member of staff came over with her sherry, who proceeded to remind her that lunch was in fifteen minutes time. Taking a gentle sip, she then resumed the conversation.

"My husband and I had lived in the house a good two or three years before we even knew the thing existed. Then one night we got home late as we'd been to the opera with friends, I forget which opera it was now, but we stopped off at our friends for drinks on the way back. You see, the chaps were both judges and had worked together for years, so we would quite often socialise with them. It must've been about one in the morning and we were both sat in the kitchen with some cocoa, musing over our evening out, when we saw the most unpleasant looking creature walk merrily through the kitchen, go over to the cellar door and go down it. I simply couldn't believe it, at first I thought it was some kind of brazen thief, although I didn't understand why it had gone past us as if it hadn't even noticed we were there."

"That's the fella! No doubt about it, we're on the same lines and he's still there now doing the same," I exclaimed excitedly.

"Was it a Friday night you were at the Opera Mrs Booth-Rogers?" asked Stephen intelligently. "It's just that we wondered if it was only on a Friday night that this thing appears."

"Oh no young man, it's every day, night in, night out, without fail. My husband should know." She stopped as if we ought to know what she meant.

"How's that?" I enquired.

"He was a sensitive man Mr Thorne, a lovely, kind, sensitive man. He just had this kind of ability to pick up on things that others couldn't. I'm not saying he was clairvoyant or anything of that nature, but there were a couple of other times in our years together, long before we moved to Edinburgh, that he seemed to be able to sense visitations from the spirit world. But I will tell you this much. My husband was a high court judge for many, many years and very much respected. He presided over a lot of cases dealing with the most wicked and vicious elements that society could produce. I think this helped him to become an even better judge of character too, if you'll excuse the pun, and as such, he could sense without any question that the soul, both as a living person and now in spirit, of that apparition was pure evil. The nastiest piece of work you could ever be unfortunate enough to come across, was how he used to put it."

"Did you see the ghost much?" asked Fran.

"No, my dear, after seeing it that evening it was quite enough for me. My darling husband was very protective of his wife, and never allowed one to go into the kitchen late at night. I think he saw it a couple of other times, if we were late in from a function or dinner party, but I only know that from overhearing a conversation he had with one of his close friends. As time went by, such was his unease about the entity, that by nightfall he wouldn't even allow me in the kitchen, which in the winter months was quite inconvenient, you know, with the nights drawing in early. In fact, eventually, such was his discomfort he began adding basic kitchen items into the drawing room, such as a kettle, toaster, small fridge, that sort of thing, to reduce the need to even go out there. Not the most rational way of living I know, but like I say, he was a bit sensitive in these things. And then, just over a year ago now, the poor dear passed away and I simply couldn't stay there on my own. Hence, I sold it and here I am in this place, waiting for my turn to be called up for judgement."

I told Henrietta about the dog bones under a flagstone in the centre of the cellar floor, to which she was most surprised.

"Goodness me! All the times we must've walked across them, unaware what lay beneath. How very odd, and you say this apparition seemed intent on getting them?"

"Well that's how it looked."

"Of course, neither of us ever went down to the cellar when that horrid ghost went down there, so we wouldn't have known."

"We have a theory it might be the case that this unpleasant looking entity is simply, even after his own death, in mourning for his much loved, departed pet," I suggested.

"No, Mr. Thorne, one simply couldn't concur. I trust the judgement of my husband and if he said that ghost is evil, then it is. Would an evil man, in life or death, really care for a dead animal? I rather think not. And if you did love your pet, wouldn't you bury it somewhere altogether more fitting than under the floor of a cellar? I think if anything is buried in such a place, it must be related to something altogether more nefarious than that."

I couldn't deny, this wily old gal had a good point and advanced age hadn't addled her brain in any way, in fact such a reasoned argument made me want to kick myself for being so stupid.

As I briefly pondered this thought, there was the sound of someone bashing a gong three times.

"Oh, I do believe lunch is about to be served, so I fear we must end our discussion there. I'm sorry I don't have very much more I can add, but I hope I have been of some good service to your investigation." Henrietta was a very elegant lady in both speech and manner.

"You have been very illuminating, thank you so much for seeing us," I responded.

We accompanied her to the dining room, which was now filling up with hungry residents, probably nigh on twenty by now. The tables were laid with crisp white linen, and silver condiment bowls with both mint sauce and redcurrant jelly confirmed my earlier estimate that it was indeed roast lamb today. So, we bid her farewell and went out to the car to find Stuart fast asleep having only reached the second page of his newspaper.

"Ah, time to be going already? Was it a useful chat?" he asked dozily, having been woken up by the sound of the car doors opening and then trying to pretend that he hadn't nodded off.

"Certainly gave us something to think about. Still, better get into the city and find where we're meeting Stephen's pal. Apart from anything else, I'm starving." With that, he fired up the motor and we headed off.

~ ~ ~

During the drive back into the city, my explanation of all Henrietta had told us certainly gave Stuart something to ponder over and not unsurprisingly, the update wasn't sweet news to his ears. He murmured something about not being especially pleased he'd bought a house with a sitting tenant and what a shame it was that such things weren't picked up on a survey.

However, he dropped us off outside the trendy wine bar café where we were due to meet up with Stephens mate and he then went off to a nearby golf course to cogitate further on the subject, most probably taking out his frustration of the matter on his nine iron.

We went in and were duly shown over to the table where our new acquaintance was already waiting for us. I immediately thought, even before introductions, that the guy wasn't what I would've expected as a friend of Stephens, in that he was hip, trendy, well-groomed and I rather suspected he fancied himself too.

"Well everybody, this is Rob," said Stephen, almost a tad nervously.

This Rob fellow, greeted us all warmly enough, in a loud extroverted way, and we sat down, Rob moving his position so as to sit next to Fran – who had clearly caught his eye.

"I got myself a lager while I was waiting and set up a tab at the bar, so can I get any of you's a drink?" he boomed in a broad Scottish vernacular and went off to get our order.

"He's a bit of all right," Frankie whispered with a broad grin, looking after him as he went over to the bar. "You never said he was so gorgeous Stephen."

"I seem to recall he was always a bit of a hit with the ladies," he responded dryly.

I must admit to only half paying attention as I was busy looking over the menu card, or more specifically the prices, which given the chairs were so uncomfortable and they didn't even give you a table cloth, I thought were a bit steep.

"Right then Stevie boy, are you rebelling against the cause!?" Rob asked, as he returned with some drinks.

"Err, not sure what you mean?" said Stephen uneasily.

"Well, you're supposed to be a man of the cloth, aren't you? Should you really be dabbling in this sort of thing? I would've thought it was a bit off limits for that old-fashioned religion of yours."

My opinion of Rob was not improving but Stephen seemed happy enough to take this man's witticisms, or mocking, whatever you like to call it, in his stride.

"I have special dispensation," Stephen replied coolly.

"Over the centuries, there have been many members of the clergy who have written about their own, or other peoples, accounts of the paranormal," I chipped in, at the defence of my young friend.

"Aye well, right enough." Rob turned toward Frankie. "So where do you fit in to all this then beautiful?"

"I just tag along with my uncle now and then. It can be quite interesting at times, believe it or not."

"He's your uncle, is he!? I see you don't get your good looks from his side of the family then!"

My opinion of Rob was now getting as low as a snakes bumhole. The temptation to smack him in the mouth was ever increasing but Stephen broke the silence by suggesting we should order our food. A minute or two more of pointless small talk continued until a bonny wee lassie came and took our order. When she departed I decided it was the time to be getting on to the nitty gritty. After all, if he had nothing to tell us of any use, there didn't seem much point in making it a lengthy luncheon.

"Rob, I understand Stephen has given you the full story, so were you able to find anything out for us?"

"Aye well since you mention it... I have," he said boastfully, reaching down to a carrier bag on the floor by his chair, and producing a handful of notepaper.

"It took me a bit of time at the university archives but I found a document which mentions the address you're researching. Basically, it's from a city magistrates journal, which is dated 14th November 1802, but it's a bit brief mind you's. It talks about a Cecil Herbert McKintosh, who evaded custody for blackmail, theft and even mentions conspiracy to murder charges, which they were unable to get sufficient evidence for. Unfortunately, I couldn't find anything to do with his trial, just that there was a warrant for his arrest after he did a bunk."

We were all interested but I pointed out there was nothing to say this Cecil Herbert chappy was our man.

"True, but what I'm saying, is that to have a big house like the one you're after knowing about, he wasn't exactly your everyday thief and blackmailer. He must've been into some pretty big deals. My guess is that he was a scandal merchant and mischief maker among the upper classes." He took a mighty swig of his drink, wiping his mouth with the back of his hand. "In fact, I'm pretty convinced of it, because I've also got something else to tell ya."

We paused our discussions as the pretty and petite waitress returned with some bread and little packs of foreign butter. I noticed that lascivious Rob was eyeing up her slender tanned legs as she departed with an almost salivating look on his face. Then he turned back to us and we all sat forward to hear the next part of his discovery.

"Anyways... I had a glance over some society news sheets from about that period, you know the thing, who was marrying who, which big house was having the glitziest ball and all that snooty class crap. Well, the lead piece on one of them was about the suicide of a Lady Emily Jane Fort-Hamilton, a young heiress who was due to marry the dashing Lieutenant something or other, double-barrelled ponsy name; I cannai remember. Whatever. Basically, something made me read the article to the end, not sure why, but I was just finding it interesting and am I glad I did!"

He paused again, taking another big swig of his lager.

"And what about it?" questioned Frankie, keen to hear the outcome.

"Hold on wee hen, its thirsty work this research."

Stephen took the hint better than I did and attracted the attention of the waitress to order Rob another drink. When she was despatched, we got to hear the next instalment.

"Seems she was racked with fear over scandal to the good name of her family, because after a big party she was giving at her house, she discovered the jewels she'd left in her bedroom were missing, as was a lot of 'private and personal' correspondence. Now if you ask me, their use of the phrase 'private and personal' was a euphemism for 'hot, naughty and dirty'. And if these x-rated billet-doux were not between her and her intended, but some other lucky fella, then you could see why she would be crapping herself over a possible family scandal."

"That is only guesswork," stated Stephen, quite reasonably.

"Aye, right enough, but there's nothing to say I'm not spot on, is there?"

"There's nothing to say you're right either," I stated haughtily.

"Whatever. All I'm saying is if it was enough for her to kill herself, they must've been pretty steamy. You wouldn't finish it all for a few jewels, would you? No matter how much they're worth."

The waitress returned with the lager just as Rob said the word 'kill' and she looked suitably startled, presumably wondering who on earth we all were.

"That's lovely darlin'," said Rob, winking and grinning at her.

"Maybe she was a lesbian," remarked Fran casually. For a second or so, I thought she meant the waitress, but realised she meant this Lady Emily that Rob was spouting about.

"Now that would've been a scandal back then," she added.

Unconvinced by yet more speculation, I felt we were digressing so decided to get things back on track.

"That was all very useful, thanks for looking into it for us…" But he interrupted.

"I still haven't told you the last bit yet. The article finished by saying that this Cecil, of the abode you're looking into, was a guest at this shindig of hers and when she took her own life, she left a note, making special mention of this guy, decrying him as nefarious and villainous. As a result, they concluded the piece with the open question; was he the thief? And did he have something on her, which made her make such a statement? Was it blackmail? Did he take her jewels? Then it finished by saying he hadn't been seen for some time. I'm afraid that was as far as I could go with it. Mind you, I did pretty well, even if I do say so myself."

We all dutifully thanked him for his efforts, as I could see he had a big ego which needed polishing. I don't know how much truth was in any of what he said, but it was intriguing information nonetheless although I couldn't at that point decide if it helped our investigation or not.

Our meals arrived, if that's the word to use, I would've said snacks was a better description given the lousy portion size against price, but there you go. Given my belly only had a bit of toast and a mouthful of salty porridge for breakfast, it was ready for something more substantial. We continued the debate about Stuart's grand house for a little while, mainly by telling Rob about the recent experiences there, but I felt he eyed us disbelievingly although didn't admit it. The remainder of the meal consisted of Rob telling us stories from when Stephen and he were at university together. It seemed to me that they were hardly close and given some of the practical jokes that Rob played on Stephen in that time, I'm surprised my ecclesiastical friend would even give this loud mouth the time of day.

For instance, Stephen was pushed off his bike down an embankment by him. A second 'amusing' story was that a rumour was started by Rob that Stephen had herpes which circulated the entire campus. Then another prank involved a store detective, where a group of these students were at a big department store and Rob told one of the security people that he'd seen Stephen shop lifting, leaving him to be dragged up to the manager's office. These are just three of the tales we were told by the talkative Rob, and all of which he found extremely amusing.

Poor Stephen. He took it all on the chin, probably much like when he was a student, politely smiling as Rob recounted his tales with much enthusiasm, taking great pleasure in the humiliation caused.

I couldn't stand very much more of this Rob character and when the lovely little waitress came back with dessert menus, before anyone had chance to take one, I said we had to be going and were ready to pay.

She said the bill would be ready at the bar and as she left us, Rob chipped in that he'd very much like to pay half.

"Thank you, that's kind," I replied graciously and indeed, somewhat surprised.

"Thing is though, I was in such a rush to get here on time, I've left my wallet at home and I've nothing with me," he then added.

What a dirty, no good waster! My low opinion of the man was forever being justified. I told him not to worry, secretly wanting to smack him about the head with my dessert cutlery, and went to the bar to settle up the tab. The bill, in all its high sterling value magnificence, was laid before me and I reached for my wallet feeling overcharged and underfed. I was getting my debit card out, when Stephen presented himself alongside.

"Let me get this Jerry."

"Absolutely not young man, call it my treat."

Glancing down at the bill, he took out cash from his own wallet to just over half the value of our bill, and immediately thrust it in my top pocket.

"I'll cover half then – no arguments."

"Thanks Stephen, you're a good egg. Not like that pal of yours, didn't take to him at all."

"Maybe this lunch has reminded me that he wasn't that great a friend after all," and glanced back to our table as he spoke. "Still, at least we've got some information which may be relevant."

"Maybe. Maybe not. I need to give it some thought when we get back to Stuart's. I feel tired now I've had something to eat, that is to say, a bloody small something to eat. So I might ponder it over while I have a lay down."

We made our way back to the table and I noted with displeasure that Frankie and Rob were sat extremely close to each other and that he had his hand on top of hers.

"Well thanks for everything Rob, nice to meet you and all that, but we had better be getting along," trying my best to sound masterful.

"Actually Jerry, I've just offered to show Frankie some of the sights, so if you've no objections, I'm going to be borrowing her for the next few hours."

"You won't need me until tonight will you Unc?" added Fran. To be honest, this took me completely by surprise and so I couldn't muster up any worthy objection.

"No, no, that's fine, you go, enjoy yourself. So long as you're back for tonight though."

"Of course, I will be!" She turned to Rob and explained we were going to have another vigil tonight to try and see Cecil the ghost again, if indeed, that is who it was.

"Oh great. If that's how you want to spend a Saturday night in a vibrant place like Edinburgh. But I'll see if I can tempt you otherwise!" he added smugly.

You better bloody not, I thought. We have a job to do.

The four of us left the bistro, at which point Fran and Rob went off on their separate way, leaving myself and Stephen to wander down to a nearby taxi rank.

"You don't seem very happy?" I said.

"You don't look full of the joy of life either," he retorted.

"I must admit to feeling a tad ripped off by that restaurant, although less so thanks to you. And I really didn't like Fran going off with that mate of yours either."

"Yeah, well, I'm a bit disappointed about that too, but what can I say, I never knew how he did it when we were students, and I still don't, but one click of his fingers and women just go for him."

We'd almost walked to the neat line of waiting cabs and I glanced around at the magnificent historic buildings all around us and felt guilty for not having a little explore of this city myself whilst I had the opportunity, without Cynthia holding my lead like I was her pet poodle. But the streets were busy with shoppers, tourists and workers so I decided to stick with plan A and the two of us gave Stuart's address to the driver and got in the taxi. Stephen looked thoughtful.

"I'm not sure how he can show her the sights, if he hasn't got any money with him. But he always was a sponger."

"That's no surprise," I said, equally peevish. "If it was anybody taking her around the city, I would've preferred it to have been you. That's what my niece needs, a calming, sensible influence like you around her."

"Yeah, so I read into that, boring you mean...!?"

"No! I didn't mean that at all. She likes you, and I trust you, so all I was saying was that it would've been nice if the two of you could've gone off for a while. Gotten to know each other better. Apart from anything else, if I'd have gotten rid of the both of you, I could've had an afternoon nap!"

He chuckled.

"Ah so that's the real plan. You go and have your sleep; I'll maybe have another scan through the video of last night." He paused. "You know, I wish I had asked Fran to have a look around the city with me. It would've been interesting for me too, having not been up here for a while, and she's always good company, in a live wire kind of way. But hey, that's the story of my life; I've always been too slow off the mark."

We said no more about it and both of us spent the rest of the short journey back deep in thought, though I suspect, perusing different things.

~ ~ ~

Although I tried to chew over the information that Rob had provided us with, unfortunately my sleeping system took over, which, given I was lying down on a very comfortable bed with the curtains drawn, was hardly very surprising.

Also, not very surprising, was the fact that ugly Cecil had found himself in my dreams, insofar as I was a guest at a big country house ball and presumably so was he. Everyone had the most elegant Georgian party outfits on, except I was wearing the same old scruffy clothes I always wear, but hey, I like a wax jacket / bushman's hat combo. The next thing I knew I was dancing across a huge ballroom but all the guests had disappeared, with the exception of my dance partner, who was none other than Cecil! He looked far more glam than the occasions I'd seen him since, although he was still unpleasant to the eye but he had some colour to his cheeks, which seemed to make his wild, ginger hair look all the more vivid. However, the next thing I knew he produced a short, shiny dagger and was plunging it deeply and ferociously between my ribs.

Therefore, I was pretty glad at this point to be woken up by the sound of Frankie entering the bedroom, not to mention the burst of light streaming across my face as she left the door open.

"All right?" she asked. "I suppose you're going to saying 'no' because I woke you up."

"Actually, I'm pretty glad you did. Wasn't having the nicest of dreams, to say the least," I replied, whilst rubbing away the sleepiness from my stressed-out skull.

"Stuart's not back yet I see," she observed.

"What time is it then?"

"Bout half six."

"He'll be in the golf club bar if he's got any sense. How was your afternoon with that cocksure, intellectual yob?"

"You mean Rob?"

"Yes, I do mean Rob, the yob, who acts like a knob."

I thought that was quite quick for a man who's just woken up.

"Actually, I wasn't with him long. I've been looking around the shops on my own. You know, they've pretty much got exactly the same shops up here selling pretty much the same stuff as we have down south. But with tins of shortbread. Even in the clothes shops; shortbread gift boxes everywhere!"

"I like shortbread, don't suppose you bought me any though?" I said, sitting up in the bed, yawning.

"No," came the short and sweet reply.

"So how come you've been on your own. I thought you were going to see the sights with 'Rob'?" I made sure I said his name with a tone of distaste.

"Oh him. Well sight number one turned out to be his flat, so I knew what he was after, and he wasn't getting it from me! Bloody front of him. We'd only known him five minutes and he thinks I'm just going to get straight into bed with him! What does he think, he's God's gift or something?"

Clearly, I was right about the man, and I felt half inclined to go around to his place and punch him, such was my rage at what Fran had told me.

"I knew he was up himself," I ranted. "Still, just you make sure you tell Stephen about it. I think he's been feeling a bit inferior, which is hardly surprising given all that unpleasant mickey-taking."

"Don't know why, he's a much nicer bloke than that Rob any day. Despite his wacky job."

I was warmed to hear her say so. "Perhaps you could be nice for a change and tell him that."

"Perhaps," she replied coolly, at which point speaking of the said Stephen, I could hear someone coming along the corridor, and in he came.

"Hi guys, have I got something to show you!"

I looked him up and down in surprise. "Given your hands and knees are covered in dirt, can I assume you didn't bother looking over the film from last night?"

"You assume correctly Jerry. Come on, come with me!"

He buzzed off excitedly, leaving a puzzled Fran and I looking at each other as if searching for the answer which clearly was only available by going with him. So, we did, downstairs to the kitchen, where we caught up with him as he stood waiting by the cellar door.

"Down here, quickly!" And the three of us descended the stairs to the basement.

To my surprise Stephen had taken up the broken flagstone from the night before and had completely unearthed the skeleton of the dog, which he'd laid to the left side of the hole.

"What on earth have you been up to?" I asked, although I could see the answer in front of me so it was a slightly silly question.

"I wondered if there was anything under the dog, so I dug it up with the intention of laying it out neatly on the cloth there at the side, so I could poke around in the dirt underneath."

"And was there anything?" asked Fran, kneeling down next to the hole, and looking in.

"No nothing under the dog," at which he grinned widely, and quite theatrically reached into his top shirt pocket, adding "but there was something *inside* the dog!"

Myself and Fran looked on open mouthed as he presented a dark coloured gem, almost as big as the palm of his hand on which he was displaying it. Then he shone his torch at it, and it gleamed and glistened as it's prettily cut surface reflected the light and showed up its rich verdant green colouring.

"Bloody hell!" screamed Fran breathlessly, "tell me that's not a bloody great emerald!"

"I can't tell you that because I think it is," replied Stephen smiling back at us.

"Blimey... No wonder Cecil keeps coming down here. It's absolutely beautiful! And you say it was inside the dog?" I asked.

"Yep, and I suppose we didn't notice it the first time we dug down to the skeleton because we didn't remove the bones from the soil. It was only when I did that, I saw it. Sort of dropped through its rib cage when I lifted the bones out. I thought it was just a stone at first!"

"It is I suppose, in a manner of speaking. Do you think Cecil forced it down the animal's throat and then killed it, so it didn't come out the other end of its digestive system? One way of hiding a precious jewel, no one's going to poke around with a dead dog, are they?"

"Except Stephen," grinned Fran. "Oh, the poor little thing!" she continued, turning towards the dogs remains. Even she can, at times, be a bit soft when it came to all things fish, fur and feathers.

"Probably something along those lines, I should think," pondered Stephen, who had clearly been musing about my emerald concealment theory and wasn't paying attention to Frankie's animal mourning.

We were all extremely keen to give the gem closer inspection, and with Fran's usual keenness and familiarity, she was first to get her hands on the goods, holding it up to the ceiling light.

"Wow, it's such a lovely colour!" she exclaimed with desire. "Can we have it?"

"Goodness me no!" I said, "This is Stuarts house, we have to give it to him."

"What!? He's got enough money as it is. And what about 'finders keepers, loser's weepers' eh? Surely that means it's ours, else why would anyone make up a saying like that?"

"So that people like you dearest niece, can lay claims on things that aren't theirs!"

"That is so rubbish! Stuart doesn't need the money, does he? Think about it! We sell it, split it three ways, and off we go with tens of thousands of pounds we didn't have yesterday! What's complicated about that?"

All the while she was speaking she was clutching the jewel close to her chest, with a wild twinkle in her eye like a woman possessed.

"Come on Frankie, give it here. It's not ours to sell," added Stephen calmly and with his usual good sense.

"Oh, not you as well Stevie...! You know, you don't have to keep your share, you could give it to the church, or a charity; whatever." She was trying her best to sound perfectly reasonable.

"You've a crazy look in your eye; exactly the same wild, covetous look as nasty Cecil had when I saw him," I told her.

"That's how it goes Fran. That's how the devil works, he takes over, fills someone with greed and avarice, until all reasonable thinking is long gone," added Stephen, with some not very subtle comments about Satan to stir things up a bit.

Frankie just looked at each of us in turn and with a sad, disappointed look on her face, handed the precious stone back to Stephen, who deposited it back in his top pocket.

"S'pose" she muttered dejectedly.

"Well done sweetheart. You know it's the right thing, to hand it over to Stuart, it's his house, so his choice as to what he wants to do with it."

"Are we still going to do the vigil tonight then? Now we have this..." said Stephen, tapping his shirt pocket, "will the ghost bother to come back?"

"He doesn't know we've got the gem, does he? So, in answer to your question, yes, we go ahead as planned. It would be interesting to see if that ugly little crook notices the flagstone's been interfered with. I'd love to know what his reaction would be, if indeed, he even notices."

"Should I put everything back in place then?" asked Stephen.

"No. Let's leave the hole and this mess, so he can see his treasure has been disturbed. That'll stir things up a bit."

"Unc, are you sure that's a good idea?" Fran had a somewhat uneasy facial expression.

"Of course, trust me, when have I ever let you down?" I asked. Although I was somewhat perturbed that nobody responded with anything positive to pacify me.

Everything was left as it was and we went back upstairs. Shortly afterwards Stuart returned from his afternoon of golf, much cheered for having won. He was even more elated when we told him the story of Stephen's find in his cellar and just stared at the stunning emerald in disbelief. But then he frowned in panic.

"Ah, but Jerry, what am I to say to Agnes? How will I explain why you lot are here, digging a hole in our cellar? She'll be furious."

"She gets a bloody nice emerald to play with, so I don't see what she's got to complain about," exclaimed Fran bitterly.

"Don't worry Stuart; I don't think anyone needs to know we were here." I turned to Stephen, who was looking at my brother in law sympathetically. "You don't mind not taking the credit for the find, do you Stephen?"

"Suits me fine. I'm more than happy to be out of the limelight. I just don't have the *X-Factor*."

"There you go then; no one need know we were anywhere near here."

"Aye, but what about the hole in the floor? What possible reason would I have for digging a hole in the cellar and, quite by chance at that exact spot, finding the remains of a dog with an emerald in its stomach? You know what Agnes is like Jerry; she has that piercing, inquisitive look with the penetrating eyes of a Gestapo officer."

Before I had chance to respond, not that I could think of anything comforting to respond with, Stephen came to the rescue.

"Can't you just say you were in the cellar looking for something and as you crossed the floor, that particular flagstone just gave way under your foot? And that's when you looked for the reason it broke. Then you found the bones and then the emerald? All sorted."

Coming from a clergyman, I was surprised by how convincing a lie Stephen was suggesting and there was a momentary silence in the room, while all present chewed this over in their heads.

"Actually, that's not bad," announced Stuart suddenly, then slowly nodding, as if in further appreciation of the fib.

"What will you do with it then?" Frankie was clearly inquisitive. "S'pose you'll sell it?"

"Oh no, it won't be sold! It's not as if we need the money after all."

At this, Fran gave Stephen and me a disapproving look which very much stated 'told you' with thorough rebuke in its silent glare.

"It's an historic find," he continued. "I shall donate it to the museum, or university, something like that. It might even find its way back to the descendants of whoever the rightful owner might've been. Still, I think for now, the thing to do is get it locked up in the safe."

At which point, Stuart went off to secure the beautiful gem away, as Fran looked on longingly at it.

~ ~ ~

It was nearly one o'clock in the morning, and all three of us were camped out in the dim, candlelit cellar. Once again, our host had retired to bed early to keep out of our way, but not before serving us up a supper of oatcakes, Scottish cheeses and port. After the pitiful luncheon, I would've preferred something more substantial, but I didn't want the hassle of going off to a local takeaway, so I packed an awful lot of cheese in the JT belly. Which was probably why I had a bit of a headache and nothing whatsoever to do with all the port I'd drunk while we had our simple supper. Surely not. Either way, I was thinking a lot about finding a pub when we got home, somewhere I could order a full mixed grill and substantial dessert!

"I could murder a ciggie," whispered Frankie, the coldness on her breath being visible even in the little light we had.

"Now is hardly a good time is it? It's nearly one and the whole point of all of us being down here was so we all get to see his reaction to his swag being gone."

"Yeah I know. It's just that the cold is really..."

"Cold?" I muttered, taking advantage of her pause in the sentence.

"I was going to say 'sending a chill around my nooks and crannies' but given Stephens present, I need to be careful how I phrase it."

"Don't mind me," Stephen whispered, "say what you like, you normally do," he added, grinning. "You should've brought some thermal knickers."

I was most surprised to hear a member of the clergy bringing up the subject of lady's undergarments, but it was time to bring order to the proceedings.

"Ssshh, we've got to start being quiet. The lovely Cecil might show up at any moment."

"If he's not shown his ugly mug by half past, I'm off upstairs to get warm," she moaned, with an exaggerated shiver.

As it was, hardly ten minutes went by before we all heard the distant and quiet workings of the door mechanism at the top of the staircase... We were hiding behind the dust sheet covered, superfluous junk and watching out for our ghost with trepidation, through any convenient little gaps. I think we were all holding our breath, trying to be as silent as possible, even though my heart beat was so pronounced I worried it was probably audible a mile away.

The spirit itself, seemed almost silent. The only sound seemed to come from the staircase, which creaked as he made his way slowly down. I had thought with his old fashioned buckled clompers, he would've made more noise. He seemed to pause as he reached the floor and I adjusted my hiding position to get a better view of his face. When I did so, I saw he wore an expression of utter shock and was simply standing there, in his diminutive proportions staring now with features of both alarm and confusion at the unearthed flagstone. Just looking at him was sending icy shivers shooting up my spine and we continued to watch him as he slowly made his way to what had been the site of his treasure. This certainly answered one of my queries, in that it would seem he had indeed noticed the hole, which meant he was very much linked to the time and not merely a replay of energy from a previous age. I was desperate not to lose sight of him, and unknowingly my body was leaning more and more to the right. In the corner of my eye I caught sight of Stephen gesturing at me, which I subsequently discovered albeit too late, was my clerical team mate trying to warn me what I was about to do. Unfortunately, by accident, I managed to do it anyway, as the weight of my body from my ever-increasing lean starboard, dislodged a pile of half empty cardboard boxes, which had been somewhat precariously left on a plastic garden chair missing a leg and as such, the lot toppled over with an almighty crash.

"Subtle. Really subtle," uttered Fran critically.

My little misdemeanour had left the three of us somewhat exposed, and the ghost immediately turned and faced us, which revealed just how unsightly and unattractive he was, although to be fair, given how many years he'd been dead I'm sure he could've looked worse.

"Oh, hello," I uttered weakly.

At first, he calmly eyed us up and down as if we were the oddities in this little tête-à-tête, which I have to admit was a bit of a sauce. Then the cogs of his long-deceased brain started to turn and he'd obviously realised we were responsible for the messy opening in the floor, or more specifically the theft of what he himself had probably stolen.

His right hand with great speed reached down to his somewhat decayed waist belt and he produced a fierce looking dagger which he rather skilfully wielded in front of us. I hadn't before noticed he kept a weapon close to hand like that, but to my surprise more than horror, I remembered the look of his weapon was exactly like the one in my bizarre dream earlier in the afternoon. But at that point in time, it wasn't really a convenient moment to be thinking about the weirdness of this coincidence (although when I think back to how this could've been possible, it leaves me very dumbfounded. Presumably though, I wouldn't now be going off to have a dance with him somewhere, as in the dream. Well, hopefully not.) The pertinent issue in hand was one of avoiding the knife of a very upset phantom, with a reputation for truculent evil.

As such, I therefore thought now was a good time to kiss arse.

"Do I have the honour of addressing Mr. Cecil Herbert McKintosh perchance?"

"Are you responsible *for this*?!" came the reply in a deep, broad Scottish drawl, the tone of the last two words rising with anger, as he gestured toward the hole with the end of his dagger.

"Errr. Responsible for what?" I replied trying to sound as innocent as possible.

He didn't verbally respond, but simply thrust his knife forward to his full, stubby arm's length and grunted. On reflection, I should've just said no and told him we didn't know anything about the floor disarray. I'm just too honest for my own good though, and apart from anything else I wanted to investigate his responses and pursue this interaction further. Conversations with ghosts tend to be few and far between after all.

"Yes, indeed, since you mention it, I believe we may have accidentally made a slight imprint on the flooring."

He ebbed closer and jerked his knife threateningly. The cellar was cold before we saw him, but now it was positively arctic.

"Did you take anything?" he snorted uneasily.

"No, no, nothing of interest. Just a dead dog wasn't there Stephen?" I turned to my friend for some backup to try and divert some of this dialogue to another party.

"Um yes, that's right," with fingers crossed behind his back, "sorry we haven't had chance to put the bones back, been a bit busy doing... stuff. Err, you know, we were tidying up this mess behind here...Weren't we Jerry?"

"Yes, indeed, and then you came in."

"You took nothing?" he snorted.

"No, absolutely nothing at all," I assured him or it, whatever you want to call the thing. The phantom then seemed to be marginally calmer, and his knife wielding arm lowered a few inches. Until, Frankie decided to join the discussion...

"Except for that big, shiny emerald of course. We didn't hang around whipping that beauty away."

Her comment was in such a nonchalant, matter of fact manner that for a second or so, I believe both Stephen and I just stared at her in disbelief, our mouths hanging open. I turned back to the apparition however, in time to see his eyes widen and his face become a pretty vivid rubicund. This was quickly followed an unintelligible imprecation on us, at which point he raised his weapon wielding arm in the air and charged at us in an absolutely apoplectic rage. Given his diminutive height, odd shape, dirty, warty skin and glowing ginger hair, it might've actually been quite comical to watch, but the danger of his knife was all too real. And after we all darted in different directions at the frenzy of his attack, I glanced around to notice the spectre had all the agility of a martial arts master, because at the point where we'd been standing, he forward rolled, got back on his feet and turned around in the space of a second. He was like a Scottish Jackie Chan.

My heart was pounding, as this was not an outcome I'd considered at any point in the proceedings. The mad wrath of the wraith was all too apparent in his ugly, grotesque face as he quickly switched his glance between the three of us while he evaluated whom should be on the receiving end of his attack first. I was convinced that now was a time for diplomatic negotiations, especially as none of us, being in different corners of the cellar by now, were anywhere near the staircase to make a swift retreat.

Angry Cecil had obviously thought Frankie was soft pickings and with great deftness shot forward in her general direction. What he hadn't anticipated was how close her hand was to the handle of an empty suitcase, so that just as he approached her, she swung the side of the case against his orange mopped head. This in turn unbalanced him and he fell over, dropping the knife which enabled Fran to run across and join Stephen in the corner he'd taken refuge. As her uncle, I was very pleased that she had been able to join forces with another warrior in this bizarre underground battle. I was quickly reminded though, of my solitary position, as the now wailing spectre was running hot foot straight at me and because I'd spent so long looking in the direction of Fran and Stephen I was somewhat at a loss as to know how to defend myself. Although to be honest, the horror of my predicament had frozen me completely, it really was like in the movies insofar as it felt like I'd drifted out of my own reality. Sound was no longer being received by my ears and the advancing ghost seemed to be in slow motion, although in reality not so. My head knew I had to do something to protect myself or at the very least, dive out of its path, but my body was so rigid I may as well have been a lump of clay. Looking back, I truly think I might've been a goner.

However, my motionless state was brought back to consciousness by the realisation of something flying through the air in front of my face.

~ ~ ~

Thank heavens for a quick-thinking Stephen. He had obviously noted my useless frozen body in the face of the knife wielding, fast approaching ghost on the attack, and leapt to the rescue. The corner of the cellar where he'd been defensively located, had like the rest of it, been a place of storage for unwanted and discarded household wares as it would seem my in-laws are even worse hoarders than myself. As it was, Stephen had noticed a long, full length hall mirror close to hand, had grabbed it when he saw my predicament, ran across to what could've been my place of execution had it not been for his quick thinking and swung the heavy mirror slap bang in the face of my assailant. As he did so, he almost knocked my own head off my shoulders, as it seemed to fly by my face awfully close. But I was not in any position to be picky.

Stephen's swing of the long mirror was made with considerable athleticism, presumably from his rugby days, and would've hit Cecil pretty damn hard. Yet he did not fall back on the floor, the mirror did not break on impact and there was no cry of pain. There was simply the sound of a heavy thud. Clearly, Stephen was braced for an impact that would stop his forceful swing, but apart from the strange noise, nothing was there to slow down his bodily movement and as a result he spun, mirror in hand, in a complete circle.

"Where'd he go!?" he asked, slowing his spin before he fell over.

"I'm not sure; there was a loud thud so I thought you'd hit him."

Frankie ran over to join us.

"When you whacked him Stephen, he just seemed to explode into a mist and disappear!" she informed us excitedly.

"We need to be on our guard then, because he might be back any second. I therefore suggest we get out of here now!"

However, as I said this, I noticed that Stephen had a somewhat perplexed look on his face and was staring down at the mirror.

"What's the matter?"

He looked back at me with a shocked and bemused expression.

"Look in the mirror," he said, turning the looking glass front to face myself and Fran.

To our complete surprise, the mirror was no longer reflective. Instead, it was like looking into a small white room, or rather a white mass, as there were no clearly defined walls or sides. And there was someone within this white mass. A short man, in old fashioned dirty clothes, with a warty face and vivid ginger hair.

"Bloody hell! He's in there... he's in the bloody mirror!"

As Frankie and I moved forward for a closer look. Within the confines of the mirror, Cecil came running up to the glass, and started angrily banging on the inside. He was shouting too by the look of it, but there was no sound whatsoever. Not his thumping on the glass, nor his cries of outrage.

"I don't believe it. This is impossible. Tell me you two can see what I can see!" I needed convincing I wasn't going mad and that I wasn't fast asleep, dreaming it all in some weird land of nod hocus pocus. I had after all, recently consumed a lot of port and cheese!

"I can see it but I can't believe it," muttered Fran, awestruck.

Stephen didn't reply, having started to examine the mirror with great thoroughness. He searched behind it, tried to find a gap, tapped it and looked about the cellar as if trying to discover a camera for a television show about practical jokes.

"I don't understand this at all, this mirror is no more than half a centimetre thick and the frame maybe an inch or so," and as he said this he was indifferent to Cecil inside the glass, shaking his fist at him for moving the mirror around so much. "It's like he's in some kind of strange white box with a glass front, yet you look behind and there's nothing there!"

As we all looked at the mirror with bewilderment, Cecil 'inside' it looked back at us angrily. For a dead man, he was extremely fit, because for all the time we stared at him in silent confusion, his stubby form was jumping up and down, his fists thumping on the glass and his mouth still moving. Not being a lip reader and not being able to hear what he was saying, I couldn't be sure what he was trying to tell us and despite all his physical jerks, silence prevailed. I think it's safe to say he wasn't saying nice things about us though and if ghosts had Christmas card lists, we three wouldn't be on his.

The thing was though; what to do now?

"Stephen, would you run up and get Stuart please? I'm too shocked to move and I don't think Fran ought to be tiptoeing into his room at this time of night, as he might think his luck is in."

"No worries," he replied obediently, and was off, leaving Frankie and I watching our Scottish 'catch of the day' rant furiously back at us, which was actually quite entertaining.

We looked on at him and I began to find it almost hypnotically relaxing. Like having a lava lamp or fish tank in your sitting room. Now that's an idea I thought. We could keep him as an ornament..!

~ ~ ~

Stuart, standing as he was in his expensive dressing gown and rich man's night attire, looked surprisingly uncomfortable at the sight of Cecil in the mirror, who with amazing energy, was still ranting and raving in whatever dimension he had found himself.

"You say it's safe Jerry, but if he got in there as quick as a flash, maybe he'll get out as quickly too."

"I think you're worrying over nothing, he hasn't managed to get out yet. I mean look at him, bouncing around in there like a demented rabbit. He's clearly stuck."

I tried to sound reassuring, but to be fair I hadn't the faintest idea how safe it was. This was a new one on me...

"Aye, stuck until he works out how to get himself out," he retorted, slyly moving all the more behind Frankie, as if she was his human shield.

"How on earth has this happened? Have any of you seen anything like this before?" Stuart asked with increasing unease.

We all shook our heads.

"The thing is what do we do now? This is pretty major stuff," I said. "To say we've caught and imprisoned a ghost, will have the world's scientists flocking for a look."

Fran's eyes lit up.

"We'll be famous! Bloody hell, we'll be on the news all over the world! I better freshen up my make up when we get back upstairs. I don't want to be plastered all over the papers looking like this!" Frankie had obviously bitten the celebrity bug and had no doubt started to fantasize about mixing with the great and the good of the world. Images of her arriving at star studded parties with paparazzi lenses going mad for a slice of her pie were no doubt passing through her head. Stuart on the other hand, even in the subtle lighting of the cellar, was looking somewhat grey in the gills.

"Oh, my word! What on earth will Agnes say!? This is a complete nightmare! What have I done to deserve this!" Panic was reverberating in his voice. "Jerry, I blame you! This was supposed to be hush-hush. Had I known you'd be putting me in such a difficult situation I would never have brought the matter up with you!"

"Calm down Stu, you'll burst a blood vessel. Now in light of what you're saying, perhaps we could keep this quiet. Maybe just tuck the mirror away and no one need know anything about it..."

"What!" exclaimed Frankie, fame and fancy frocks falling from her fantasy world.

"Hang on a minute Jerry," interjected Stephen. "You cannot deny the world this, this, this, whatever this is! I mean, look!" and he pointed to the mirror with the now more lethargic Cecil trapped within. "Scientists all around the world will be wanting to know how a man who died about two hundred years ago, has managed to avoid heaven or hell, then found himself trapped inside a gilt-edged mirror, which in turn is barely any thickness at all." But Stuart looked even more rattled.

"Whilst I appreciate why a man in your position would bring in the whole heaven and hell debate, it's still my house, my property and my privacy at stake, so surely any publicity should be on my say-so," responded Stuart somewhat huffily.

I have to admit I was torn. There was family loyalty and I could see how much trouble Stuart would be in with Agnes. I'm not sure what would be worse, the scandal of the world knowing we'd caught a ghost in their house or the scandal of him allowing me to stay without her knowledge or permission, to research a subject she doesn't approve of. I would also be in for it back home too, with Cynthia, as if life there wasn't difficult enough already.

However, there was the bigger picture to consider. This was a scientific breakthrough! Finally, after all these years of trying, I had some sort of proof to offer a sceptical world about the paranormal.

On the other hand, a sceptical world can be a cruel and judgemental place. No one would believe it. There'll be all sorts of people dismissing our grubby little mirror man as some kind of hoax. A shabby trick with film projection or a computer-generated microchip creation. Oh dear I thought, and while I'd been pondering, the exchanges between my companions were beginning to get a little heated. Fran was worried about her celebrity status, especially after losing out on a claim to a third of an emerald, Stuart was panicking about his reputation and Stephen was agonising about denying the world this extra afterlife knowledge we could afford them. Now we were the ones providing entertainment to Cecil, rather than the other way around, who was eyeing us all from his strange confines with much curiosity.

"Look!" I stated with authority, or maybe irritation and fatigue, "now isn't the time to be having this conversation. It's the middle of the night, we're all tired and stressed, and its bloody cold down here, so may I suggest we adjourn this discussion until breakfast time when we might all be able to have a more reasonable debate."

To my surprise everyone concurred. We quickly cleared up some of the mess we'd made, while Stuart who was still extremely unnerved by all the proceedings was keen to be the first up the stairs back to the kitchen door. Stephen and I did most of the work mind you and blew out the candles while Frankie merely stood holding the mirror at her arm's length, staring hard at Cecil, something he reciprocated in equal measure. Our host at the top of the staircase, quickly turned off the cellar lighting the second after we'd blown the candles out, as being a canny Scot he clearly didn't believe in wasting a single drop of electricity. This was fine for us two chaps as we were beginning to ascend the staircase anyway so being plunged into virtual darkness didn't matter. However, I had to chivvy Fran along who was completely absorbed trying to 'outstare' the ghost, an activity I remembered she used to play as a child from time to time with their family dog. Unfortunately, this meant she rushed up the stairs; the mirror wedged under her left arm, with a tad too much swiftness for someone running in the dark, the result of which was that she lost her footing part way up. Needless to say, when the human form is faced with a head first impact on stone steps, the natural bodily reaction is to put the hands out to break the fall. Unfortunately, when you've got a long mirror under your arm at the same time, something has to give. And it did. In loud and spectacular style.

~ ~ ~

Moments later we were all back in the cellar, lighting reactivated, surveying the wreckage of a gilt frame in four broken parts and mirror glass in ten thousand pieces.

"You shouldn't have rushed me!" Fran protested. "And he shouldn't have turned the bloody lights off!" giving Stuart a look of displeasure.

"I suppose accidents do happen," said Stephen reassuringly, who was obviously feeling her pain, like a good trainee vicar might act with a suffering parishioner.

"I could've been in the newspapers. My one chance of fame! 'Cos opportunities like this don't come along twice in a lifetime you know..." she whinged, utterly downcast. "And I better not get 'seven years bad luck' as well!"

"It's probably for the best" said Stuart smiling with glee, "we've never liked that mirror, that's why it was down here, so Agnes won't even notice it's gone."

But then a shot of realisation and concern was across his face.

"Good God! What do you think happened to your ghost Jerry? Is it in pieces with all this glass? It's not been freed has it!?" he asked with slight panic, looking all around him in case the fierce little ghost was about to pounce on him.

"I can't imagine so; I think if it had, we would've seen something of him by now, or felt him biting our ankles, especially given how angry he was about us stealing his knocked-off emerald. No, I think it's probably safe to say, Frankie has inadvertently killed a dead person."

"Thanks," she replied gruffly, "I'm obviously never going to live this down."

"Manslaughter, but of a ghost. Wonder what the legal business would make of that?" I muttered.

She just looked at me severely, so I decided not to add anything to my statement.

To my surprise, given how moral he was on the subject previously, Stephen was quite magnanimous about the situation.

"That aside, there'll be no point in us telling anyone about all this now we've no proof. We may as well put it down to experience and move on, because if the Lord Almighty had wanted this discovery to be known, the mirror wouldn't now be in bits under our feet."

"Oh, shut up!" said Fran abruptly.

"Well Stephen," replied Stuart, "you know my feelings on all this, so I cannot say I'm especially disappointed. But look on the bright side, once I've polished up my story on how I serendipitously found the stone, all of you will have the quiet knowledge that you were really the ones responsible for the find. Even if you can't publicly take any credit."

The three of us politely smiled at back at him, taking no comfort from what he said at all. Well, Fran didn't smile; hers was more of a scowl, but I don't think any of us were in the mood for Stuart's words of wisdom. Granted, it was all a great experience for us, but I certainly felt disappointed we weren't going to go down in history as the crew who somehow, not sure how, but somehow caught a ghost. Only for lady luck, to come along and say 'oh no you don't' and make everything come crashing to the ground – literally in this case.

There was no point in hanging around the freezing cellar, looking at the broken glass any longer. We decided to leave the final clearing up until morning, whereby we could also help Stuart with the deep clean of the house in general, insofar as making sure we removed even the slightest trace of the three of us having stayed there, so battle-axe Agnes wouldn't find out. And if that meant going all over the property on our hands and knees, looking for any stray hair, then so be it. That woman had the eyes of a hawk and a similar taste for carrion I shouldn't wonder. Therefore, defeated and dejectedly, the three of us followed Stuart up the cellar staircase, from what was to be the final night time visit to the underbelly of his old, historic Edinburgh townhouse.

As we were half way up the stairs, I thought for a second, I saw something move in one of the corners, so I stopped, turned around and stared into the darkness. Again, I wondered if there was something which ever so slightly moved behind one of the several piles of unused home wares.

"Come on Jerry, I want to shut off the light," bemoaned the skinflint homeowner.

Aware that everyone else was back in the kitchen and that Stuart didn't want to spend another penny on basement electricity; I gave up looking and joined them.

"Anything the matter? You seemed a bit preoccupied," enquired my brother in law.

"No, nothing's wrong," I replied casually, silently wondering if the movement I saw was just a shadow or perhaps a rat. Although, I'm not altogether sure that dark outline didn't have a shade of ginger about it...

~ ~ ~

Here I am, in the garden 'den', writing up my notes on our Scottish jaunt some weeks after the event but in doing so it has enabled me to tie up some of the loose ends of the trip. Agnes and my Cynthia not only had a splendid weekend away for their reunion events, they also had no idea of our visit to the Edinburgh house. Stuart has surreptitiously informed me that he was able to run off a pretty convincing story about how the flagstone in their cellar gave way under his foot, hence how he discovered the dog skeleton and the jewel within. The local Scottish press went pretty mad for the story and even a couple of the nationals had a few paragraphs. Be it some serious ramblings in the broadsheets to, in special honour of the story, a swimwear model bedecked in fake green gemstones photographed in one of the lesser articulate papers – so I hear anyway. All told, Stuart did quite well out of it. The emerald couldn't be traced for sure back to the descendants of 'Lady Emily whatever it was' although I understand there were a couple of interested parties keen to try and lay claim to it, without success. However, Agnes and Stuart generously donated it to the museum, where a multitude of display lights apparently set the sparkly surface off a treat. Needless to say, security around it is pretty tight, and although an accurate value wasn't published, the word 'priceless' was bandied around by one or two experts.

As I write this, myself and Cynthia have just returned home from our latest trip to see the in-laws. My wife and her sister were keen to get together again, with this extra trip to our normal yearly quota because of all the excitement.

"It's been such a whirlwind!" Agnes announced at dinner on the first night. "Of course, you hear stories like this, but you never expect anything to happen to you. I don't think I've taken it all in yet, even after all these weeks. I mean to say, what serendipity to buy a house with such a treasure lying beneath it. I've even been asked to give a talk at the Guild about it; my fellow members have been enthralled by the whole event. And the newspapers and local television news couldn't get enough of the story, could they darling?"

"No dear," Stuart dutifully replied, like any well-trained husband.

"We didn't take a penny for the gem either, but I have to say the trustees of the museum we donated it to were extremely kind in sending us a gift of some beautiful green wrought iron garden furniture. Just the four chairs, around a little table, but we've only a small garden here so it will look quite fitting, you know, on the edge of the patio, by my two terracotta herb pots."

I very nearly put my foot in it because I then asked if that meant they'd be getting rid of all the old plastic stuff down in the cellar. Needless to say, Agnes was somewhat taken aback and the marginally pained expression which was now across Stuart's face made me recall on my last 'official' visit up to Edinburgh with Cynthia, we didn't actually see the cellar and that my intimate knowledge of its contents are only down to my 'unofficial' visit.

"I hadn't realised you've been down to the cellar," Agnes eventually responded, eyeing me curiously.

"Well, no, but..." Then Stuart chipped in, thank goodness.

"I'd already told Jerry about the gift from the museum darling, and I said it was my intention to sort out the old stuff downstairs."

"Ahh," she simply replied, her suspicion nipped in the bud. Just as well Stuart is a quick thinker, must've been all those years as a captain of the banking industry...

If a banker can't talk his way out of trouble, who can?

After the meal, we all adjourned to the drawing room, and it was clear my invitation to Stuart's study for cognac and cigars such as that of our previous visit was a one off. But then, he didn't need my help anymore. I was a spent force. However, as the ladies led the way, deeply engrossed in conversation, I pulled my brother in law to one side as I had one question I wanted an answer to.

"Hey Stuart, just a mo."

"What is it?" he replied, clearly intrigued to understand my clandestine movements.

"Have you seen anymore of little Cecil?"

"No, I have not! I feel pretty comfortable we've seen the last of him. Or rather 'it'. Don't you? Surely he was destroyed just like the mirror?"

"To be honest I don't know. On the one hand, I think yes, on the other, I think, well, if he's a spirit, a non-physical form, why would he be destroyed?"

"Oh, I don't think we need worry," was his blasé response, with more than a hint of the supercilious.

And with that, he nonchalantly walked off with his nose in the air, joining the ladies for the coffee session. Clearly old Jeremiah Thorne had served his purpose and that was the end of our brief friendship. Wish I'd invoiced him now, but too late. I did consider going downstairs at one in the morning to see if Cecil the ginger wonder was still making his nightly trip down to the cellar. But if Stuart wasn't worried, then why should I be? And I don't particularly want to be turned into a pin cushion by that dagger. I'm not completely convinced I won't get another invite for Cognac from a worried man on a future visit and hopefully Cecil's dagger won't be lodged in Stuart's kneecaps (or somewhere far worse) when that happens. Yes, I think maybe I'll get a quote for service ready just in case, even if I don't normally charge people. Perhaps I'm just a bit bitter that he did so well out of our efforts, while I got the brush off. Therefore, he's not going to buy me off with glorified grape juice and fancy tobacco leaves next time around. Bloody banker.

About the author.

James Barr has had an interest in the paranormal since a young age. He loves a spooky story on a dark and stormy night but he really likes hearing people's real-life paranormal experiences. Being a scaredy-cat doesn't help his own paranormal investigating but he does believe he has encountered ghostly activity. A countryside fan and family man, James lives in southern England and always does what his wife tells him. Find him on twitter here: @JamesBarrJT